HIDDEN
IN THE
SHADOWS

BOOKS BY IMOGEN MATTHEWS

The Girl Across the Wire Fence

WARTIME HOLLAND SERIES

The Hidden Village

IMOGEN MATTHEWS

HIDDEN
IN THE
SHADOWS

bookouture

Published by Bookouture in 2022

An imprint of Storyfire Ltd.
Carmelite House
50 Victoria Embankment
London EC4Y 0DZ

www.bookouture.com

ISBN: 978-1-80314-375-0
eBook ISBN: 978-1-80314-374-3

Previously published by Amsterdam Publishers, 2019.

ONE

WOUTER

He never imagined it would end like this. Yet here he was, half-paralysed with fear as he tried to flee for his life. He knew he should have stayed and behaved like the leader he'd been trained to be, but he hadn't. Instead, he'd abandoned the woodland village, home to countless innocent people, when he should have been helping them to safety. What was he thinking?

Moments earlier, Wouter had noticed three figures at the corner of his vision. They were running into the yard, screaming and firing their pistols into the air. He froze. With a clatter, the wooden bowl he'd been carving dropped to the floor. He bent down quickly to retrieve it, fearful they would have heard the noise, but the three men were too intent on carrying out their deadly mission to notice.

How could he not have heard their approach? A vague sensation that he should be doing something came to him, but his mind refused to tell him what that might be. His only thought was that he was unarmed and wouldn't stand a chance. As the screams grew louder, instinct took over. He had to survive.

Peering through the rough door to his hut, Wouter saw Karl go rushing forward as if to confront the three Germans, then stop dead as more shots ripped through the air. Had he been hit? Wouter dared not look. Revealing himself would be suicide, so he waited, knowing all the while he should have been leading them to safety.

A noise behind the attackers must have distracted them, for they turned towards it. Once again, the bowl slipped from his grasp but there was no time to waste. Without a backward glance, Wouter hurled himself out of the hut and fled into the dense wood that bordered the village. Behind him came outraged cries. Bullets spattered into the ground at his feet, hurling leaves and dirt into the air. Breathing hard, he tripped, regained his balance but kept running till he could no longer hear the voices. He knew he had to put as much distance between himself and the hidden village as quickly as possible. It hurt to breathe, but he mustn't stop, even though he could no longer hear them. They could still be following him... they could still ambush him by stealth.

Every sound from the forest drove him on. The flap of wings as a bird rose out of an oak tree. The scuttling feet of darting squirrels. His own feet snapping twigs and snagging at the undergrowth.

He arrived at the other edge of the woods, skirting a large field, and sensed there must be a farmhouse close by. Fear still prevented him from formulating a plan. He, of all people, was running away when he should have been helping others in far greater need. Instead, he'd panicked.

At the far end of the field and across a low hedge was a track that led to a sprawl of deserted outbuildings. His breathing slowed as he crawled cautiously through the hedge and moved slowly towards the farm. In the distance a dog barked, but not aggressively, so he kept moving. He heard no voices as he crept soundlessly towards the open door of a barn. Inside, his eyes adjusting to the dark, he could make out a ladder leaning against a tower of hay bales. Just visible was a gap between the top one and the roof. A place to hide till he could work out what to do next. In the distance, still the listless bark of that dog. No one could have spotted him, he told himself, so he tested out the bottom rung of the ladder. It creaked. After a brief pause, he crept up rung by rung. Halfway up he heard a scrabbling sound, and froze. The noise stopped. Probably a rat, he reasoned, but as he climbed higher the rustling grew louder. There was someone in there.

'Who's that?' came a hoarse whisper from the hay.

'Wouter,' he said, without thinking, then instantly regretted it. Had he walked straight into another trap? He was about to retreat down the ladder when he heard more rustling from above. Surely, if this person was about to ambush him, he would have revealed himself by now?

'Do you need to come up?' asked the voice. For a moment, Wouter relaxed. From his position on the ladder he strained to see, but it was inky black. He guessed whoever was hiding wanted the place to himself.

'I won't stay long,' said Wouter. With a shock, he found himself being lifted by a pair of hands onto the topmost bale.

'Keep quiet,' hissed the voice. 'There's not much room up here.'

Wouter blinked hard and could just make out some shapes huddled in the hay, some larger than others. Children as well as adults. He counted six.

'Klaus.' The man who'd spoken held out his hand. It seemed a strange, polite gesture, but reassuring. He spoke in a low whisper. 'Mr and Mrs Lok and their son.' He nodded at the shapes that shifted slightly. 'And these two policemen.'

Wouter shrank back towards the ladder. Police up here in hiding?

'It's fine, we're all on the same side,' said a quiet voice from the corner. High-pitched, almost like a girl. Wouter shook his head. Nothing seemed right.

'How long have you been up here?' Wouter addressed Klaus, the spokesman for the group.

'Me, four nights. The others a couple. But we can't stay here much longer. The farmer's getting nervous we'll be discovered and he'll be arrested.'

'Or shot,' said the high-pitched voice. 'We witnessed a terrible thing close up not far from Kampenveld. Me and Bert were passing the big house with the lawn in front when we saw a *mof* shoot the owner dead on his doorstep. That did it for us. We didn't stop to see what happened and fled across the fields. It's how we landed up here.'

'What about you?' asked Klaus.

Wouter had been expecting this question. 'I've been hiding in the woods. There were quite a few others when the raid came, but I don't know how many escaped.' He was glad no one could see his face.

Laura. Her face, with those big trusting eyes, swam into his vision. The girl he'd found himself falling in love with and hadn't had a chance to tell. He swallowed as he remembered his promise to help her. But in the heat of the moment he hadn't told her and he was unable to fathom out why.

'Not Berkenhout?' said Klaus with a sharp intake of breath. 'That's where I was heading. Dick Foppen had arranged it. What happened?'

In that moment, Wouter decided to trust him. Klaus not only knew about Berkenhout but was on his way there. But what about the others up here? Did it even matter now the secret was out?

'It's over. Berkenhout's over. They came out of nowhere, shouting, shooting. I think there were three *moffen*, maybe more. I didn't wait to find out.'

'What about the rest of them? Did any others escape?' said Klaus in a low voice.

For a moment, the only sound was of Wouter taking a deep breath. 'I hope so.'

Klaus allowed him to stay but said he would have to leave at first light as nowhere would be safe. The area would be teeming with people desperate for shelter and the Germans were unlikely to show any mercy.

It was the most uncomfortable night Wouter had ever spent. He found himself longing for the comparative luxury of his underground hut where at least he had a wooden bed, a straw mattress and bedding. High up in the hayloft, he was restless, shifting his body from side to side as he tried to find a position in which to sleep. It was chilly for September, but at least the hay was warm, even though it crackled with every small movement. The little boy kept coughing and his mother's shushing only made it worse. Wouter rolled away onto his side with his arm crooked beneath his head and eventually dozed, but noises kept wrenching him awake. First an owl hooted. Then came the sound of rodent feet pattering across the barn floor. Raindrops skittered on the metal roof over their heads. Somewhere, a door started banging in the wind that had whipped up. When dawn arrived, Wouter was exhausted, his mouth dry with a raging thirst.

'Are you awake?' came a whisper close to his ear.

He groaned.

'Let's go. Now.' It was Klaus.

Wouter didn't need persuading even though he ached all over and could barely stretch out his legs. As he followed Klaus down the ladder trying not to make a noise, he noticed how quiet everything seemed after his broken night. Even the dog had ceased barking.

The rain had stopped and the track was a mosaic of muddy puddles. Wouter was relieved he was wearing his thick boots as the two men hurried away in the direction of the farmhouse.

'Stay here,' whispered Klaus, gesturing with his hand for Wouter not to follow him. He went round the back of the house and knocked softly on the door. A bark came from within and Wouter could hear a man's voice quieten the dog before opening the door. Klaus disappeared inside for what seemed like ages before coming out with a small wrapped package. He jogged back to where Wouter was standing, shivering beneath a spreading oak tree.

'We'll be safe over there,' said Klaus, heading off down the track and into a field covered in stubble. He threw himself on a patch of grass at the edge and tore open the package revealing half a loaf of bread, a chunk of cheese and two apples. '*Eet smakelijk!*' he said, tearing off a lump of bread and cramming it into his mouth.

Wouter did the same and bit into a juicy apple in an attempt to take the edge off his thirst. Greedily, they ate in silence, finishing every last scrap. Wouter let out a long sigh, enjoying the sensation of his body waking up.

'Good, *heh?*' said Klaus, his face breaking into a smile. 'The farmer's been so kind to us, bringing us food and drink twice a day. Then he'll stand watch by the barn door so each of us could stretch our legs a bit, if you know what I mean.' He grinned.

Wouter couldn't imagine staying hidden up in the hay like that for four days. Another night would have been torture.

'We can't stick around here,' said Klaus, as if reading Wouter's mind. 'The farmer told me that Dick Foppen has a place not far from here, but we need to be quick. There are bound to be others looking for somewhere they won't be caught.'

The two men set off at a brisk pace along the track that led into the woods. Wouter felt safer to be back in familiar surroundings that had been his home for the past eighteen months.

It was perfectly silent. No sounds of shooting or the rumble of army vehicles. The two men fell into easy conversation, but kept alert for anything out of the ordinary.

'I was getting quite excited about going to Berkenhout after weeks of moving from place to place. The idea of being hidden away in a community and having a roof over my head. What was it like in the camp?' asked Klaus eagerly.

Wouter raised his thick eyebrows and laughed. 'Boring really. There were long spells with nothing to do except wait for visitors. We had daily tasks, of course, but it was a strain to keep quiet so much of the time. Sounds carry in the forest and no one could afford to raise their voice, laugh or cry. You get used to it, I suppose.' Wouter glanced over at Klaus, who pulled a face. He guessed they were about the same age, though Klaus's red cheeks and sprinkling of fair stubble across his chin made him seem younger. For a moment, Wouter envied his enthusiasm and ignorance. 'Don't get me wrong,' he carried on. 'We were really well looked after and someone from the outside came to visit nearly every day bringing everything we needed. Food, clothes, tools to make stuff with. Medicines too. We felt safe. Maybe too safe.'

They walked on in silence as Wouter became lost in his own thoughts.

Gather everyone together in the reception hut. Organise people into small groups. Lead them down the escape routes at the back of the village. He shivered. He'd been wrong not to stay.

'Look there,' said Klaus, pointing ahead at a small cottage set well back from the path. 'Let's see if we can get water.'

There were no signs of life, so they crept round the side where they found a water pump. Wouter got to it first and vigorously jerked the handle, which squeaked with each attempt to get the water flowing. With a rush, it came surging out and Klaus whooped as he thrust his hands into the flow and sucked greedily.

'Hey, my turn now.' Wouter laughed and they swapped over so he could revel in the sensation of cool water in his mouth and over his head. Water had never tasted water this sweet.

'Shh,' hissed Klaus. He cupped his ear. It sounded like voices coming down the track. They needed to move fast. Edging round the back, they came across two rusty bikes leaning against a wall. Needing no encouragement, they grabbed one each, jumped on and pedalled as fast as they could back onto the track. It wasn't easy, as the tyres were so badly patched up that they might as well have been cycling on bare frames, but at least they were able to get away.

The sound of voices ceased, but they kept pressing on. Wouter had no idea where they were, but Klaus was confident they were heading due north. Months on the move had given him a strong sense of direction.

'Are you sure this is right?' said Wouter. He was struggling to keep up with Klaus. The bikes were small and Wouter, a good few inches taller than Klaus, had difficulty pedalling as quickly. Klaus was heading deeper into the woods and the track was almost impassable in places.

'Trust me,' called out Klaus over his shoulder. 'I'm sure the path widens out along here in the direction of Epe.'

Eventually, they bumped and rattled over a metal grid and onto a made-up road between a few houses. Wouter grew uneasy. Having been hidden for so long in the shelter of the woods, he imagined Germans lurking behind every wall, ready to jump out. No sooner had the thought planted itself in his mind than they saw a young man in German uniform walking towards them. He was on his own and when he spotted the two men hurtling towards him, the soldier stepped into the road and held his hand up.

'*Halt! Absteigen!*' he barked.

Wouter and Klaus skidded to a halt but had the presence of mind to throw the bikes onto the ground blocking the German's way before tearing across the road, over a ditch and into a field. Shots rang out, propelling them even faster. Breathing heavily, they plunged into the trees and kept running. They must have gone at least a couple of kilometres before feeling safe enough to collapse onto a soft mossy patch of grass.

'We did it,' said Klaus through shallow breaths as he squeezed Wouter's shoulder.

Wouter rolled onto his back and stretched out his long legs. It was the most comfortable he'd felt in days.

TWO

LAURA

I've started to worry about where I'll go when all of this is over.

I can't possibly go back home when I've no idea if our house even belongs to us anymore. And if I do manage to return, what about Mama and Papa? I can't imagine moving back without them. All I ever wanted when I arrived at Berkenhout was to be back home in my bedroom surrounded by my books and things, knowing that Mama was down in the kitchen about to call me for supper. That was back then, before I was brought to this hiding place deep in the woods in the middle of the night to be told this would be my new home. I was so scared and so alone – I didn't know how I'd survive. But Sofie was so kind and welcoming to me, sharing her own story of loss to make me feel better. We were like sisters, both separated from our parents because there wasn't enough space for them here. We still don't know when we'll see them again. She gave me hope when I so desperately needed it, making me realise that home can be anywhere as long as you have people who care about you. I still worry when I think about Mama and Papa and what they must be suffering, but it's now a dull ache that never goes away.

Recently, what worries me most is Wouter. I've tried to get

to the bottom of his moods but he brushes me off and I'm sure it's something I've said or done. Maybe he regrets the things he's said to me. They were only little things, like touching my hair and telling me I was good for him. But a few days ago I found him outside, hunched over with a cigarette and telling me he should never have come to live in Berkenhout. It scared me to see him like that. I need to know what he meant by it. Tonight, if this fine weather holds, I'll ask him to walk with me down to the boundary path. I'd rather know if he wants to call it off between us.

Corrie will soon bring in the boys for lunch. They're growing fast and need a lot more than I can give them. Today, it's my job to make the soup, and however much I try to thicken it, it looks pathetic, but what more can I do with three potatoes and a handful of brown beans? I should go over to Janneke's and see if she has any beans to spare.

Something distracts me. It could be a field mouse rustling behind the flour sack. I hesitate. I know I should investigate, but they have a habit of darting out all over the place. I have a dread one will run up my legs and I wouldn't be able to stop screaming and that wouldn't do. Imagine our village discovered after all these months because of a stupid thing like that. The rustling stops and I breathe a sigh of relief. I fill up the soup pot with a bit more water and take the cotton bag down from the peg.

I'm about to leave when loud voices stop me in my tracks. No one ever shouts – it's against the rules. Then an ear-splitting crack shakes the floor beneath my feet – it has to be a gunshot. I daren't emerge through the door with all the commotion but it seems to be coming from the reception hut.

My first thought is Wouter. There's no sign of him... what was it he said he must do... he promised to come and get me first... he promised... all those times he's gone over and over the escape plans with me... what was it he said?

My mind is in turmoil as I press myself against one wall, keeping in the shadows. Maybe the mouse will run out and distract them, I think stupidly.

The silhouette of someone appears in the doorway, but it's not Wouter. I can't make out who it is and look frantically towards the window, as if that would be any help.

'Get out! Run! It's an ambush!' It's a Dutch voice. A familiar voice, but I don't stop to check whose it is. He rushes forward and grabs my arm so roughly that my sleeve rips. 'There's no time, you have to get out.' His hoarse voice is almost a scream.

Our hut is set slightly back from the others and is in a dip so that it can't be seen. He goes first, shielding me from view. Only then do I think of the others. The twins who must still be in class. Their parents, Corrie and Kees, who were on water duty and are probably walking back towards the village right now. Sofie. Wouter. My mind twists as I try to remember what they were all doing this morning.

'Hurry!' My rescuer urges me towards the clump of trees where the children are allowed to play at certain times of the day. Half a dozen children squeeze together, trembling behind the wide trunk of the oak tree. I glance around for the twins, but they're not amongst them. 'Look after them. I'll be back as quick as I can,' he says.

There's no time to lose as I gather the children round and whisper that it's all going to be fine. The smallest is whimpering and I hold him close till he stops shaking. As I comfort them, I'm listening keenly. The crack of gunshots mixes with screams. Instinctively, I cover the ears of the little boy cowering in my arms. I can't have been here more than a minute when I hear terrified voices and a stampede of footsteps as people from the village scatter out into the undergrowth. My rescuer returns, this time limping heavily, with more youngsters and the order for us to flee. Now.

'Wouter?' I hardly dare breathe his name.

He shakes his head, his mouth set in a grim line.

I take one last look back at Berkenhout. Another bullet splits the air in two and I see someone fall to the ground. I don't stop to look who it is, but from his shape I'm convinced it's Karl.

There's nothing for it but to run for our lives.

THREE

WOUTER

The feeling of comfort didn't last long. Gradually, he became aware of a cold dampness spreading up his back, nudging him from sleep. Jumping up, he tried to stamp some feeling back into his numb feet.

Daylight was fading. Next to him, Klaus was lying on his side, arms wrapped round his body, fast asleep. Wouter prodded him, but only got a groan in response as he curled himself tighter.

'Wake up. We can't stay here,' said Wouter, shaking him by the shoulder.

Klaus rubbed his eyes and yawned. 'What time is it?'

Wouter shrugged. 'Late. We should try and find somewhere to stay for the night and search for Dick Foppen's house when it gets light.' He remembered he had half a packet of cigarettes in his pocket. 'Here, dinner,' he said, handing one to Klaus with a short laugh. They sat side by side on a fallen branch, working out what to do next. They'd come so far back into the woods that there was unlikely to be any habitation. And without the sun, they had no idea in which direction to start walking.

'Come on. Let's get going before it's completely dark,' said Klaus, stretching his arms above his head as he got to his feet.

After a while, an almost-full moon cast silvery tree shadows across their path, leading them away from the thickest part of the wood. The distant rumble of an army vehicle made them stop once or twice as it seemed to draw nearer, then fade away. They needed to keep going to find somewhere they could rest, but the going was hard after a day on the move with little to eat or drink.

They must have been trudging along for the best part of two hours when they reached a sort of T-junction leading onto a broader track. Traces of tyre marks were visible in the sandy soil.

'There must be a farmhouse or something along here,' said Klaus, striding purposefully down the track.

Wouter was too tired to question why he had chosen to go right and not left. The thought of finding a place to rest and maybe some food propelled him on. After a little way, he sniffed, detecting wood smoke on the air. 'Smell that? There's definitely something close by.'

They kept going more cautiously. A small cottage, almost entirely concealed by trees, stood back from the path.

'We must be careful and get ready to run,' warned Klaus as they approached the closed gate and walked up the path. He rapped on the door and waited. No noise from within. He knocked more quietly and a shuffling sound could be heard.

'Who's there?' said a quavering voice from behind the door.

'Two young men who need a little food and shelter,' said Klaus, eyebrows raised at Wouter as he spoke.

The door opened a crack and two eyes peered out at them.
'You're not German?'

'No. Dutch. But we've lost our way. Could we trouble you to come in?' said Klaus with a broad smile.

She was a small pale-faced woman of about twenty-five

wearing a faded striped apron. A little boy, no more than two, clung to her skirts. She hesitated before ushering them in, then quickly closed the door behind them.

'You can't be too sure round here. We haven't had any visits from Germans recently, but when they turn up you can't refuse to let them in. They expect to eat our food and drink our *jenever*. There's no point objecting because they get angry and threaten to search the house for *onderduikers*.' She peered at them closely. 'Is that what you are?'

Klaus cleared his throat. 'It got dark before we reached the place where we're meant to be staying. Sorry for the inconvenience, *mevrouw*, but would it be possible just to stay here till it gets light?' He smiled again at her.

'I suppose so. But I can't have you sleeping in the house, you understand. Please, come through for now.'

They followed her, apologising as they both stumbled over a pile of shoes in the gloomy hallway.

The kitchen was lit by a low overhead light and warmed by a black stove. The smell of soup filled the room. Gesturing for them to sit at the rough wooden table, she brought out a bottle of beer from the larder. 'My husband won't notice. He's away for a few days,' she said, pouring them each a glass. She lifted her little boy onto a chair piled up with three cushions and sat down beside him.

'I'm Griet and this is Bertje.' She rubbed the top of Bertje's head as she spoke and the little boy gave them a broad grin.

The two men introduced themselves, then both spoke at once.

'You're so kind...'

'We're so grateful to you for...'

Griet's face relaxed into a smile and she said how pleased she was to have company. Her husband worked in the forest and was often called away on jobs for days. 'I don't really like being here, it's so isolated. He worries about me and Bertje when he goes away, but what choice do we have? My parents live in Kampenveld. We were about to move there when the occupation started and we were forced to stay put. But what about you? How do you come to be wandering around these woods at this time of night?'

Wouter and Klaus exchanged glances. There seemed no point in lying.

'I've come from Berkenhout. There was a raid… no, it was more than that. The camp was stormed and I ran for my life. I fear people were shot dead.' Wouter was unable to meet her eye, unwilling to reveal more.

Griet's hand flew to her mouth and she gasped. 'So it's true, then. There were rumours but I was never sure if the place actually existed. Bram must have known, but never talked about what happened in the woods. Out of protection for us, it was. Now, what about you?' she asked Klaus.

Bertje had been pulling at Griet's sleeve, making soft whimpering noises that grew steadily louder. Her attempts to soothe him by stroking his hair stopped having the desired effect and he began saying 'hungry' over and over. Wouter tried not to think about the pot of soup bubbling away on the stove as he took a small sip of beer. It tasted so good that he had to stop himself from emptying his glass in one gulp. Out of the corner of his eye, he could see Klaus fidgeting in his chair. It had been a long day.

'Excuse me, but I'm running late with supper as Bertje keeps reminding me.' She lifted him off the chair so he could follow her to the stove. Peering into the soup pot, she said there was just enough for them all, but would it be all right to give them bread to fill them up? Wouter had to stop himself from jumping up and hugging her, so happy was he to be offered a hot meal.

After they'd had their fill, Griet brought out a bottle of *jenever* and poured three small glasses.

'*Proost!*' they said in unison. Bertje banged the table in glee. Before long, the bottle was half-empty. Laughter filled the room.

Griet stood up and announced that she must put Bertje to bed, but that they should help themselves to more *jenever*. 'Then I'll show you where you can sleep,' she said on her way out of the room.

'She's very trusting,' said Wouter when she was out of earshot.

'Well, we're not German.' Klaus laughed, slopping some *jenever* onto the table as he missed the glass. Wouter laughed a little too loudly, knowing he'd had too much, but was unable to resist another refill. After another couple, he laid his head on the table and fell asleep. Klaus must have done the same.

He was back in Berkenhout chopping logs in the wood behind his hut. It was warm work and he stopped for a moment to wipe his brow. Behind him, he heard his name being called. It must be Laura calling him for the lunch of brown beans and potatoes she'd prepared. It was unusual to have the same meal two days running but Nico, the delivery boy, hadn't turned up that morning. No cause for concern just yet, but if no contact was made the following morning, Wouter would have to break curfew and go and find out what was happening. It had only happened once before. The boy had lost his way through the thick undergrowth and dense trees. He'd arrived the next day accompanied by Jan, who knew the woods like the back of his hand. He'd claimed no one from the camp had heard his whistles, probably because he hadn't been anywhere close by. The relief among the inhabitants had been palpable when the boys turned up. The idea of being abandoned had been as acute as being discovered.

There was Laura's voice again, more urgent. He wanted to

run to her, to hold her in an embrace and tell her he loved her. Instead, he remained rooted to the spot. A feeling of unease slid up his body. Why wasn't he able to reach her? He thought he must have sat down and closed his eyes for a moment till he became aware his arm was being shaken. Forcing open his eyes, there was the dark silhouette of Laura standing over him. With a gasp, he remembered he'd done her wrong and he needed to make amends. 'I'm so sorry,' he said, and tried to pull her into his arms.

'Stop it!' shouted Griet, pushing him away from her. 'After all the hospitality I've given you. Get out!' She dragged Wouter to his feet and shoved him towards the door.

Still coming to, Wouter didn't resist. 'I'm sorry, *mevrouw*...'

'What's happening?' said Klaus, awakened by the noise.

'He tried it on. Now both of you, out!' A deep flush spread across her face and neck. From upstairs came Bertje's cries.

'I'm sorry...' began Klaus as he stumbled out after Wouter into the night.

The door slammed shut with a thud behind them.

FOUR

LAURA

I'm handed a bowl of potato and brown bean soup. It's like the soup I abandoned, but I'm pleased to see there's enough of this one to go round. We all attack it like wolves. The first food we've tasted in two days. Two of the children squabble over a chunk of bread. A good sign. The rest of us are just grateful to be somewhere with a roof over our heads. The outhouse is big enough for the seven of us – five children, me and Janneke – and she was among the last people to get out with me. It'll be a squash, but no one cares, as long as we're safe.

When I've finished eating, Henk comes over to me and Janneke and asks us for a word outside. My insides clench as all kinds of situations flood my brain, the worst being he's heard news about Wouter and it's bad. I glance over at Janneke and she nods, as if she knows what he's going to say.

Lately, I've come to rely on her. She has this ability to stay calm when everything around her is in chaos. It's what comes of having been a head teacher. She rarely talks about it, but she must miss her school, the children. Only once did she open up, telling me about the morning she arrived at school and found someone had replaced her because she was a Jew. She'd had no warning but she knew she had to leave quickly before they came to arrest her. It still makes no sense to me why they picked on her. She's kind, hard-working and would never do anyone harm. In fact, much like everyone close to me.

We step outside. It's warm for September, even this late in the evening, and it reminds me of being allowed to stay up late during the long summer evenings. I'd hide away with my friend Norah in the little summer house at the bottom of the garden when Mama and Papa were holding one of their parties. We'd drink lemonade out of chipped cups and laugh at the murmur of voices and tinkle of glasses on the terrace, breathing in the scent of Papa's cigar that Mama only allowed him to smoke outside. I push away the memory of school holidays, friends staying over, freedom.

We walk a little way from the house to a roughly carved wooden bench. He comes limping towards us and gestures for us to sit down. I notice a slight chill in the air and realise it's not as warm as I first thought.

'I'm sorry, but I can't have so many staying here. It's too dangerous, so tomorrow the group will have to split up. I want to know how we should deal with the children.' I can hear the anxiety in Henk's voice and realise he never expected to play this part in our escape. His role was to organise the building of the huts in the village and make sure that supplies got through. It was pure luck he'd been in the vicinity of Berkenhout and was able to rescue us. Since hurting his ankle in the escape, he must find it hard to cope. He made light of it at the time, but every so often I notice the way he winces. He's already done so much for us, but sending us away does seems cruel after all we've been through. Instinctively, I turn to Janneke for her advice. She looks thoughtful and takes a moment to answer.

'Obviously the children can't be asked to fend for them-selves, so I will take three. Laura, you will have to take the two older ones.' She looks at me, trust in her eyes, even though she knows I'm only sixteen. Under normal circumstances, I'd be considered a child myself, but this war has added years to us all.

I'm still anxious though. 'Where will we go?' I ask him.

'You don't need to worry. We've been getting offers of help from people with space in cellars, attics, sheds. It seems that the whole of the Veluwe is hiding *onderduikers*.' He smiles and I see him for the kind man that he is.

I lie awake for a long time, unable to sleep. Several children are restless and need comforting. I wait to hear their steady breathing, but it doesn't calm me. I must have dropped off, though, because I'm woken by the crowing of the cockerel he keeps in the yard. A sliver of light seeps under the crack of the door and I can see Janneke's silhouette as she sits up.

'We must wake the children and leave before the sun is fully up,' she whispers, her voice close to my ear. I nod and try to ignore how tired I feel.

It's hot and noisy in the back of his van. I keep reminding the children not to pull back the blanket covering us. They think this is all a game and want to stick up their heads so they can look out of the square window. I try to distract them by singing quietly. At least it helps to steady my nerves. The windows rattle every time we pass over a bump in the track.

The van stops and I hear his sigh from the front. The clang as he slams the door, then daylight and a gust of fresh air.

'Keep quiet and follow me,' he instructs us. Janneke and I hug each other before I scramble out with the two boys, glad to stretch our legs after the cramped space.

He raps out a beat on the door of the cottage and a plump woman with a cheerful smile opens up. I guess she must be about my mother's age. He doesn't come in, but shakes my hand

and wishes me luck. I notice he seems anxious to go and have to remind myself we could never have done any of this without him. But I can't help feeling abandoned, me with two children I barely know. I'm not entirely sure I know what's going on but am relieved to step into the warm hallway, which smells of baking bread. For now, this is the nearest to the home I used to know. And Mevrouw Schaft is so welcoming. Not only is there fresh bread and butter, but cinnamon cake, which we wash down with cold milk. From a cupboard under the stairs, she fetches a box of puzzles and settles the boys on a rug by the stove.

'I've sorted out some clothes my daughter has grown out of. I can see they'd fit you. Would you like them?' She hands me a neatly folded pile and when I press my nose against it the clothes smell as if they've been drying outside in the breeze. I can't explain why but when I look up my eyes are full of tears and she leans towards me to give me a hug. I cling to her and try to control my sobs, but the warmth of her touch makes me want to cry more. Out of the corner of my eye, I see one of the boys look up quizzically, and I pull away to smile through my tears at him.

Her kindness doesn't stop there and she insists I take a bath. I simply cannot remember when I last had such a luxury. As I sink down into the warm scented water and let my hair float out behind me, I have a moment of peace, knowing Mevrouw Schaft is going to look after us. For now, everything feels a bit more normal.

Behind the bathroom door and away from the others, Wouter's kind face swims into view and I clasp my arms tight around my body until the tears begin to flow.

FIVE

WOUTER

'It wasn't like that, honestly,' he called out. He was furious with himself for losing the chance of having a proper roof over their heads. But Laura had seemed so real. He'd trembled when she'd appeared before him, her lips pursed tightly in anger as she'd lunged to grab his arm. He'd just wanted to stop her so he could explain and beg her forgiveness for all he'd done. Then she'd started hitting him. Or so he thought. Of course he would never have made a move towards Griet.

Klaus didn't stop to listen and strode away as if he couldn't bear to be in Wouter's company. Right now, Wouter couldn't even bear himself, but there was no point falling out when he had no idea where they were. Reluctantly, he ran to catch him up.

'Please, let me explain.'

Klaus shot him a furious look. 'Listen, I don't care if you did or you didn't. But now we don't have anywhere to stay and I'm sick of it. Sick of sleeping out in the open. Sick of being stuck with you. So clear off.' He set off at a brisk pace, anger rising off him as he disappeared into the distance.

There seemed to be little point trying to patch things up. If

Klaus was merely angry in the heat of the moment, he'd eventually calm down. But Wouter had no desire to apologise for something he hadn't done. *I'll just carry on alone*, he thought bitterly as he trudged forlornly along the unlit path.

The moon had long disappeared. Wouter's pace slowed as he strained to look for a place to stop, until all at once something small and dark shot across his path, its hooves making a slippery clattering noise. Wouter cried out in shock, his heart pounding, his mouth dry. In a flash he was fleeing for his life, blood roaring in his head, the crack of bullets bouncing off the ground around his feet. He imagined Laura crying out to him in a panicked voice and the image filled his head. Why hadn't he waited for her or gone back to help? Like before, guilt flooded his body and his knees gave way. He collapsed onto damp grass and stayed unmoving, while his breathing slowed. The echo of Laura's cry kept on in his head, as if he was noticing it for the very first time.

He must have fallen asleep. From deep in the undergrowth came a rustling, scuffling noise. Scrambling to his feet and ready to run, he saw the pale rump of a small deer bob away into a clump of pine trees. He fell back onto the grass with a grunt. He was still lost with not even Klaus to share his misery. When would it ever end?

He fell into a fitful sleep, punctuated with vivid images of his escape, Griet's shouts and Klaus's angry face. After what seemed an eternity, it was morning. He'd survived the night but had no desire to move. Apart from a raging thirst, he didn't feel as bad as the night before, already a lifetime away. The sun was just starting to poke through the leaves above him and he lifted his face towards it. If he kept his eyes closed he could imagine that none of this had happened and that he was still in Berkenhout, sitting with Petr who was whittling a piece of birch wood into a toy bird on wheels for one of the children. Petr had few words of Dutch, but somehow it never mattered. He always made encouraging noises when Wouter asked to have a go,

Petr's tobacco-stained teeth visible when he smiled. Sometimes, he'd stop to correct Wouter's efforts, but mostly they'd sit in silence, sometimes sharing a cigarette. Then Petr would start to sing Russian folksongs to himself and Wouter would hum along. His attempts at the words were as laughable as Petr's efforts in Dutch.

Half dreaming, Wouter smiled to himself. Funny, how the idea of being back in Berkenhout now seemed so appealing. He missed the daily deliveries of fresh bread and vegetables brought by young Jan and Nico, and visits every Sunday by Tante Else, one of the organisers. She'd made sure they never went hungry, even when food shortages throughout Holland were starting to hit. Sundays were the highlight of the week, when she'd come with baskets of cake and cookies and her secret supply of real coffee. By the end there were nearly eighty of them living in the village, and there'd only be enough for one small taste, but the smell alone had always been enough to buoy him up and give him hope that things would return to normal.

It was over coffee and cake that Wouter had fallen for Laura. He'd hardly noticed her before, apart from witnessing her arrival late one evening. He'd gone outside to smoke a cigarette when he'd heard quiet footsteps approach the village. It'd been late in the evening, so was unlikely to be a German, but he couldn't be sure. He'd slunk behind a tree to watch. It was Henk, the forester, one of the few people who could find their way to the village in the dark. Next to him had been Laura, though he didn't know that at the time. She'd been enveloped in a slightly too-large grey coat, her dark hair covered by a blue scarf. Two of the organisers had come forward to meet her and escorted her to the Janssens' hut, home to their family of four plus Sofie. He remembered being amused at how Sofie, who'd at first been so uncooperative and moody, would react to having another person joining them, when space was already so confined.

He saw little of Laura in the following days, but when he did, she was always staring at her hands while Sofie talked at whoever was prepared to listen. Gradually the two girls had become friends. Sofie had found an unlikely ally in Laura, as there were no other teenage girls forced to live in Berkenhout. Sofie was so feisty and furious, determined to show everyone she knew how hard done by she was as she riled against the camp rules that restricted her freedom. On one occasion, when passing their hut, he'd heard Sofie in full flow, complaining rather too loudly about the lack of space and that she had no privacy. He'd glimpsed Laura through the hut opening, her head bowed in concentration over a stocking she was darning. She'd seemed lost in her own thoughts, oblivious to Sofie's rantings. Then she'd looked up and given him a small smile. Straightaway, he'd been struck by her dark, brooding eyes and wondered what lay behind them. In that moment, he'd felt his heart lurch, triggering feelings he'd never experienced, even with Francine, the girl he'd intended to marry before all this had happened. Then, as his eyes had met Laura's, he realised that she was the one he wanted to spend the rest of his life with.

One Sunday, it was warm enough to sit outside. Wouter and three other young men had been felling a tree for firewood and pulled some logs into a semicircle for the weekly meeting. They knew it wouldn't matter if their voices carried as the Germans were never out patrolling on a Sunday. Everyone was relaxed, passing round coffee and slices of cinnamon apple cake and chatting to their neighbour. Wouter sat down on the last free seat next to Laura.

'Hello, I'm Wouter,' he said with a smile. She turned her soulful dark eyes towards him and smiled back. Briefly, her face lit up and, in that moment, she was the most beautiful girl he'd ever seen.

'I'm Laura.' Her voice was so quiet he had to lean in close to hear her. She shrank away as if he'd invaded her personal space.

'I'm sorry,' he said quickly, and made things worse by placing a hand on her arm. He looked up and was relieved to see Tante Else standing before them holding a plate with cake. 'Wouter, can you hold this a minute? I've got a letter for Laura.'

Laura snatched the letter and hurried off to her hut.

'I'm hoping it's good news about her parents. She hasn't heard from them since the family was split up.' Else sighed, her eyes on Laura's dwelling. 'There was room for just one of them here so that went to Laura. A place was found for her parents in Friesland. It's a long way from Ghent where they lived. It was all so sudden and a great shock for her.'

Wouter was silent as he listened to Laura's story, typical of so many who'd come to Berkenhout. His own was quite different. For a start, he wasn't Jewish, but, like many young men of his age, had chosen to go into hiding. As he was a postman, it wouldn't have taken much for the Germans to seize him and send him across the border to work in their factories. Conditions there were terrible and he'd heard of how the starving workers missed out on food coupons when they failed to achieve their work targets. Not that the coupons were worth having. One coupon barely provided enough for a watery bowl of soup. Wouter struggled to understand why his best friend, Tim, had been so eager to leave to put himself through such hardship. Tim's lack of hatred for what the *moffen* were doing to Holland was incomprehensible to Wouter. Tim never let on, but Wouter suspected a mutual acquaintance who'd signed up to the Waffen SS was behind his friend's fervour to get away. Tim seemed blind to the dangers, particularly of the likelihood that he wouldn't be working in a factory at all but transported straight to a labour camp. But Tim was not to be persuaded and kept on about how much better life would be by supporting the work done by the Germans. After that, Wouter was careful not to tell him of his intention to go into hiding. He no longer trusted his oldest friend.

The day Tim left was a sad one. Wouter stayed home and couldn't bring himself to say goodbye. Later, he discovered that Tim's own family had turned their backs on him. Within a month of his arriving in Lübeck, word reached Wouter that Tim had become a recruit for the Waffen SS. At that moment, Wouter knew for certain that he needed to disappear.

At first, Dick Foppen had been reluctant to allow Wouter to go to Berkenhout. Naturally, Jews were given priority with so many inundating Kampenveld and the surrounding towns from all over Holland. Why should he give him a place? Wouter argued that his contribution would be enormous. He was young and strong, capable of putting his shoulder to any manual task and he'd be willing to be involved with the organisation of the village. He convinced himself and Dick of his worth, but once he'd arrived at Berkenhout, things had been different. There was plenty of work to be done to keep things running smoothly, but he couldn't help feel guilty that he'd snatched a place from someone more needy than himself, maybe a Jewish person in danger of being arrested, shot or transported to a labour camp.

This thought had run through his head again as he'd looked up to see Laura emerging from the doorway of her hut. Her dark hair was a mess as if she'd been thrusting her fingers through it. She'd looked straight at him with huge unfathomable eyes. He'd lifted his hand to wave, rose from his seat and walked towards her. Whatever her news, he wanted to be the one to comfort her.

SIX

WOUTER

He blinked awake, vaguely aware of a tinkling sound reminding him of how dry his mouth felt. Following the sound, he found a pond through the trees where the deer had fled. It was almost hidden by reeds, fed by a trickle of water. He fell to his knees, scooping great handfuls into his mouth and vigorously rubbing his face. It tasted wonderful. He slooshed water over his head and raked his fingers through his thick hair. Refreshed, he dragged off his boots, socks and the rest of his clothes before plunging in. A duck flapped out of the reeds and flew off, loudly quacking. Wouter laughed and beat the water with the palms of his hands. It was his first wash in days. He rinsed out his clothes, hanging them on some nearby branches in the sunshine. Leaning against a tree, he enjoyed the warmth from the sun's rays, until the hunger he'd been trying to ignore became too much to bear. Nearby he discovered a clump of bilberry bushes, which were laden with tiny purple berries. Handfuls of the juicy berries were enough to revive him, but served as a reminder he'd barely eaten since escaping from Berkenhout. He tried to savour the rush of sweetness, but it was short-lived. He knew he had to get out of the woods and find help. Too impatient to wait for his clothes to dry, he tugged them off the makeshift clothesline, but the dampness made him realise he hadn't made such a good job of cleaning them after all. Maybe the smell wouldn't seem so bad once he got going.

Using the position of the sun as a guide, he set off purposefully. The terrors of the last two days had receded along with the constant crack of gunshot. The Germans had either grown tired of the hunt or were simply too lazy to get going this early. Wouter's breathing slowed as he listened out for sounds – the occasional burst of birdsong in the tops of the trees, the crunch of twigs and rustle of dry leaves below his feet. He sensed he couldn't be that far from Dick Foppen's house, but what kind of a welcome would he receive? He hoped that in the chaos that ensued, no one would have mentioned his disappearance to Foppen. *I'll explain everything*, he thought. *All in good time*.

After he had been walking for what seemed like hours through dense woodland, the trees thinned out to reveal a path leading onto a lane. As he approached it, he could discern a couple of large houses set well back amongst tall pine trees. He glanced about him, anxious not to be spotted. After his near-disastrous encounter with the German – could it only have been the day before? – he couldn't be too careful.

Quickening his step, he approached the first of the two houses and glimpsed a woman hanging out washing round the back. He knew he must have looked and smelled like a tramp, so kept his distance while he smoothed his still-damp clothes as best he could.

'Good morning, *mevrouw*. Could I stop here a little while?' he said, a little nervously.

The woman stopped pegging out the sheet she was holding and dropped it into the laundry basket. 'Berkenhout?' she said curtly.

Wouter nodded.

'Wait here a minute,' she said, and disappeared into the house.

Wouter looked around him but there was no one to be seen and no sound from within. But that single word had reassured him and suggested others might be sheltering here. He turned back to the house to see the tall confident figure of Dick Foppen marching towards him with a broad smile on his face. Wouter couldn't help himself from rushing to embrace him like a long-lost friend.

'Sorry. I must stink,' said Wouter, pulling back, embarrassed by the sight he must present.

'I've seen and smelled a lot worse.' Dick chuckled. 'It's good to see you. I didn't think you'd made it. What took you so long?'

'I got lost in the woods and it took a while to find my way out,' said Wouter, not untruthfully.

'But surely you were with others? How did that happen?'

'It's complicated,' began Wouter, searching Dick's face for any signs.

Dick didn't seem to be listening as he said, 'We're nearly all accounted for. Now come in. You'll be surprised who's here.'

At the door, they passed the woman who'd been hanging out the washing. She stepped aside without looking up.

'Don't worry, Hennie. Wouter is the last. There won't be any others,' said Dick. 'I'm sure there'll be enough soup for everyone, but some will have to wait their turn as we've run out of bowls. Can you serve it up in ten minutes?'

The woman nodded and hurried away to the kitchen.

'The last couple of days have been madness with all the people arriving,' Dick told Wouter.

'All from Berkenhout?'

'Mainly, but one or two others were hiding in the woods when they heard all those shots being fired. Come along, I think they'll be pleased to see you.'

Would they really? Wouter was overcome by sudden

nerves. Dick obviously had no idea about Wouter's failure to pull his weight when it mattered most. Perhaps no one else had noticed among the chaos. As he followed Dick, his hands grew damp at the prospect that one of these people might be Laura.

Dick opened the door to a room packed with men, women and children. There must have been at least twenty. Some looked exhausted and were slumped silently on seats. Others, mainly the younger ones, were standing in clusters, talking animatedly and loudly. Wouter scanned the room, recognising several from Berkenhout, including Petr, standing apart and staring out of the window. Wouter's spirits lifted on seeing his old friend, but his nerves returned on realising that Laura wasn't one of the gathering. Moments earlier, he'd been worried about finding Laura here and the excuses he'd be forced to make. Now, he'd have given anything to be safely in the same room with her, even if it meant putting up with her staring reproachfully at him with those big dark eyes.

'Everyone, please be quiet for a moment and look who's arrived.'

The room fell silent as all eyes turned towards Wouter, who quickly looked at his feet as he waited for Dick to continue.

'Where did you get to?' asked Otto, with a challenging look. He was a stocky fair-haired man with unfriendly blue eyes. Otto had been put in charge of organising and running meetings in Berkenhout, but he ran them like the bank manager he was, ordering people around rather than trying to win them over. There had been complaints to Dick who sought to smooth things over by appointing Wouter as leader. Inevitably, it had led to arguments between the two of them and Dick was forever being brought in to calm things down. Tensions in the village were a frequent occurrence due to the harsh conditions and limits to everyone's freedom, but the friction between Wouter and Otto went beyond this.

'Yeah, I thought you were meant to be leading everyone to

safety,' said a man next to Otto. A murmur rippled through the room and Wouter could feel all eyes on him, judging him.

Dick ignored the remark and carried on before Wouter could answer. 'I'm pleased that Wouter has made it here in one piece. These are difficult times, so let's not make things worse,' he said with a little cough. 'But now that everyone is here, I want to tell you what will happen next. In a little while, Else and her colleagues will come with instructions to move you all to designated safe houses in Kampenveld and nearby villages.'

Several people began to murmur among themselves. Dick lifted a hand for silence. 'I know it's not ideal, but returning to Berkenhout is no longer an option. There's a rumour the Germans are drafting in many more soldiers to search the woods for *onderduikers*. You are all lucky to have escaped but the danger is by no means over. It's not possible to have so many of you staying here under one roof. I'm sure you understand that. I'm doing my best to find temporary accommodation and we all hope it won't be for long. Now, I have some good news.'

The murmuring started again, this time more animatedly. Wouter shot a glance at Dick who was smiling. He hardly dared think it might involve Laura.

'News has come through that Breda has been liberated by the Allies. They're taking other towns as they move across the country. It seems the Germans have been defeated.'

A cheer went up and they all began hugging one another and shaking Dick's hand as if he were personally responsible. Hennie came running in at the commotion and to her surprise was swept up by Otto who planted kisses all over her face.

Of course Wouter was pleased it was soon going to be over. He joined in with the rest of them as best he could, but felt sick at the prospect that Laura might not have made it. Making his way across the crowded room, he headed over to Petr who was smiling and nodding. It wasn't his way to jump around like the younger ones.

'Petr. What will you do now? Go home to Russia?' Wouter squeezed his friend's hand with both of his.

Petr's face clouded over. 'No, I must stay here. Too dangerous to go home. But one day. Maybe.'

'You're right. We shouldn't believe that everything will return to normal just like that. You heard what Dick said about the Germans sending more troops into the woods. I can't imagine they won't want revenge for all those months we stayed hidden.'

Dick was at Wouter's shoulder. 'No, it's far from over,' he said in a low voice. 'People have been celebrating in the streets all over Holland expecting the Allies to turn up to liberate them at any time. But I have a bad feeling about it. At first Radio Oranje was so upbeat with reports of the Germans making a hasty escape back over the border, but there's been no further news. It makes me think the Germans have seized the initiative.'

'Why did you tell us it was good news?' Wouter turned to stare at Dick.

'To give us all hope. This situation can't last forever.'

'But to give us false hope?' Wouter shook his head in anguish. The day, which started out with so much optimism, was turning into a nightmare. He had to know. 'Not everyone made it out of Berkenhout, did they?'

Dick took Wouter's arm and led him to where they wouldn't be overheard. Petr shrugged and turned to gaze out of the window.

'We haven't had confirmation but it seems that six were shot when trying to escape. They didn't have a chance. I'm so sorry.' Dick took a handkerchief from his pocket and blew his nose.

'I need to know... was Laura one of them?' said Wouter in a shaky voice.

'I don't think so, but she's unaccounted for. She was seen running along one of the escape routes, but I've had no further news.'

Wouter heaved out a long sigh. So there was a still a chance she was alive.

'We're doing all we can to find her and also several others. It's early days.' Dick smiled encouragingly. 'I don't suppose you will have heard about Sofie.'

Wouter shook his head. Surely not Sofie? He could imagine her putting up a fight and being gunned down for her insolence, but could she have been so foolish?

'She was the last to leave. In fact, she didn't leave when you all did. We found her the next day in her hut.'

'But why? How did she manage to hide?' asked Wouter incredulously.

'She didn't. She was attacked but was spared. She's extremely traumatised and won't talk about what happened. I fear she was sexually assaulted.' He spoke in a low voice.

Wouter felt as if he'd been punched in the belly. 'The bastards,' he spat. 'You don't think Laura...'

Dick laid a hand on his arm. 'I don't know, but sincerely hope not. My feeling is she wouldn't have made it far if the Germans had caught up with her and we would have... found her by now if that was the case.'

It was small consolation. Briefly, Wouter turned away and looked around at all these people who were just pleased to have escaped unscathed. Perhaps Dick was right not to say much more, especially when details were so sketchy. He wished he could be as happy as they looked.

SEVEN

LAURA

All I've been given is a day's warning to prepare myself for the next move. It doesn't seem fair, just as we were all beginning to settle. I've even got used to sleeping in the cellar. It's dark, but not at all cramped and I feel safe on the other side of the hidden door behind the potato sacks. The brothers love their space, high up in the attic where no one can hear them playing their games. I've watched their anxiety lessen over these last days. If only it were possible to give them the stability they so need.

Pia, Mevrouw Schaft's daughter, is a few years older than me and was preparing to go to Leiden when the *moffen* closed the university. There's nothing more to do than wait until it's all over, but she's been waiting two years. I'm not sure I'd be as patient as her. But I can tell her mother is pleased to have her around, the way they chat together and share the household tasks. Just like I used to do with Mama. It makes me realise how much I miss her, when we used to sit together at the kitchen table chatting away peeling and chopping potatoes and carrots for dinner. And listening to Papa's soft whistling in the background as he tinkered with his tools, finding small jobs that needed doing around the house. I try not to dwell on these bittersweet memories. I turn my attention to the jobs that need doing here and try my best to help as I don't see why they should provide me with everything for nothing in return. When I'm not polishing the furniture or digging up vegetables in the back garden for dinner, I'm keeping the boys occupied with small tasks. During class in Berkenhout, the younger one was always a bit of a handful. Back then, he'd joke with the other children and wouldn't settle to his work. Now, since getting all my attention, he's a lot more conscientious, but I worry he's losing his spontaneous joyfulness. Being cooped up is hard for us all. So I've been setting the boys a story to write every day and asking them to read it aloud. It's a delight to hear how eager they are to outdo the other and to set their imaginations running free.

I tell the boys I'll be up to check on them and expect them to finish the task I've set. They shoot up the stairs, two at a time, making me smile. As I start to wash up the breakfast things, Mevrouw Schaft comes into the kitchen and asks me to sit down at the table with her.

'I'm afraid it's time for the boys to move on,' she says, not quite looking me in the eye.

'But why? Surely they're safe here?' I say, not understanding.

'It's not just about safety, Laura. It costs too much to look after two of them. One perhaps, but I don't want to split up the brothers. All they have is each other.'

I'm determined not to cry in front of her. First, they lose their parents and now me, just as they were growing to trust me.

'Who decided this?' It comes out a bit more sharply than I mean it to. It's not her fault but I can't help feel the injustice of it all.

A look of pain crosses her face as she sighs, but she doesn't answer my question. 'They'll be safe and well looked after, I can assure you of that. I've met the woman who has kindly offered to take them in. She's the mother of a friend of Pia and has a smallholding in a small village near Groningen.' She shrugs and tries to smile.

'Have you told them yet?' I ask.

'No. You're close to them so I hoped you would.'

I have a lump in my throat as I climb through the secret door into the attic. The boys come into view, their dark heads bent in concentration over their work. Jacob, the younger one, looks up and runs over to me, holding up his exercise book to show the picture he's drawn. It's of a boy sitting with his arm round a small brown dog who is looking up at him.

'That's me and that's Fido. Mama doesn't like it when he sleeps on my bed.'

''Cos he's smelly,' says Aaron, who is colouring in his own picture.

'No, he isn't. You just say that 'cos he likes me, not you.'

'Shh, boys. That's enough. Now sit down. I have something to tell you.'

I can't quite make out the look in their eyes as they both turn their wide-eyed gaze on me. It's as if they have guessed what I'm going to say.

EIGHT

WOUTER

Several weeks of working alongside Dick to rehouse Berkenhout evacuees gave Wouter a renewed sense of purpose and helped to assuage his feeling of guilt that he'd failed as a camp leader. Dick insisted, not unkindly, that whatever happened that day was done – Wouter should put the past behind him and move on. The threat of discovery was still at a critical level and Dick needed all the support he could get in ensuring that the dozens left homeless were given a safe haven. Wouter was grateful for Dick's continuing trust and belief in him. In return, Dick said he would do all he could to discover what had happened to Laura, but it was no easy task.

Rumours were circulating about Laura and others who were still missing. She was last seen heading south after escaping the woods with several others, unidentified, on the back of a farmer's truck. She'd made it back over the border to Belgium. No, the network had arranged for her to travel to Friesland where she'd been reunited with her parents. With each piece of news, Wouter clung to the possibility she was still alive, until another rumour dashed his hopes. He must have written at least three letters to her, which he passed on to one of Dick's colleagues in the network. But he received nothing back. He knew in all likelihood his letters would be intercepted by the Germans, so he'd been careful not to say anything that would incriminate either of them or reveal his whereabouts. Had she even received them? Each day without news convinced him that Laura was angry with him for running away without her, as well she might have. So he kept on, burying himself in useful work for Dick who let him stay at his woodland house, though it wasn't where he wanted to be.

After one long day spent driving Berkenhout evacuees to new temporary places of safety, Wouter broached the subject of returning home to Kampenveld.

'You'd be better off staying here for the time being,' warned Dick. 'Kampenveld is swarming with Nazis. Some of the big houses on the outskirts have been commandeered for their officers and they've taken over the primary school as their base. So much for it all being over. I had a feeling that all the excitement and dancing in the streets was premature. All of us stupidly imagining the *moffen* were giving up and going back home. God, what a mistake it was to believe the Allies were on the verge of freeing us,' he said with a shake of his head.

'Do you believe this can really go on any longer? It's been nearly five years, for God's sake,' said Wouter, tired out with it all.

'When I believed we had a chance of defying them, that's what gave me hope and optimism to carry on. But now that Berkenhout's gone and all the people we were helping are scattered... well, I don't know what to believe anymore.'

Wouter had never seen Dick talk like this and it shocked him. Dick had always been so upbeat, but if he was losing faith now, surely so close to the end of hostilities, Wouter knew it was right for him to leave.

'I don't know either, but I must return home and do what I can to support my parents,' said Wouter. 'I'm sorry, Dick, but I've done everything I can here.' He hesitated as he dwelt on the real reason for wanting to leave.

'It's Laura, isn't it?' said Dick, as if reading his mind. 'I'm so sorry I can't do more to help.'

Overwhelmed by all Dick had done for him, Wouter grabbed Dick's hands and held them between his own. 'You're a good man, Dick, and I know you couldn't have done more. But if there's even the smallest chance of finding Laura, I have to leave now.'

The reception he received from his father was not one he'd been expecting. Still fearful that he might run into a German or someone who bore him a grudge, Wouter arrived late one evening and crept round to the back of the house. Knocking gently on the windowpane, he waited. On hearing his father's low hesitant voice he replied in as loud a whisper as he dared. He could discern the shape of his father through the frosted glass as he unlocked the door.

'Come in quickly.' His father, greyer and smaller than the last time Wouter had seen him, ushered him through the open door before locking it again. He looked his son up and down. 'So, what made you return?'

'You must have heard that Berkenhout's over. Aren't you pleased to see me?' Under his father's gaze, Wouter looked at his feet, just like when he was a boy and was being reprimanded for some misdemeanour or other.

They were interrupted by Wouter's mother who came hurrying from the kitchen at the sound of her son's voice. 'Wouter! You're safe!' she cried, hugging him with all her might. 'But you look so thin and you need a haircut.' She tugged at his hair, which fell untidily over his face. Her own face was damp with tears. 'Come and sit down and I'll find you something to eat. You must be starving.'

She hurried away to prepare some food, leaving Wouter and his father awkwardly facing each other. His father was the first to speak and what he said came as a shock. 'The *moffen* came knocking not long after you left and took me away for questioning. I said nothing, of course. They let me go, but the raids never stopped. Every few weeks they come and turn the place upside down. What do you think of that?' He furrowed his brow in anguish, but his tone was one of defeat.

'I... I heard. Someone got a message through to me just before Berkenhout was ambushed. I wanted to come immediately but have been on the run ever since.' He stared at his father, who didn't answer, merely nodding his head. Wouter was struck by an impulse to hug him. But he didn't. That wasn't the kind of thing they did. Instead, he remembered why he'd come and asked if he could stay, at least for a night or two.

'It's not possible, can't you see that?' said his father, narrowing his eyes in what seemed like irritation.

Wouter closed his own as he tried to calm himself before speaking. 'I don't have much alternative, Father. I can no longer be an *onderduiker*. Since Berkenhout was taken, there aren't enough safe hiding places for everyone. The Jews must be given first choice.'

'But what if they find out you're back? There'll be no second chance for me and they'll probably take your mother this time too.'

'I'm sorry, I really am, but what do you expect me to do? Hide out in the woods in some cold and dilapidated barn crammed in with a whole load of others? Because that's what I did after I fled Berkenhout. It's finished. It's not safe to be anywhere in those woods while the Germans are still sniffing around in there. And if they find me, do you honestly believe they'll show me any mercy?' He spoke these last words force-fully, but then immediately regretted them, knowing he was the cause of all this trouble. How tired and old his father looked, the price of worrying about his only son.

'Sit down, son, and tell me about it.' His father spoke in a gruff voice as he led the way into the small front room, bending down to pick up a book from his armchair.

'It's fine, I'll sit over here,' said Wouter, taking a less comfortable seat across from his father's chair.

His father went to the old oak sideboard and brought out the remains of some *jenever* and two small glasses. Without asking, he handed Wouter one. '*Proost*,' he said, chinking glasses. 'It's the last of the *jenever*, I'm afraid. There's been none in the shops so I've been holding on to this for... well, just in case.'

'*Proost*,' said Wouter, enjoying the burning sensation as he swallowed the fiery liquid. 'It's good to be home.' In that moment, he meant it.

Wouter noticed his father's eyes were shining as he recounted his escape and the difficulties of the past days and weeks. Somewhat guiltily, he omitted to tell him how his only thoughts when he escaped were for his own safety. He also decided to hold back saying anything about Laura, realising he hadn't had an opportunity to tell them it was over between him and Francine. 'Everyone panicked when the shots started. We blindly ran towards the escape route into the forest before the *moffen* realised what was happening. But they kept on firing and the noise was so deafening that it seemed as if they were right behind us.' We... us... he'd said. How could he admit he'd been alone? Wouter took another sip of *jenever* to calm his stomach that had gone tight again. It was with a sense of relief that he looked up to see his mother come into the room and place a bowl of steaming soup on the low table in front of him. He smiled up at her and immediately tucked in. The *jenever* made him realise how ravenous he was and he wolfed down his food, causing his mother more worry that he was near starving. Wouter assured her he'd been well looked after by Dick. 'It's being home that's brought my appetite back, Mum,' he lied through a mouthful of bread.

His father cleared his throat as he prepared to speak. 'Like I said, it's not safe for you here.'

'What are you saying, Len? Turn your own son out?' Wouter's mother said in a shocked voice. Wouter kept quiet, relieved his mother was on his side.

'You know we discussed this. We agreed it would be bad for all of us if Wouter came home while there was still a threat.'

'After all he's been through, do you still believe that?'

Wouter stood up to leave. His mother tried to make him sit down. 'Don't listen to your father. He doesn't mean it...'

'I do. Now, just listen.' His father raised his voice almost to a shout and Wouter sat back down. 'It's not that I want to throw you out. Wait, I have something.' He went over to the bureau and rummaged among some papers till he found what he was looking for. Meanwhile Wouter sat silently with his mother who gripped his hand. When he held out the letter Wouter saw how his hand was shaking. The envelope was addressed to Wouter.

'I held on to it for you,' his father said.

Wouter tugged the sheet of paper from the envelope, which had been opened, presumably by his father. It was dated three months previously and was from his friend, Tim. The hand-writing was a scrawl as if he'd had to finish it quickly, making it hard to make out the words in places. When Wouter finished reading, he folded it back in two and replaced it in the envelope. His face had gone pale.

'Is that what you want to happen to you? Now, do you see?' His father stood looming over him.

'Pa, you had no right to open my post and read it. And jump to all your pessimistic conclusions.' Wouter took to his feet again, ready to leave. 'Tim made his choices and he's suffered for it. He signed up to work in a car factory. How were any of us to know he intended to join the Waffen SS all along? Surely you know me well enough that I'd never ever do such a thing.' Wouter's eyes blazed at the idea that his father could even consider such a notion.

'Can't you see what this is about? Tim must have tipped off the *moffen* about you and it's why they came searching for you.'

'No, I don't believe he'd do that. I'm his best friend, for God's sake.'

'Wouter, listen,' said his father, blocking Wouter's exit to the door. 'I've tried to protect you with my silence but I don't know how much more I can take. Can't you see I want to help you? Now, please. Stay a while so we can discuss this rationally.'

'No, it's best for all of us that I go.' Wouter's mind was in turmoil with images of Tim reporting Wouter to the police, Nazi sympathisers, who could come crashing into his home and accuse his parents of concealing him. He had to get away, not only for his own sake but to save his parents.

'Please, Wouter. Your father's upset. He doesn't mean it,' pleaded his mother, clinging to his arm. 'The attic, you can stay in the attic tonight till we can work something out. Where will you go if you leave now?'

'Back to Dick's or to Else. Anyone who's prepared to help me.' The words came out more harshly than he meant them to and he knew they would sting his mother. He didn't want to hurt her; he had no choice but to leave.

He strode to the back door, but his father halted him with a hand to his shoulder. Before Wouter could argue, there came a loud drumming on the front door and shouts of '*Aufmachen!*' For a moment, the three of them stood rigid as the German voices grew more insistent they open up. Wouter mouthed to his father to get the key, which hung on a hook beside the door. Snatching it, he rattled the lock open. With a quick glance at his parents, he slipped out into the darkness.

NINE

LAURA

Last night, I heard soft voices from the kitchen. Perhaps I shouldn't have, but I crept up the stairs and put my ear against the cellar door. Mevrouw Schaft was talking to Pia. I couldn't hear everything, but what I heard was enough. She'd only taken me and the boys as a favour to Dick Foppen, who was a friend of the family. It wasn't meant to be for this long. From the tone of her voice I could tell she was too frightened to carry on. The worst of it was I could hear Pia agreeing with her, and I thought she was my friend.

How stupid of me not to realise that Mevrouw Schaft wants to get rid of me. And after all these weeks of comparative normality. I don't doubt her kindness, but the strain of hiding two children and me has clearly got to her. I realise now that the signs were already there. Her nerviness whenever there's a knock at the door and the way she avoids my questions when I ask her how long I can remain here.

I lie awake, wishing I was back at Berkenhout among my real friends. Would I ever see Sofie again – did she even survive? And Karl, poor Karl. I prayed she hadn't seen him being gunned down and gone to save him. But there's been so little news that now I fear the worst. I squeeze my eyes shut and try to blank out the screams and thump as Karl hit the ground. Did no one hear them coming? How can it have happened so fast?

It's my turn now. I'm to leave at daybreak and no one will tell me where I'm going or how. All I know is that I'll be one of a group, mainly from Berkenhout. Where we'll be staying is anyone's guess. It makes me feel like a piece of cargo shunted around without any thought as to what I might want.

As soon as I learn the others are from Berkenhout, my heart jumps. Could Wouter be one of them? I don't think it's possible as I'd surely have had news from him by now. But what if he is? I start to tremble inside. What could I possibly say to him, and in front of all the others? This wasn't how it was meant to be.

I've tried so often to make sense of my escape. I ran and left everyone I loved behind because I had no choice. That wasn't the case as far as Wouter was concerned. He could have come to me but chose to put the safety of others first. But I can't help believing it's because of the argument we'd had that morning. I should never have nagged him but couldn't bear his dark mood. I thought we were happy but it was like he didn't want to be with me. So I stormed off in a strop, I admit, fully intending to make it up to him later. Only there wasn't any later and now I fear it is too late.

All I know is if he turns up now, I'll forgive him for everything.

TEN

WOUTER

Wouter sucked in the cool night air, damp with the smell of autumn. From the street, he could hear German voices, shouting, laughing, thumping on doors, clearly enjoying their nocturnal entertainment. Wouter felt strangely safe out here in the cold, perhaps a legacy of his time spent at Berkenhout hiding out in the woods. For a moment, he hesitated, worried for his parents having to endure another nightly raid, but he knew he couldn't be of any help. Quite the contrary, he justified to himself, as he felt his way along the fence for the panel he knew opened onto next door's garden. Finding the one he wanted, he pushed gently and the pretend door made a slight squeak. Looking round to see he wasn't being followed, he risked creaking it open and was careful to put it back in place behind him. A cat slunk past, its belly close to the ground as it stalked something in the bushes. It leaped away as Wouter crept across the grass towards the next fence. This opening was easy to find, as the wood hung slightly loose and buckled outwards. Once through, he blew out a sigh. No signs of life other than a rustling at ground level in the flowerbed, suggesting a mouse or rat. Wouter shuddered, but kept on. Two more gardens, then a gap in the hedge onto a path that led away from the houses. He just hoped there'd be no one in wait when he got there.

Glancing back at the row of houses, hardly visible with their blacked-out windows, he was satisfied he was on his own. He hadn't formulated a plan but knew he needed to put some distance between himself and the marauding Germans, their voices still just about audible from the street. The gap he was searching for was more overgrown than he remembered but he managed to squeeze through, catching his sleeve on twigs and scratching his hand in the process. On the other side, as he staggered slightly to his feet and brushed the dirt from his trousers, he froze. The noise he heard couldn't be an animal, but a person. He shrank back along the hedge, but it was too late. A dark shape rushed at him, knocking him to the ground and causing him to shout out loud.

'Shut up,' hissed a voice. A gloved hand clamped Wouter's mouth. In shock, he shook his head violently in a bid to gasp for air. It was then he realised he knew that voice. Struggling even harder and with a huge effort he pushed the man over.

'What the hell do you think you're doing?' he panted as he held his rival down by his shoulders.

'Let go, you idiot. How was I to know it was you?'

Wouter released his grip and watched as Klaus rolled over onto all fours.

'What are you doing here?' wheezed Wouter, attempting to catch his breath.

'What are *you* doing here?' gasped Klaus with a furious sideways glance.

Wouter hesitated. He was reluctant to say this was where he lived, in case Klaus expected a free bed for the night, something that was definitely not going to happen now or any time soon.

'Getting away from that lot.' He jerked his thumb in the direction of his parents' street. 'Isn't that what you're doing?'

Klaus cocked his ear as if he'd only just noticed the commotion. 'A raid,' he said in a matter-of-fact voice. 'We'd better get out of here. Are you coming?' He turned to Wouter, who was hesitating as he weighed up his options. Get entangled with Klaus again after what happened last time, or return home? Neither was appealing. But maybe, with his gift of the gab, Klaus had contacts and could find them a place to hide out. Wouter's main concern now was finding somewhere to sleep for the night.

'It's a while since I stayed with old Kappen, so I'm sure he won't mind if I turn up again. I'm not sure about you, though.' Klaus looked Wouter up and down with a grin.

Kappen? That was a name Wouter knew. He hadn't seen his old violin teacher for at least ten years, nor given him even a passing thought. Wouter had been a great disappointment, never taking his lessons or practice seriously despite Mr Kappen's constant encouragement. Both of them knew Wouter wasn't cut out for the violin and he only kept on at his father's insistence. And after failing his exam for the second time, he was elated to be allowed to give it up. It was the look of disappointment on his teacher's face he remembered now. He hoped he wouldn't recognise him after all this time.

At first he didn't. Nor did he seem pleased to see Klaus, who stepped inside the door before Mr Kappen had a chance to shut it. Wouter followed him in and greeted Mr Kappen while trying not to catch his eye.

'My friend and I were on our way to stay with my uncle in the centre when we heard there was a raid on. We had to get away, I'm sure you understand. As you're the only other person I know I can trust in Kampenveld, we were hoping we could stay just for tonight,' said Klaus, with a winning smile.

'Well, I'm not sure it's possible,' began Mr Kappen, looking quickly over his shoulder. 'My wife's not well...'

'We'd be no trouble at all and don't even need to come into the house,' said Klaus.

Mr Kappen then seemed to notice Wouter and his expression changed. 'Why, hello, isn't it young Wouter Brand? What are you doing with this troublemaker?'

Wouter shrugged and stretched out his hand in greeting. 'It's very good to see you, Mr Kappen. I'm sorry for the intrusion.'

'Always so polite,' said Mr Kappen slowly, shaking his hand warmly. 'But you live just two streets away. Surely you can't be wanting a bed for the night?'

Wouter caught Klaus's eye. He didn't look pleased.

'It's a bit complicated, but it's not safe to stay at home at the moment. Like Klaus said, if you'd be so kind to let us stay just for tonight, we'll be gone in the morning. We won't be any trouble.'

'Well, for old time's sake I'll let you stay. But mind, it can only be for tonight. As I say, my wife's poorly and mustn't have the anxiety of unexpected visitors. It was the news of her brother's arrest that sent her to her bed. The poor man is blameless, we all know that, so why the *moffen* picked on him, I don't think we'll ever know.' The old man's shoulders drooped as he spoke quietly of his wife. 'I suppose we're fortunate we haven't had the *moffen* calling round here. They don't seem to bother with our street, but no one's safe, are they? I hope you see now why I don't want her to suffer any more upset.'

Wouter nodded, slightly shamefaced. This was not the lively, upright man with a booming voice that Wouter remembered from his school days. The teacher, who'd tried so hard with jokes and encouragement, but failed to engage with his reluctant pupil who imagined he had better things to do than scrape away at the violin handed on to him by his father, a passable player in his youth. Wouter tried to work out how old his teacher must be. Surely no more than fifty, but he gave a much older impression as he shuffled to the back door and fumbled with the key in the lock. Wouter really had no desire to put his old teacher to any trouble and was about to say something when Klaus gave him a warning look.

'Leave it,' he mouthed, and roughly pulled him back by his sleeve.

Oblivious to the tension between the two young men, Mr Kappen led the way along the path to the summer house at the far end of the garden. It was an old wooden building and the front was almost entirely covered by some kind of creeper. It was certainly well hidden from any prying eyes. Inside, Mr Kappen lit an oil lamp, which cast soft shadows across a surprisingly tidy room. There were two camp beds, neatly made up as if visitors were expected. In one corner was an old trunk with labels stuck all over, evidence that someone had spent time travelling abroad. The walls were covered in paintings. Wouter went over to look at one of a mountain scene. 'Did you paint this?'

'A lifetime ago,' said Mr Kappen with a sigh. 'I haven't painted since before the war. Now, I hope this will be comfortable enough for you. Don't come to the house in the morning. I'll come and fetch you.' He shut the door behind him with a quiet click.

ELEVEN

WOUTER

'Easy, wasn't it?' said Klaus, flopping onto one of the beds. 'This is certainly the best place I've stayed in for a while. Play our cards right and he'll let us stay here.'

Wouter stood with his back to Klaus, pretending to examine another of the paintings. He thought of Mr Kappen, trudging back to the house, bowed down with worry over his wife and the prospect of a raid. Then the image of his own parents came into his head, also racked with worry. 'Didn't you hear what he said? It would be wrong to push his hospitality. I can't keep on like this, fleeing from house to house. I'm tired out with it all. It just seems such a cowardly thing to do. Here we are, quite safe with no responsibilities, while they get raided, searched, questioned, even arrested. It's not right.'

'So what do you suggest? Sit around and wait your turn to get hauled off? There's no alternative. You know that. You may as well go and hand yourself over and get shot. That's what keeps me going. I've been on the run for six months now and it'd be impossible to go back to my old life.'

'Well, you're obviously harder than me.'

'What's stopping you from going home? Or don't your parents want you there?'

'I could ask you the same question.' Wouter's eyes blazed.

Klaus, who had propped himself up for this exchange, slumped back on the bed. It was as if all the air had been let out of him.

'What?' said Wouter, still angry.

'Six months ago, my father was called up to go and work over the border. He's a doctor and didn't have any choice. My mother told me to leave home, maybe go and help with the Resistance. She managed to get to Belgium where her sister lives. So you see, there is no family for me to go back to.' Klaus spoke staring blankly at the ceiling.

Wouter sat down on the edge of his bed, gripping his hands together. 'Have you had news from either of them?'

'Pa wrote to my uncle and told him he had a chest infection he couldn't shake off. Of course he couldn't say too much in that letter as there was a strong chance the *moffen* would open it. But it was obvious they've been working him hard. Way too hard. And my mother... well, I haven't heard from her, which I suppose must be good in a way.' He sighed.

'And your uncle, can't he help you?'

Klaus made a scoffing sound. 'He's got his own problems. Invalid, he is. Weak heart. But at least they don't bother him. I only turn up when I've run out of places to hide.' Klaus propped himself up again onto his elbow. 'Go on, tell me about your family.'

'They keep getting raided. My pa reckons it's because someone's told them about me. I can't see how, because I left long before the raids became a regular thing. They march in, turn the house upside down looking for me and threaten Pa and Ma with arrest. I only heard it was happening just before Berkenhout got ambushed. This young lad, Jan, he used to deliver food and stuff and came one day with a letter from a family friend back home. She wrote that my parents were finding it hard to cope with the raids and that she feared for their health. It unnerved me and I knew I had to return and do something to help. But before I got a chance, Berkenhout was attacked and I knew I had to get out fast. You know the rest, because that's when I ran into you.' Wouter took shallow breaths before continuing. 'So when I turned up tonight, I was the last person my parents wanted to see. At least, that's the impression I got from Pa. Ma would have me back like a shot. So, it doesn't look good for either of us, does it?'

Klaus was right, it was the most comfortable place they'd stayed in for some time, even better than Foppen's woodland house, where Wouter had been forced to sleep on the floor of the living room along with several others. By comparison, this place seemed like a hotel with its neatly made-up beds. He'd forgotten what it was like to lie down on a bed with a mattress covered in sheets and blankets. Gratefully, he fell into a deep sleep, the best he'd had in months.

Early next morning, he woke with a start to a soft rap on the door. The shock had both men leaping out of bed, ready to make a run for it.

'Oh, thank God, it's you,' said Wouter, his heart pounding. 'I thought we were done for.'

'I'm sorry, I didn't mean to disturb you.' Mr Kappen smiled as he entered the room. 'But I can assure you the coast is clear. You needn't worry about sudden attacks this early. The *moffen* are lazy layabouts. Never see them on the streets till midday at the earliest. Now, if you're quite wide awake, I've come to invite you up to the house for some breakfast. I realised I didn't offer you anything last night and it was most remiss of me.'

The anxious, bent old man from the night before had vanished. The cheerful man who stood before them was more like the teacher Wouter remembered from his school days. Wouter guessed his wife must have spent a better night. Either that, or perhaps having company had improved his mood.

It was warm as they left the summer house. An early autumn day with a soft breeze rustling the remaining dry leaves high up in the trees. It was perfectly quiet, hard to believe that this was a country at war and in constant fear of the enemy. More than four years of occupation. Surely it had to be over soon?

As they sat at Mr Kappen's kitchen table, chatting, sipping tea and eating bread and jam, Wouter felt happier and more relaxed than he had in months. His anger at Klaus for walking off and abandoning him in the woods had dissipated now he'd heard his story, which wasn't so different from his own. How many young men were hiding in attics, cellars, outhouses, coal bunkers because they refused to bow down to the Germans? He used to believe it was a proper act of defiance, a way of beating the Germans at their own game, but now he wasn't so sure. After months of hiding and fleeing, he felt as if he'd achieved nothing. It was more like cowardice than defiance.

But there was worse to come. Mr Kappen was quiet as the two men described life on the run. Once they'd finished he announced that Berkenhout had been burnt down.

'When did this happen?' said Wouter, white-faced. Had Dick Foppen known and not told him? It seemed unlikely.

'The news came from Henk Hauer just yesterday. He was on his way to Kampenveld when he smelled smoke and went to investigate. When he got to Berkenhout, all that was left were the smouldering remains. A petrol can kicked into the bushes was enough evidence. We can only assume the Germans were so angry this secret had been going on right under their noses, that they went mad and tried to eradicate all signs of it. It shows you what they're capable of and that they have no intention of stopping now.'

Henk Hauer. Wouter had always been wary of the forester who had been put in charge of the building of the huts. He'd been seen having dealings with Germans but, when questioned by the organisers of the village, always denied it. Everyone knew he had a bigger stash of *jenever* than anyone else and he was the man who persuaded Dick Foppen to allow that German defector, Karl, into the camp. It was hard to know where his loyalties lay.

'Do you believe his story? I never did trust him,' said Wouter, his expression hardening. He could just imagine Henk, with a smirk on his face, passing information in exchange for another case of *jenever* with absolutely no thought for the community he'd protected for so long and now callously discarded. But was Henk even capable of being complicit in this latest awful deed? As unlikely as it seemed, the thought enraged him.

'Why wouldn't I?' said Mr Kappen, looking surprised. 'Henk has no reason to betray the village he's been instrumental in building up and protecting. There was always a strong chance it would be discovered and it was a miracle it lasted as long as it did. No, Henk's a bit of a dark horse. But that doesn't make him bad.'

Mr Kappen continued to tell them other news. 'We should consider ourselves fortunate we haven't got it as bad as those living in the west of Holland. The Germans there are ruthlessly stealing all the food. Everything. There's virtually nothing left and people are starving. There are meant to be daily rations for everyone but the coupons are worthless. No food, no rations. They've taken the lot. We can count ourselves lucky that we produce enough to survive, but if it carries on, they'll take ours as well.'

The three of them stared at the crumbs of bread on their plates as if it might be the last food they would ever see. Wouter let out an exasperated sigh, pushed his plate aside and stood up.

'Mr Kappen, you must look after your wife and yourself. It's not right that we're receiving your hospitality at such a desperate time.'

The old man raised his hand as if he couldn't bear to hear what Wouter might say next. 'No, no, my dear boy. You mustn't think that. You've no idea what a tonic it's been to meet you again and to have the company. Will you please consider staying for a while longer?'

Klaus, who had been quiet during this exchange, cleared his throat. 'Of course, what Wouter means is that we will do all we can to help you and your wife in exchange for a bed. I'm sure it can't be for long, can it?'

Wouter turned his head away, reluctant to engage further in conversation. It dawned on him that staying with Kappen wasn't a solution, for him at least, after his ill-fated visit to his parents. How could he go into hiding only two streets away knowing they were in danger because of him? He'd always be at risk of being caught and the truth was it didn't bring him any closer to Laura. This life spent ducking and diving from the enemy had to stop. He needed to take control.

TWELVE

ELSE

It wasn't the quantity of supplies that worried her, as she pored over the accounts. She no longer had to ask. Every morning crates of vegetables and neatly packed boxes of flour, sugar, eggs, dried fruit, beans, tea and ersatz coffee would appear as if by magic in the rundown shed behind a large sycamore tree at the back of her long garden. One morning, the door appeared stuck and she realised it was blocked by a stack of crates yet to be distributed. As she gazed at the abundance of food before her, she felt a pang for the thousands of people in the west of Holland left to starve. The winter had arrived suddenly with cold air sweeping in from the east, freezing over the canals and turning the ground rock hard. Else's own sister and family in Delft were just about coping thanks to her food parcels, but it was dangerous work getting them delivered. Else relied heavily on her underground contacts to get the parcels through without a hitch. Once the packets had passed through Gerrit's hands and on to Oscar and his contacts in Utrecht, she had to hope and pray they would reach her sister without being intercepted. They only had to fall into the wrong hands for her role in the Resistance to be exposed.

Since Berkenhout had been broken up, people were scattered across the Veluwe, hidden in farm buildings and rural houses, many cramped into every available attic space and cellar. Most were provided for by the families hiding them, but Else still had to make sure these clusters of kind people didn't go short. The burden had increased with every additional person who needed her help.

At the click of the gate, Else paused, pen in hand, and looked up from her ledger. These days, she'd become more wary about covering her tracks. The Germans were swarming the village, determined to expose the network that had allowed Berkenhout to survive as long as it had. Days ago, she'd received news that they'd stormed Berkenhout and set fire to the abandoned huts, a futile act in itself but intended to send a strong message to show who was boss. Now was not the time for weakness.

She was shaken from her thoughts by the appearance of two young men who arrived with a gust of bitterly cold air. First one removed his hat, followed by the other.

'Wouter! You're safe!' Else's chair fell backwards as she recognised him. 'And who is this?'

'Klaus, *mevrouw*. We're friends.' Klaus bowed his head.

Else noticed Wouter purse his lips as if about to say something, but he decided better of it.

Another click of the gate announced the arrival of Liesbeth, who ran straight to Wouter and threw her arms round his neck. 'I thought it was you. Where have you been all this time? We've been so worried.'

Wouter couldn't keep the smile off his face as he took her hands and held her at arm's length. 'I've been fine. Well looked after, in fact, but I'm back now and hope to be of some use,' he said, with a hopeful glance at Else.

'You've turned up just at the right time. I need all the help I can get,' she said, pleased to find him safe and well. Dick had often told her what an asset Wouter had been to the Berkenhout community. He'd taken his role seriously, keeping himself apart. His growing friendship with Laura had been a source of speculation, because he'd made it known he had a fiancée on the outside, not that Else minded. People should be allowed to fall in love, whatever the circumstances.

'I don't know if you've heard, but the *moffen* have destroyed Berkenhout,' she said with a heavy sigh.

Wouter nodded briefly and gazed at her, waiting for her to say more.

'It's a terrible thing. They'll stop at nothing and it seems they're determined to flush out anyone who escaped or who's been involved.'

'But that also means you. Aren't you worried?' asked Wouter.

'It's too late for that. Over twenty families depend on our network. I can't let them all down.' She waved her hand to stop the conversation. 'Would you put on the coffee?' she asked Liesbeth. Warming themselves round the *kachel* and exchanging stories would be a comforting reminder of happier times and right now that was all she wanted. She watched as Wouter went over to help Liesbeth ostensibly prepare the coffee, while chatting quietly. Else eased herself back in her big armchair and closed her eyes, letting her mind slip back to the times when she and Liesbeth used to visit Berkenhout with baskets of fresh cakes and gossip. Wouter always sat next to Laura in the semicircle for their weekly gatherings. On Laura's other side was Liesbeth's best friend, Sofie, who to start with would be indignant at some injustice or other, but she usually calmed down once she had a slice of apple cake inside her. A smile lifted Else's lips at the memory. Then, as if Wouter could read her thoughts, he placed a cup in her hands and asked softly if she knew anything of Laura's whereabouts.

'I'm sorry, I don't have any news, but it's likely she managed to get out, probably on a truck owned by a local farmer. He drove several families to relatives of his near Zwolle,' she said. 'It's the most likely explanation.'

'But if she didn't escape, is there a chance the Germans caught her?' Wouter spoke with a hoarseness to his voice.

She sensed he was unwilling to believe her theory. 'Anything's possible, but you mustn't think that. I have de Boer's address somewhere. Perhaps you can go and visit him,' said Else, reaching for his hand.

All the while, Klaus had been sitting quietly, sipping his coffee. Else wondered what part he had to play. She'd come across his type before, keen to keep out of the clutches of the Germans but not so keen to take an active part in undermining them. She hoped he wasn't just a hanger-on. But if he showed commitment to hard work, she could use the extra pair of hands.

The purpose of Wouter and Klaus's visit soon became clear – a place to stay out of sight of the Germans in exchange for work. It was an arrangement that had worked well at Berkenhout's peak. Young people came and went all the time, some staying days, others weeks. The majority were too young to have bothered the Germans and were excited to lend a hand helping with the war effort. Liesbeth was the only one to stay on, providing Else with much more than a capable pair of hands. Since her father had taken up with their housekeeper, Liesbeth treated Else's house like home. The two had grown close and Else dreaded the moment when Liesbeth decided to move on. At seventeen, that time must surely come soon. Else knew only too well that Liesbeth's situation at home was another example of the stress of war breaking up families and causing people to behave differently to normal.

'It would help if you can drive,' said Else, weighing up how these two strapping young men could best be put to work.

'Deliveries have become a bit of a nightmare now that we're supplying families across the area. Even more so since Henk is no longer driving as much.'

'I thought he was your main courier. What's happened?' said Wouter, stiffening slightly.

'On the day of the raid, he hurt his ankle leading the Bartfeld family to safety,' said Else. 'But he's made of sterner stuff and kept on fleeing. He got quite a few out, children too, which is the main thing. Anyway, he's decided to take a step back from deliveries, so I'd be grateful for the help. My van's a bit battered, but that won't be a problem, will it?'

'Of course not. I haven't done much driving but I'm sure I can pick it up,' said Klaus, perking up at Else's offer.

'I've been driving the post van since I was eighteen. And I know how to get it started if it breaks down,' said Wouter.

Else smiled at Wouter's obvious irritation at being upstaged by Klaus. 'That's settled. I'm putting you, Klaus, in charge of sorting deliveries and Wouter can do the driving. Now, I need to work out who needs what or else these poor people won't get anything tomorrow. Liesbeth, can you show the boys where they'll be sleeping? Don't forget to tell them the rules. We can't afford to be found out now.'

THIRTEEN

LAURA

I nearly didn't make it on the last journey out of Kampenveld. As I'm getting ready to leave, Mevrouw Schaft comes down to the cellar, her arms piled high with more of Pia's cast-offs. Two thick jumpers, woollen stockings and the kind of frumpy skirt I'd never dream of wearing. I'm about to open my mouth to object.

'Please, do take these. You'll need them. It's turning cold with a bitter easterly wind.' She puts the pile down on the bed next to the canvas bag she's also given me. I can see they won't fit in. 'You could put the sweaters on. You will thank me for it,' she says with a weak smile.

'Thank you for all you've done, *mevrouw*.' My voice catches as I'm suddenly overcome by her generosity. In that moment I believe she really does want the best for me.

We laugh together as I tug the second sweater over my head and fail to find the armholes. I feel her hands guide my own and it takes me back to when I was little and my mother used to do the same for me. When my head emerges, I pretend my tears are of laughter.

I suppose I'm not surprised to see Henk's van draw up, as

he's the only one the Germans ignore round here. But I hadn't expected to see him after he'd been so keen to move us on. He doesn't say much as he climbs out and stumbles slightly and winces. His ankle must still be troubling him. He takes my bag and swings it into the back. All he says is that I'll be going to a safer place. He catches my eye only briefly and looks away. I'm about to ask him where I'll be going, but he's already shutting the van door on me. Among the blankets I can just make out the shape of a young man. I say hello and when he replies I wonder if he's German, so decide to keep myself to myself. I'm grateful our journey isn't too far. Another trip bumping over ruts would simply be too much.

But then to my dismay I discover I'm to be loaded onto a trailer pulled by a tractor. There must be ten others packed in under the tarpaulin. How can I be expected to crawl in under that? I turn to confront Henk but he is back in his van and already driving away.

The farmer's face is damp with sweat even though it's freezing out here. His voice is panicky and I have a horrible feeling of dread. Did Henk know something and didn't want to say? If I get in there, how do I know the farmer's not a sympathiser and won't hand us straight over to the Germans? I look nervously at the man I've been travelling with, but he looks as scared as me. I stand back, hugging my bag, as he clambers aboard.

The farmer shouts at me, 'Quick! Get in. There's no time to lose.' He holds out his hand and I accept the gesture as one of kindness. I have no choice but to go. I squeeze in between two women who turn their faces away from me and lie down with my bag still clutched to my body.

FOURTEEN

WOUTER

Wouter walked slowly round the van, kicking each of the tyres and examining the windscreen for chips and cracks. He peered at the faded paintwork for any signs of rust. He knew he couldn't be too fussy, but it was a miracle the vehicle was still serviceable. The tyres were so patched up it was hard to see any of the original rubber. He was doubtful they'd make it over the unmade-up roads, but Else assured him that she'd never had any trouble. The trick, she'd told him, was to take it gently over the bumps and tree roots. Besides, a rickety old van was unlikely to attract the attention of any interfering Germans.

A bitter wind blew as Wouter scraped the overnight frost from the windscreen. Klaus loaded up the back with the crates and slammed the doors shut before jumping into the passenger seat.

'Great, just what we need,' said Wouter, wiping away a snowflake that landed on his cheek. First, the worry over the roadworthiness of the van and now the possibility that they'd be stranded in the woods.

'It doesn't look as if it'll amount to much. Let's go,' said Klaus, blowing onto his hands.

Their first delivery was to a farm not far from Berkenhout. Wouter had been mulling over whether to go and see the burnt-out village for himself but it would mean leaving the van and walking the last half mile into dense woods. A parked or abandoned van in the middle of nowhere would itself arouse suspicion, especially if found to be full of supplies.

Wouter sat behind the wheel and turned the ignition. It took several attempts but when it fired both men looked at each other and grinned in relief.

The sky was still dark. At least the roads were empty of any vehicles. It had been Else's idea to leave early to avoid suspicion. She said he must not turn on his headlights under any circumstance. Gradually, the grey dawn cast a thin light and there were only a few snow flurries. But once they got to the start of the woods under the thick canopy of the tall trees, it grew darker and became heavy going. Even though they did not pass a soul, Wouter dared not turn on his headlights. The track was uneven and he was unable to prevent the van from bouncing over the tree roots.

'Can't you go a bit slower?' said Klaus, jolting awake after the van rattled over a particularly large bump.

'Sorry, I didn't see that one,' said Wouter, peering at the road.

'You should've let me drive,' grumbled Klaus, holding on to the passenger door in an exaggerated fashion.

Wouter ignored him as he concentrated on following Else's directions. Soon, Klaus's head was lolling against the door until the next thud jerked him awake. A fork in the road loomed up ahead and Wouter recognised the house with the pump out front where he and others from Berkenhout had walked after dark each day to fetch water. He drew the van to a halt by the side of the unmade-up road and looked over at Klaus.

'Stay here a moment. I'm just going to see if an old friend of mine still lives here.'

'What if the *moffen* turn up?' said Klaus, rubbing his eyes and peering down the track.

'I'm only going to be a couple of minutes.'

The early morning light filtered through the trees as Wouter sprinted up the overgrown path and knocked on the door. 'Hello? Mr Hendrik? Are you there?' He cocked his ear and picked up the sound of shuffling steps approaching the door. It opened a crack.

'Who is it?' came a croaky voice.

'It's me, Wouter, Remember me? From Berkenhout? I was passing and wanted to see how you are.'

The door opened a crack to reveal a shrunken figure with sparse grey hair that stood up in messy clumps from his scalp. The old man fumbled with the belt of his threadbare dressing gown and drew it around himself. Despite his tired appearance, his face lit up as he took Wouter's hand in his own gnarled one. He held on to it as Wouter explained how he was now working for Else.

'And what about you? Have you had any trouble?' asked Wouter.

'Not much, but that's because I've nothing to hide,' said the old man with a sly smile. 'They never did catch anyone at the pump, though it was close on more than one occasion. Then after all that business over at Berkenhout, they were banging on my door all hours of the day and night, searching the house and questioning me about my pump, but there's nothing to say.' He tapped the side of his nose knowingly and began to laugh, but it turned into a cough that he was unable to control. He swayed a little before steadying himself against the door frame.

'Have you got anything for that?' Wouter moved forward to help him.

The old man waved Wouter away, but his coughing fit continued until he brought up a few gobbets of phlegm, which he spat onto the bare earth beside the front door. Repelled, Wouter looked away but couldn't help feel sorry for his old acquaintance.

'You be careful,' croaked Mr Hendrik. 'There's still loads of them searching these woods. If they catch you in that' – he waved his hand towards the van – 'you'll stand no chance.'

'I'll be careful. I promise,' said Wouter. 'I'll call again and bring you something for that cough of yours.'

Mr Hendrik turned round and shuffled back into the house with a flap of his hand as if he were ridding himself of an irksome fly.

'He was friendly,' said Klaus as Wouter climbed back into the van. Wouter stared back at the closed door, wondering how the old man managed living out here on his own. He didn't seem to have anyone to look after him, not that it seemed to bother him.

At that moment, they could hear the distant rumble of an engine and two faint spots of light appeared through the trees.

'Come on. Out,' said Wouter on the spur of the moment.

'Are you mad? They're heading straight for us,' shouted Klaus, ducking his head between his knees. Wouter hesitated before deciding to make a dash for it, but it was too late. The distinctive shape of a military vehicle came roaring through the trees, throwing up clouds of dust. It stopped abruptly next to the van and two uniformed soldiers jumped out, each holding a pistol.

'Just get out and don't say a thing. Leave this to me,' whispered Wouter. He stepped out and greeted the soldiers in German.

'*Heil Hitler!*' the soldiers said in unison, each snapping the heels of their shiny knee-length boots to attention.

'*Was machen Sie hier?*' demanded the taller one, who wore a visor cap with the distinctive eagle insignia.

In faltering German, Wouter explained that they were on their way to visit their sick uncle when their van broke down. Would they be so kind as to take a look at the engine? It was a risky thing to do but he couldn't think how else to deflect their attention from searching in the back and discovering enough food for what must seem like half the Veluwe. The two soldiers muttered something between themselves. The one in charge waved his pistol at him to open up the bonnet. While he fiddled with the catch, the other stood pointing his pistol at Klaus. Wouter was preparing what he'd say once they saw there was nothing wrong with the engine, when the crack of a bullet made him jump. He let the bonnet drop back down with a crash. Then Wouter saw Mr Hendrik standing at the door pointing a rifle at the two soldiers.

'Get away from my property,' Mr Hendrik growled in perfect German, and took another shot at the ground by their feet. Wouter heard two clicks as the men trained their pistols on the old man, but he was unfazed and walked toward them. Rubbing his eyes with his free hand, he seemed to recognise them. He let his rifle drop by his side and greeted the two men warmly.

'What are you doing with my two friends here? They've done nothing wrong. Just visiting an old man in need of a bit of company.'

Wouter pieced together what the old man said and could hardly believe it. This wasn't the churlish man who had waved him away in irritation only moments before. Instead, here stood a man at ease with these Germans. Who obviously knew them.

'Herr Hendrik, you mustn't go around firing your rifle like that. You might kill someone,' said the one with the visor. 'But really, are you telling me these men are your friends?' He turned his cold eyes onto Wouter. 'Why didn't you say?' he addressed Wouter in a thick Dutch accent.

'*Ach*, Fritz, leave him alone. Why don't you come in and have a *jenever* with an old man, hmm?'

'Not today,' the German said, pressing his lips into a thin line. He clicked his heels once more and returned with his accomplice to their vehicle. Before getting in, he gave Wouter a disdainful look. 'Don't let us find you here again. Next time there will be consequences.'

Without another word, Wouter and Klaus turned towards their van. It started first time and Wouter fumbled to find the gear so he could get away quickly. He glanced in the mirror and thought he saw one of the soldiers raise his pistol. Not wanting to waste another second, he pushed his foot down on the accelerator and prayed they wouldn't come after them. Only when he was sure they were out of sight did he take a breath.

Klaus burst into laughter and stretched his hands behind his head.

'It's not funny,' said Wouter, still anxious. The soldiers knew the direction they were heading. He now berated himself for not having the presence of mind to mislead them by taking a different turning at the crossroads.

'Did you see the look on his face? I've seen it before. When those *moffen* think they've been wronged they'll do anything to get the upper hand.'

'Come on, stop exaggerating. We didn't exactly do anything,' said Klaus.

'We didn't have to. Thanks to old Hendrik, they didn't check what we were up to. But they knew. I wouldn't put it past them to come looking for us.'

Wouter decided to take a detour, soon losing his bearings when the track almost petered out. With no landmarks or distinctive features to guide them, he drove the van off the track into a small clearing. 'We'll just have to go back the way we came. Let's wait here and hope they get bored and hunt down someone else.'

They got out to stretch their legs. 'Cigarette?' Klaus took two from a pack and handed one to Wouter, who shook his head.

The sun was breaking through the mist hanging in the tree-tops, but the temperature remained icy cold. Wouter tramped up and down to get some feeling back into his feet, while he pondered what to do next. The crazy thing was he knew they were probably only a mile away from their first drop-off point. They had two other outlying farms to reach after that. He glanced at his watch, telling him they'd already been on the road for almost two hours.

'Do you have a girl?' said Klaus all at once, with his back to a tree.

'What?'

'Do you have a girl?' repeated Klaus, sighing out a plume of smoke.

Wouter stared at the ground as he thought about Klaus's question. Francine, his ex-fiancée, had been his last proper girl-friend. Sweet Francine. He'd been fond of her but never loved her. He'd asked her to marry her because it had seemed the right thing to do before going away, but once he'd arrived in Berkenhout he realised it had been a mistake. Meeting Laura only confirmed his feelings about the situation. 'No, not really. There was a girl, but the war screwed it all up,' he said, though he wasn't thinking of Francine. 'I'd be married by now. Probably with a kid on the way,' he said as he forced his thoughts back to his ex-fiancée.

'What happened to her?'

'Francine? She went to live with an aunt in Venlo, I think. I don't actually know. We didn't keep in touch.' Wouter remem-bered how understanding she'd been when he'd told her, though he suspected she was more upset than she'd ever let on.

'Do you miss her?' Klaus asked, sucking on the last of his cigarette and grinding out the glowing tip with his heel.

Guiltily, Wouter realised he'd barely given Francine a thought since the day he'd arrived at Berkenhout. 'No,' he said, looking Klaus in the eye. 'Why do you ask?'

'There was this girl, sister of my best friend at school. She was a year above me. Of course she never gave me a second glance. Anyway, she had a boyfriend, but he was a Nazi sympathiser and signed up with the NSB at the start of the war. I saw my chance and she became my girl for a while, but I always knew she loved him. She never got over his death. He drove a motorbike and skidded off the road in bad weather. Tragic it was. For her.' Klaus walked back onto the road and peered down for any signs of life.

'Do you ever see her?'

Klaus made a scoffing sound.

Wouter took a deep breath. 'There was someone else. I met her in Berkenhout. Laura was always so trusting but I couldn't show my feelings. It wasn't just because of Francine. I'd already been planning to leave home and should never gone to Berkenhout. Then I met Laura, which hit me hard, but I didn't want to hurt her. In my head I had to get out, but in my heart I couldn't bear to leave her behind. And then, when the ambush came, I did leave her behind. I still don't know why. Panic, I suppose. But if I really cared for her, don't you think I would have gone back for her?' He shook his head at his own weakness. 'And now I've no idea if she even made it. For all I know, she was caught and deported God knows where. I've written letters hoping they'll somehow reach her, but without an address, what's the point? It's not as if I can say anything much in case the letters are intercepted and I end up putting us both in danger. Else has this notion she may have managed to get away to Zwolle, but I'm not sure it's possible.'

'Zwolle's not that far away. Perhaps you can go and look for her.'

It was Wouter's turn to scoff. 'What, just turn up and knock on doors and alert everyone to a Jewish woman hiding in their midst?'

But Klaus wasn't deterred. 'I've got a cousin who lives there. She might be able to help. You know, if you don't try, you'll never know.'

FIFTEEN

LAURA

We stop abruptly in front of a grim grey church and the farmer orders us to get out. It's a scramble and I'm fearful for the elderly couple who have been clasping one another silently in one corner. A scrawny man I vaguely recognise clambers down and helps them onto the road. As we huddle together, I look around and take in our sorry group, shivering in the cold, eyes full of fear. I hold my bag against me for comfort. No one wants to make a move, but as the farmer clangs shut the back of the trailer, a man hunched up in a shabby coat with his cap pulled over his ears emerges from the church. It could be so much worse, I think, willing myself to trust this man who nods in our direction. He briefly embraces the farmer who grunts and holds himself stiffly. He seems in a hurry to leave.

The man who has come to greet us introduces himself as Hans. He tells us that he's in charge of making sure we reach our accommodation safely, but that we must stay in the church overnight. It's all been arranged with the pastor who has been busy bringing in bedding and food for our supper. I know I should be grateful, but it's the first anybody has told us anything about this latest move. People are shuffling, murmuring, but I must speak. I fold my arms before taking a deep breath. 'Can you tell us what's going to happen to us?'

He looks surprised and I'm sure he hasn't noticed me standing there. 'I have a list with where each of you will be staying. If you tell me your name, I'll look it up.'

'Laura Wechsler,' I say in a louder voice, then I feel slightly foolish for being the only one to speak up. Perhaps they all know what's going on. Then, one of the women I'd been pressed up against in the trailer gives me a quick smile and pipes up too.

'You can look me up on your list – Bets de Jong.'

We all troop in after him and our voices fill the church. It's as if everyone has woken up and is grumbling. We crowd round Hans and crane to see our names on his list.

The pastor arrives through a back door and we all go quiet at the squeak of his shoes as he approaches us across the cold stone floor.

'Welcome to Zwolle,' he announces, to my surprise.

'This is Zwolle?' I say, emboldened by having spoken earlier. 'Is this where we'll be staying?'

'Why, yes. We have a strong network of families providing shelter for people such as yourselves. So far, no one we've looked after has been discovered by the Germans,' says the pastor, folding his hands in front of him, looking pleased with himself.

'So why do we have to stay in your church?' I ask boldly.

The pastor raises his hand to cover his mouth as he clears his throat. I sense his discomfort. 'There's been a slight delay in finding you all accommodation. It's unusual to have so many arrive at one time. Unfortunately for yourselves, we have to see to the earlier arrivals first. Now, I can assure you it will be perfectly warm and comfortable for you here.'

'And then what happens?' I persist.

Hans shuffles forward, holding up his list. 'It's all in order and you have no need to worry. We'll have you away from here by six in the morning.'

I turn to Bets, who shrugs, and I take that as a sign that we should just put up with it. 'I've got my eye on a place we can rest at the back. Do you want to join me?' she whispers.

We wait patiently in line as the pastor hands each of us a small package of food, two cushions and a blanket. I follow Bets and we settle down with our blankets round our shoulders. After we've eaten the bread, cheese, boiled egg and apple and drunk the lukewarm tea that's handed round, we tell each other our stories. She tells me she's also from Belgium and that makes me glad. Bets lived in Antwerp until the Germans smashed up her father's jewellery shop that had been in his family for generations. Together with her parents, Bets fled to Maastricht where they stayed with relatives until it became too dangerous to stay. Bets' parents sent her on to a close friend in Apeldoorn, saying they would follow on. They never arrived. That was over a year ago and Bets has received no further communication from them. A week ago, the friend, already frail from a long-term illness, announced she could no longer give Bets the security she needed. Bets found herself travelling on the same truck as me after a brief stay with someone who worked for a Resistance group outside Kampenveld.

It's unnerving the way she recounts her journey, laughing quietly in places, smiling. You'd have no idea of how awful it must have been moving from place to place and staying with total strangers. Her smile drops, though, when I tell her about my pain in being wrenched away from my parents and ending up in Berkenhout. I speak in a soft voice so we're not overheard. 'I had no idea what hit me when I arrived in the dead of night. It was so scary being dropped by car in the middle of the woods. We had to walk a mile in the pitch dark. I remember a man and a woman escorting me, lighting the way with torches. The woman – I can't remember her name – held my hand as I kept tripping over tree roots. They called it a village, but I could see next to nothing. Just a couple of huts that could have belonged to the forester. And there was no sound. I thought they were playing some awful trick on me. Then the man kept whistling a few notes until someone appeared out of the darkness. It was unreal. I didn't realise it then, but he came out of an underground hut.'

Bets shakes her head in disbelief. 'I heard rumours that there was a big community of *onderduikers* living somewhere on the Veluwe, but no one had any idea where it was or who was supporting them. Was it true you lived underground?'

'I hated it, being cooped up with five strangers. If I'd been able to, I would have run away, but where to? Those early days were hard, even though everyone around me was incredibly kind. But it wasn't as bad as you might imagine. We had oil lamps and a *kachel*, which was always on, so the hut was warm and dry.'

'Sounds quite *gezellig*. But seriously, how did you get through it?'

'By making friends. Really good friends.' I drop my eyes so she can't see them well up with tears. Bets puts her arm round me and we sit in silence listening to the soft murmurings of the others, the children bedded down between the pews and others side by side in the aisle. After a while like this, she asks if I want to tell her how I've come to be here. I shake my head and I think she must sense my tiredness. 'Tell me another time,' she whispers against my hair. It's obvious she's heard nothing about Berkenhout's demise.

SIXTEEN
WOUTER

Wrestling with his thoughts, Wouter drove through the woods in silence. His conversation with Klaus had stirred up emotions he'd long been trying to bury. What if he never found Laura, or worse, discovered she was dead? He'd heard rumours about the Nazis cramming Jews onto cattle trains for deportation to brutal work camps. How could he live with the knowledge that Laura had been amongst them? And if he did find her, would she even want to see him after learning about his cowardly escape from Berkenhout? He imagined she'd want to put the whole horrible experience behind her. And with it, him.

His mind wandered to the first time they'd met. He'd known nothing about Laura's past until Else had spoken to him the day she came with a note for Laura. After she'd emerged from her hut, he'd wanted to comfort her and taken her round the back where the men always went to smoke. Wouter had kicked a few cigarette stubs aside and sat Laura down.

'What does it say?' he'd hardly dared ask.

'It's from my dad,' Laura had begun, twisting her fingers in her lap. 'They were living in Friesland but have moved on. He won't say where.'

'That's good news, isn't it?'

Laura had shot him a dark look. 'I was told Friesland was safe, but not anymore. It seems the *moffen* are everywhere. Here, read it yourself.'

Wouter had scanned the one-sided letter. It had read like a telegram.

> *A raid took place last week. Nothing taken, but too risky to stay. Will send news when we arrive.*

'It's so unlike Dad to write in haste like that. All his other letters were long chatty ones. Do you think he was forced to write it?'

'More like he didn't want to say too much in case the letter fell into the wrong hands. At least he wrote to you.'

'How can you say that? For all I know they're in great danger. They might even have been caught.'

'There you are.' Tante Else was walking through the trees towards them. 'Is everything all right?'

Laura's eyes had brimmed with tears as she'd handed Else the letter. 'Did you know my parents are on the run again?'

Else had shaken her head as she'd read the few lines on the sheet. 'No, but it sounds like your father had to write it quickly before leaving. Gerrit asked me to give you the letter when I came today. Nothing more. He didn't indicate he knew what it was about. I'm so sorry. I'll do all I can to find out where they've gone.'

It was the last letter Laura had received from her parents. From time to time, sketchy details came through from various members of the underground who'd helped them escape, but nothing firm on her parents' whereabouts. That day, Wouter did try to comfort Laura. He hadn't meant to be unsympathetic, but he was unable to understand what she was going through.

The fear, the loss of her parents, the threat to her own safety. Nothing Wouter had ever experienced came close.

When they reached the edge of the woods, Wouter took a deep breath. Beyond was open farmland spelling potential danger. The only signs of life were one or two figures bent over their work in the potato fields. He had just asked Klaus to scour the area for anything unusual when someone waving their arms came running down the middle of the road.

'*Verdorie!* What's this all about?' Wouter shouted, slamming on the brakes and coming to a halt in front of the dishevelled young woman. Her face was streaked with tears and her faded blue dress was ripped under one arm. Wouter and Klaus looked at each other in astonishment.

'It's Griet. Whatever is she doing here?' said Klaus.

The woman pulled Wouter's door open with a cry. 'Please, can you take me away from here?' Fear was etched on her face. She kept glancing over at the people working in the field but no one looked up.

Wouter jumped out and tried to put a hand on her shoulder to reassure her, but the gesture made her flinch. 'I have to get away from here. Please take me.' In her distress, she hurried to the back of the van and wrenched open the door. When she saw it was filled to the top with crates she stifled a cry with her hand.

Klaus moved towards her, uttering reassurances and ushering her into the passenger seat before squeezing in next to her. She sat hunched, shaking and sobbing. At the sound of a horse and cart clopping and rattling along the road, her sobbing grew louder.

'Go, go, can't you?' she urged Wouter, who was attempting to restart the engine, which kept stalling. At the third attempt it caught and he wasted no time in moving off before the farmer could draw level and accost them.

'We're close to the farm. She may find shelter there,' Wouter told Klaus.

'Wait. We need to ask her what's going on first,' said Klaus. 'Let me.' He gently laid a hand on her arm. 'Griet, do you remember us? We turned up at your house and you shared your meal with us.'

She halted her sobbing and gazed through her tears at Klaus, then Wouter. 'No! Let me out!' Leaning across Klaus, she leant over and grasped at the door handle but he grabbed her wrist to restrain her.

'Stop it! We won't take you anywhere unless you tell us what's going on,' said Klaus, raising his voice.

It was enough to calm her down, but it was a while till she was able to speak. She twisted her body away from Wouter, who was concentrating on the road ahead and the occasional farm vehicle trundling past. He had no desire to involve himself in the conversation.

'Tell me, where is your family? Your little boy?' asked Klaus.

Griet wiped her eyes with her sleeve. 'He's safe. Bram took him to my parents before his arrest. He saw it coming and we rowed. He was so stubborn and refused to talk about where he went in the evenings. It was something about passing on ammunition dropped by the Allies, but something must have gone wrong. If only he'd shared what he was doing with me, none of this would have happened.' Her voice grew less shaky as she related her story, though she kept taking long shuddering breaths.

'So he was arrested? When was this?'

'Last night. We'd only just gone to bed when they banged on the door. Bram made me put the pouch with our ID and money under my clothes before he opened up. There were four, maybe five *moffen*, all shouting at the tops of their voices and pushing Bram aside. I was frightened and hoped it was just another raid. I knew they wouldn't find anything. But it made them really angry when they didn't find what they were looking for. They ordered Bram to get dressed and two of them forced him out of the house and into the van. They wouldn't let me say goodbye or tell me where they were taking him. Just that he was under arrest for betrayal. After they left I didn't know what to do. I was frightened they'd come back to arrest me. I couldn't sleep and sat in a chair near the door, waiting for something terrible to happen. Every rattle from the windows and every creak made me more nervous. By morning I was exhausted, but I had to leave.'

'Do you have any idea how you ended up here?' asked Klaus.

'Of course,' she retorted, and, for the first time, seemed in control of herself as she resumed her tale. 'Bram's sister and husband live on a farm a mile or two from our house. I thought she could help me, but I never made it that far.' She took several jerky breaths with her hand over her mouth.

'Take your time,' said Klaus, touching her arm once more.

'I... I started to pack a bag with a few clothes. Then the door flew open and they were back. Just two of them this time. They demanded I give them papers or something. I don't really remember. They were so rough and ripped my dress as they pulled me over to my father's old desk, shouting at me to unlock it. All I could think of was Bram. They'd come back to get proof he was a Resistance fighter. I knew he kept stuff locked in that desk but never suspected he'd been involved in anything like that. One began hitting me and threatened to take me away too. I had no choice but to open the desk. They pulled out all the correspondence we keep in there, letters, papers, documents. Lots of stuff I didn't know was there that Bram must have hidden. They took the lot, piling it into their canvas bags. Everything. Even the letters we wrote to each other before we were married. I tried to plead with them to tell me where they'd taken Bram, but they just laughed in my face. What could I do?'

'So you left the house?' said Klaus in a coaxing voice.

She nodded. 'As soon as I heard their motorbike had gone. I was in a panic and forgot my bag. I just started running in the direction of Bram's sister's house. But I heard them coming back. I'm sure they were coming to arrest me too. I managed to crouch down in a ditch at the side of the road but they kept driving up and down. I don't know how long I was in there, but it was a long time before I could be sure they'd gone. That's when I saw you.'

'You'll be fine now,' said Klaus, patting her hand.

Up ahead and set back from the road was a farm. Wouter slowed the van. He eased it off the road onto a rubble track that ran parallel to a field. He was concentrating hard on not getting stuck and wished he had a more robust vehicle. As they approached the farm, a skinny brown dog came rushing towards them, yapping furiously. Instinctively, Wouter shrank into his seat, as the dog rushed at them. The farmer came limping towards them, shouting at his dog to cut it out. Griet began to whimper.

'Wait here. He should remember me. I used to come with my pa to buy meat from him,' said Klaus, jumping out of the van. The dog immediately stopped its yapping and cowered, allowing Klaus to pat it on the head. Wouter watched as Klaus greeted the farmer, whose set face relaxed into a smile. He grabbed hold of the dog by the scruff of the neck and slipped a chain over its head. The dog settled down quietly next to its owner.

Wouter ventured out of the car and the dog started up again.

'Be quiet, you idiot,' shouted the farmer, yanking the dog's chain. 'I'm glad you've turned up. I've got three families in there and had no deliveries from Else for days.'

Wouter glanced back at the car where Griet sat white-faced and unmoving.

He cleared his throat. 'You wouldn't have room for one more, would you? We've just picked up this woman and she's in a great deal of distress. She's running away from a couple of *moffen* who've taken her husband on suspicion of working for the underground.'

The farmer sucked in his breath and pursed his lips. 'I suppose one more won't hurt but it's getting to be quite a squeeze in there.' He pointed his head towards the barn where Wouter and Klaus had slept. The memory of crouching in amongst the prickly hay bales next to strangers sprung into Wouter's head. He shuddered.

'Did they all come from Berkenhout?' asked Wouter, trying not to think how crowded it must be in the hay loft. He went round to the back of the van and began lifting the crates down.

'Some, I think. They're all just *onderduikers* to me. Come over and meet them.' The farmer hoisted a crate onto his shoulder while keeping one hand on the dog's chain.

Klaus went back to Griet and spoke quietly to her before she got out. Side by side, they followed the farmer who limped over to the door of the barn, depositing the crate on the ground. Wouter followed, carrying two crates, one on top of the other. At the barn entrance, the farmer tied his dog to a post, loudly scolding when it started its barking again. Muttering to himself, he went inside and took a torch off a shelf and swung the beam around the barn. There was nothing to be seen and no sounds apart from the farmer's voice telling them to keep quiet. Wouter expected him to lead the way to the ladder leading up to the hayrick, but he walked over to a corner of the barn piled up with rusty farmyard implements. He nodded to the men to help him move them aside. On the back wall was a wooden door. The farmer rapped softly and opened it with a creak.

'Must get that oiled,' he said, stooping down to go through.

The others followed him in. Wouter didn't know what to expect, certainly not a large room full of people. The room had probably once been a storage facility of some sort and was lit by several lamps. Along one wall was a pile of mattresses with bedding on top. The floor had been swept clean and was strewn with cushions. In the centre stood a large table piled high with books. At one end sat four children who looked up from their schoolwork. Two adults stood at their shoulders, supervising. The rest of the group were sitting on the floor carving pieces of wood with Petr in their midst. He raised his hand when he saw it was Wouter and carried on with his work. Wouter was struck by how quiet the barn was, despite being filled with adults and children.

'I see you're passing on your skills,' said Wouter, clapping a hand on his dear Russian friend's shoulder, before crouching down to pick up a half-painted blue wooden bird on wheels. He was glad to see he was still engaged in making his beautiful wooden toys that had cheered the children at Berkenhout. Petr was showing a boy of about ten how to smooth the wood before applying the bright paint. He laid down his sanding paper with a warning to the others not to touch it. Taking a cigarette from his pocket, he examined it between his fingers without lighting it. He walked with Wouter to the door.

'Hey, watch out, will you. You don't want to be seen,' said the farmer, who was busy with Klaus unloading carrots and potatoes into a makeshift cupboard.

'I need a smoke. I'll be fine,' said Petr, raising his eyebrows at Wouter as they walked outside.

'How did you come to be here?' asked Wouter, as they stood in front of the barn.

'Dick moved me here last week. He thinks it safer than staying at his place. It's all right here. A bit cramped but will do till I work out what I do next. Who's the woman?' He glanced sideways at Wouter while taking a drag on his cigarette.

'She'll be joining you. Her husband was taken late last night and she's too scared to stay in her own house. We met her running down the road on our way here. She was distraught.' Wouter shook his head. 'Is it safe here?'

Petr snorted out a plume of smoke. 'Safe enough. But is anywhere safe these days?'

Both men turned their heads at the sound of a sputtering engine. A motorbike with sidecar was turning up the track from the road. Petr grabbed Wouter's arm and pulled him back inside the barn. Before he could adjust his eyes to the dark, Wouter accidentally kicked something that flipped over with a metallic clang. It set the dog off again and its yaps grew more frantic at the sound of the motorbike drawing into the yard. The commotion alerted the farmer who came rushing and swearing out of the room at the far end. Hurriedly he pulled the door shut and shoved a pile of empty crates in front.

Two figures appeared silhouetted against the opening to the barn. From the shape of their helmets, there was no mistaking who they were. Wouter shrank back into the shadows and felt Petr's steadying hand on his back, sensing this wasn't the first time Petr had been in danger here.

The farmer stepped forward out of the gloom, demanding to know what they wanted.

'We have information that there are *onderduikers* hiding on this farm. Explain,' said one of the men, flicking on a torch and shining it round the barn. It came to rest first on Wouter, then Petr. 'So!' he barked.

'You're wrong. These are two of my workers I asked to clear the barn before bringing in the hay. We're running low, as you can see,' said the farmer, nodding towards the hay bales that occupied about a third of the space.

'We'll see.' Grim-faced, he gave a short nod to his companion as he flicked his beam towards the ladder. He climbed up while the other man stood with his legs apart, keeping an eye on the farmer, Wouter and Petr, who all remained silent.

Soon, clumps of hay flew down from the top of the bales along with angry shouts. '*Unglaublich! Hier gibt es nichts zu sehen,*' he called out in fury at finding nothing, before thundering back down the ladder.

'I told you. There's no one hiding here,' said the farmer, folding his arms.

'All of you. Come outside where I can see you.' The soldier marched out, setting the dog's barking off again. '*Verdammt!*' He turned on the dog and kicked it, making it cower and squeal.

'Well, well. I think we have met before,' said the angry German, prodding Petr in the chest. Petr's face remained unmoving.

'There's no point speaking to him. He's deaf and can't speak,' said the farmer.

This seemed to make the German even more angry. He put his face close to Petr's and spat '*Onderduiker*' at him. Petr managed not to flinch as spittle landed on his cheek.

Wouter, who was standing behind the two men, quietly moved towards the dog and slipped the chain off its neck. With a ferocious growl, it launched itself at the angry German, grabbed hold of his trouser leg in its teeth and wouldn't let go. Cursing loudly, the man swung round, shouting at the farmer to get the dog off him. The farmer sauntered over and grabbed the animal by the scruff of its neck while speaking in soothing tones, quite unlike those he'd used when Wouter and Klaus had turned up earlier. The dog held on, its growls growing in intensity. With a roar, the other soldier lifted the butt of his rifle and brought it down on the back of dog's head. Too surprised to scream, the dog loosened its grip and dropped limply to the ground.

'You've killed my dog! Get off my land!' yelled the farmer, bending over his inert dog.

The one who'd struck the animal spoke in urgent tones to his mate who was cursing and examining bloody tooth marks above his ankle. Without another word they returned to the motorbike. All at once, the injured man turned, drew his pistol from his belt and fired a warning shot onto the ground close to where the dog lay. Wouter and Petr flinched. The farmer glanced up briefly but continued to crouch over the lifeless body of his dog.

Once the motorbike was out of sight and the rumble of the engine had ceased, Wouter knelt next to the farmer and gazed down at the dog. After a moment he said, 'Look, it's still breathing.' He placed his hand on the dog's chest. Its snout began to twitch and it opened its eyes, before struggling to its feet. The three men laughed in surprise and relief as the dog began to stagger into a run round and round the yard, sniffing the ground while making little yelping noises. The farmer let it carry on for a minute or so before grabbing the loose skin on its neck and slipping the chain back on. 'Enough, you stupid animal!' he scolded, and tied it back up to the post where it lay down with a whimper, head on its paws. As the farmer stood up, he frowned at Wouter and said, 'You must go. And take the woman with you. It's too risky for me to take in more.'

SEVENTEEN

LAURA

'It can't be for long,' says the woman, blocking the doorway. She glares at us, arms folded across her body. She's certainly no Mevrouw Schaft.

'Of course, of course. It'll only be until I can arrange a more permanent solution,' says Hans, darting an apologetic look at her. 'I wish I could say when, but it won't be long. We're so grateful that you can help.'

Well, I don't feel grateful. It's as if we're invisible. Like I'm a beggar who's turned up on her doorstep wanting shelter. I look down at my shoe, the one where the sole is coming off, and feel ashamed. Isn't that what I am now, a beggar? Have I any right to complain? Maybe that's what I am, but it doesn't stop me being furious. I want to scream at her, tell her it's not my fault I'm here and that I'd rather sleep in the street. But of course, I don't. Instead, I stand and wait. Timid, shy Laura, who is so grateful to be given shelter.

It's Bets who speaks up. 'We'll go back to the church and sleep on the stone floor if it's inconvenient. Would you prefer that?'

Silently, I will Bets on as she juts her chin forward. I'm pleased we're in this together.

'It won't be necessary,' says the woman, and her voice is softer. 'But, Hans, I put my name down for one and now two of them show up. That's not what we agreed.' She spreads her hands and gives Hans a pleading look.

'Just a few days, Liv, I promise. I'll sort it out,' says Hans, not quite catching her eye. He wipes the sweat from his forehead, though it's icy out here.

She's not to be placated and makes an exaggerated sniff before turning to go inside. Hans whispers an apology to us but we stand tight-lipped. Why she's so ungracious I can't imagine, but, once Hans has gone, she becomes a bit more friendly, asking our names, where we're from, that sort of thing. I wonder if she's had an argument with Hans over us, or maybe a lovers' tiff, but I push the idea aside.

Her friendliness, if that's what you can call it, doesn't last long as she leads the way into the kitchen, which is as unwelcoming as she is. I swear I can see my breath and wonder how often she comes in here. I shiver when I see the tightly shut curtains and the unlit *kachel* in the corner. Liv busies herself taking dishes from the larder and placing them in front of us. Cold potatoes and fatty meat. It could be worse but it does little to warm us up on such a cold day.

We eat in silence. Occasionally, I allow myself a quick glance at Bets who looks as uncomfortable as I'm feeling. Neither of us is willing to start a conversation with Liv in case of upsetting her again.

'Finished?' She whisks away our plates as soon as we put down our knives and forks. "I'll show you where you'll be hiding,' she says, without so much as a smile. She walks over to the back of the kitchen and drags a small chest across the floor. She's down on her hands and knees, feeling along the line of a floorboard till her nail catches on a groove. There's nothing to see till it lifts in her hand to reveal wooden steps leading down into the darkness. She goes first, the steps creaking a little as she descends. We're meant to follow. I adjust my eyes at the bottom and see a long low room, which must run the length of the kitchen above. My first thought is how stuffy and dark it is down here, but once she switches on a lamp, it doesn't seem as bad. Then Liv sees me look at a window with the curtains pulled firmly across. 'I'd show you the view of the garden, but the curtains must remain shut, even during the day. We don't want to arouse any suspicion. Now, when you're ready, come up so I can tell you the house rules.'

After she's disappeared back up the steps, Bets and I stare at one another in disbelief.

'Do you get the feeling we're not welcome?' I say, listening to Liv's footsteps walking across the kitchen above our heads.

Bets's face looks pale in the half light. 'Definitely. Let's hope it's only for a day or two.'

It becomes obvious why Liv was prepared to tolerate us being in her house, despite the risks of being found out. We're set to work immediately, scrubbing the kitchen floor and washing the sheets from the couple who'd stayed before us. They've only left this morning. Bets is upstairs, cleaning the bathroom. Of course, I'm not allowed out into the garden to hang up the sheets in case I'm spotted from the street. It's unlikely, because there's a thick hedge all the way round.

'Get back from the window. Do you want to get us into trouble?' Liv blazes. She's been prowling round us all day, watching us, pulling us up on inconsequential things. I flinch at the vehemence of her tone and drop the bundle of wet laundry into the basket, pushing it towards her. We stare at one another until she grunts, sweeps up the basket and stomps out into the garden.

I'm on my own for the first time that day. I sit down at the kitchen table and rest my head on my arms. How I long to be back in the woods, smelling the sweet scent of unfurling bracken as the sun sets and feeling the breeze on my face. Wouter next to me, taking my hand in his and kissing each of my fingers till I shiver. I try to summon up his features, but all I get is an indistinct image of his face, and the more I focus on him the more he seems to fade from my mind. His deep voice that made me melt whenever he directed his words to me – how did it sound? My chest tightens at the thought that I'll end up forgetting him and all the times we spent together, gazing into each other's eyes. The realisation hits me hard that he's gone and that I may never see him again. And if he is still alive, somewhere, have I also faded from his life?

EIGHTEEN

ELSE

It was after 10 p.m. when Else heard the back gate click. With the hint of a smile, she looked up from her darning and nodded towards Liesbeth. 'They're back.'

Nothing much surprised Else these days, but as it had been their first trip out as couriers, she'd hoped they would avoid any trouble. In all the months she'd been organising supplies, she'd lost no one. So much was based on trust and there was never time to check out people's reliability. With so many mouths to feed, it was essential to keep boxing up food and get it delivered as quickly as possible. So when help was offered, she had to take it. Like Henk. Without him, Berkenhout would never have been built and the refugees would never have reached the village in safety. His van had been a familiar sight in the woods and he was used to deflecting anyone from stopping and searching him. He'd made countless trips with whole families crammed in under sacking and not once did he arouse any suspicion. On the occasions that he'd been flagged down, he'd provide a perfectly reasonable explanation that he was moving timber on behalf of the authorities. And he'd done so much more. There was the time he arranged for Kees to be taken from Berkenhout to hospital in secret after his terrible accident. Somehow, Henk had managed to drive his van off road through the thickest part of the wood so that the men didn't have too far to move the injured man who had a suspected fracture after falling from the roof of one of the huts. The operation had taken place at nightfall to reduce the risk of being caught. Even Henk would have found it difficult to explain the presence of an injured man in the back of his van if he'd been stopped. Nothing deterred him and his willingness to help his fellow people was remarkable, but still Else had her worries about that man. At the precise moment that Berkenhout had been ambushed he'd happened to be in the vicinity, so she'd been told, arousing suspicion of his involvement. Then the stories came through about Henk leading so many to safety. Surely that made him a good man? Living alone as he did in the woods, he was bound to have connections with anyone who could do him favours. But where did his loyalties lie? At times like these, Else wondered whose side he really was on.

'We have another visitor,' said Liesbeth, followed into the kitchen by Wouter, Klaus and Griet.

'Griet, what a surprise! But where's Bertje? And Bram?' Else started up from her chair and put an arm round the dishevelled woman, while issuing instructions to Liesbeth to fetch her a hot drink. 'Don't cry, you're safe here,' said Else, warming Griet's hands between her own. 'Sit down, you two, and tell me what's going on.'

'No, let me,' Griet spoke up, after blowing her nose on the handkerchief Else handed her. 'Bertje's safe with my parents. But this... it's all my fault. I didn't know what else to do. I was trying to get away from the *moffen*. They'd already taken Bram but came back looking for me. I was running along the road to Bram's sister when I recognised the motorbike. They were coming back for me, I'm sure of it. So I hid, and when these two turned up I knew it was my only chance. How was I to know the *moffen* would still be after me?'

'It wasn't like that,' said Wouter. 'The *moffen* didn't come till long after you'd gone into the barn. And they never asked after you. They were more interested in finding a load of *onderduikers*. Someone must have tipped them off and they were probably searching all the farms.'

Else looked grave. 'I'm afraid Wouter is right. I received news this morning that the Bakkers in Epe were raided and seven members of one Jewish family were discovered in their cellar. It doesn't look good for those poor people. They were arrested and taken away. They only moved there a few days ago after weeks of hiding out in the woods. It makes you wonder who must have been passing on intelligence.' She sighed wearily. 'It's inevitable now there are so many on the run, so we have to be extra vigilant. I have a way of dealing with them when they come calling. Thankfully, it hasn't happened for a long time. It's Jews they're after, so you'll be safe with us here for the time being.' Else smiled at Griet, who stared back with fear in her eyes.

'You can share my room. It's a bit small but you're lucky there's no one else with me at the moment,' said Liesbeth, handing her a cup of ersatz coffee.

'But I must go to Bertje and find Bram,' said Griet, her voice breaking.

'Tomorrow, after a night's sleep,' said Else. 'We'll fetch Dick Foppen. He'll be able to help.'

Now wasn't the right time to voice her concern that Bram might already be on his way to a work camp.

It was late before Else had the chance to get on with her calculations. Every couple of days she received stacks of coupons organised by the *LO*, the Resistance organisation, which needed reconciling with the goods waiting to be distributed. But today something wasn't quite right. She was convinced there'd been sufficient quantities of cheese, butter and eggs when she'd checked that morning, but the columns still didn't add up. Numbers weren't her strong point and the discrepancy was only slight. She yawned and rubbed her eyes, but however many times she ran her pencil over the columns the totals were under.

A creak on the staircase signalled Wouter tiptoeing back downstairs. Apologising for the disturbance, he asked for a glass of water, but took his time at the sink while she tried to concentrate. He appeared to have no intention of moving.

'Is everything all right?' she said, snapping her ledger shut. The numbers would have to wait until morning. When he didn't answer she asked, 'Is it Laura?'

Nodding, he ran a hand through his unruly hair. 'It's over a month now and still there's no news. Everyone I speak to claims to have seen her or heard of her whereabouts, but there's been nothing definite. What am I to believe?'

Else went over to the dresser and rummaged in a drawer, overflowing with papers. 'I'm so sorry. I meant to dig out de Boer's address for you. It's here somewhere,' she said, eventually finding a black leather book held together with a rubber band to stop the pages falling out. 'Ah, here we are. De heer de Boer, Apeldoornseweg 19. And there's a telephone number. You can call him in the morning.' She unscrewed her pen and wrote the details on a scrap of paper.

'What about you? You seem distracted. Are you all right?' frowned Wouter.

'Me? Oh, it's nothing. I need to get my figures to reconcile, but I'm having trouble with them. Probably because I'm tired.' She stifled a yawn as she fingered the ledger.

'This distribution of food. I can see it's taking up more of your time. You're not just helping the people from Berkenhout, are you?'

Else sighed. 'There are so many being hounded from their homes in the west of Holland and they think they'll be safer here. I wish it were true. All we can do is try and find them safe houses, but how are we to feed them as well? The *moffen* think they can come in and take our food. We've been all right up to now, but we're getting overstretched.' Tiredness washed over her. Now she'd started talking she didn't want to stop. Wouter was a willing listener and she knew she could trust him.

'Wouter, please share a *jenever* with me.'

She reached up to the top shelf of the dresser for the bottle, which was covered in a film of greasy dust. Henk had given her it over a year ago in exchange for a sack of dried peas. It was the currency he used when he wanted some extra for himself. She hadn't had the heart to tell him she rarely touched the stuff. And all this time the stone bottle had stood unopened. Easing out the cork, she poured a thimble of the fiery liquid into two small glasses.

'*Proost!*' they both said as they chinked the glasses together.

'This is a good one,' said Wouter, lifting the bottle so he could examine it.

'Is it? I don't know much about these things. I never normally drink,' said Else, taking a tiny sip and immediately coughing. After a couple more attempts she began to enjoy the sensation of the warm liquid sliding down.

She sat back in her armchair with her eyes closed. 'I received a letter from the pastor who is on the committee for the LO. He wants my help to find more hiding places. He knows about my work with Berkenhout.' She opened her eyes and gazed straight at Wouter. 'As you know, people in hiding need food, but also a lot more. Coupons, identity papers. More to the point, forged identity papers to help them cross borders. But I don't have a good enough or reliable network to supply these.'

She paused as a thought passed through her mind. 'The pastor knows Oscar Mulder and tells me he's been officially acknowledged by the *LO* in his role providing documentation to Jews in Utrecht.'

'Oscar? Isn't he Jan's older brother?'

'That's right. And doing great things now. He's quite an expert in forgeries and I'm keen to use his skills. You see, there are at least twenty-five people in hiding in the Veluwe who need new identities, but I don't have the time to sort these out. I'm thinking you could go to Oscar in Utrecht and get hold of the printed documents and more ration books. That would help me enormously.' Else smiled. She met Wouter's eyes and a thread of understanding passed between them.

'But first, you must see if Mr de Boer has any news about Laura. Don't worry if he hasn't. I'm sure Oscar will be able to help you.'

NINETEEN

WOUTER

It was difficult to sleep and it wasn't just the effects of the *jenever*. He was excited at the prospect of getting closer to Laura, but he kept jolting awake with a dread that something terrible had happened to her. One moment it seemed as if she was next to him, the next she'd gone. He clutched the pillow to his chest and screwed up his eyes, trying hard to conjure up her warm body. But why would he be able to? He had no memory to help him as they'd only just begun kissing like a proper couple days before they were forced apart. Wouter buried his head under the pillow – it was he who had run away from her.

Later, when he woke again, the memory of Laura had gone. He rolled onto his back and rested his hand across his eyes. His mind was clearer, despite only sleeping for a few hours. He decided he wouldn't ring Mr de Boer in case their conversation was overheard by any German listening in. Better to go to him in person, he thought.

Careful not to disturb Klaus sleeping on the opposite side of the room, Wouter got up. He quickly ran a razor over his face and washed at the small basin. Not wanting to turn on a light, he felt his way downstairs. The half-finished *jenever* was still on the table. He hesitated before slipping it into his jacket pocket. It might prove useful.

It was just starting to get light. He remembered there was a bike inside the shed that no one ever used. Hidden from view and out of temptation's way, it had terrible tyres, but that was nothing unusual. It would have to do and was unlikely to attract attention should he run into anybody.

As he set off, the only sound was the loud squeak of the bike every time he turned the pedals. After a while the squeak wore off and he was able to relax. It was just him on his bike pedalling along beyond the houses and out onto the open road. A harsh northerly wind bit into his face and made his eyes water. No wonder there was no one out this early. As he got near to the farmer's house, he noticed field after field all empty of crops. A light dusting of ice covered the frozen furrows. He was glad to stop and rubbed his hands to get some feeling back into them. Wheeling the bike out of view, he walked round to the front where he rang the door-bell. Somewhere from up the road he heard a car coming. Seconds passed as he willed Mr de Boer, or anyone, to open up.

'Who is it?' came an irritated voice from within.

Wouter cleared his throat. 'My name's Wouter Brand. A friend of Else. I'm sorry to bother you so early, but could I please have a word?'

A shuffling sound and the scrape of a key in the lock, and the door opened. Wouter quickly stepped inside as the car drove past. He inhaled with relief, then remembering his manners, removed his cap and introduced himself.

'I don't usually open the door to strangers, so I hope you are who you say.' The farmer gave Wouter a challenging look. 'Do you see that?' He pointed to the desolate fields out of a side window. 'They took the lot. When I protested, they threatened me. Said they'd send me to a camp over the border if I didn't comply. They couldn't care less about the people I feed through my efforts.'

'When did this happen?' Wouter wished he could offer some words of comfort. It didn't seem right to start asking about Laura.

Mr de Boer, a man of about forty who moved as if he were seventy, slumped into an armchair beside an unlit fireplace. 'Two weeks after all the celebrations on Dolle Dinsdag when everyone foolishly believed the war was at an end. A week after I was stopped returning from Zwolle.' He looked warily at Wouter and paused as if he realised he'd revealed too much.

Wouter cleared his throat. 'Else told me about what you did. You were very brave. I was one of those who escaped from Berkenhout that night.'

The farmer leant his elbows on the arms of the chair to get a better look at Wouter. 'I never wanted to get involved, but Dick, he's so persuasive. He said I was the only one with a big enough trailer and that he needed my help right then. I knew it would lead to trouble. Thank God I managed three journeys before they stopped me. Fortunately, the search happened on the way back when the trailer was empty.'

'Three journeys? How many did you bring to safety?'

Mr de Boer stared into space. 'Nineteen. Maybe twenty. Not all from Berkenhout.'

'Else didn't know the details. That's why she said I should come. I'm looking for a girl who was at Berkenhout. I've had no news, only a rumour she might have made it to Zwolle. Laura is her name. She's slightly built and has big dark eyes and straight black hair. Was she one of them?' Wouter held his breath.

The man shook his head. 'I didn't ask anyone's name. I just wanted to get the job done. Wait, let me think.' He rubbed the greying stubble on his chin. 'Yes, there was a girl of that description. I nearly didn't take her as the trailer was full. Everyone had to lie flat, side by side like sardines with the tarpaulin pulled over. This girl, Laura, did you say? Slip of a thing. I thought she could squeeze in. Otherwise she'd have been left behind and I wouldn't have known what to do with her.'

It was the first bit of news that made sense. It had to be her. 'So she made it to Zwolle?'

'Oh yes, along with all the others. I took them to the Protestant church on the canal and from there my brother arranged for them to go to safe hiding places. Hans is remarkable. Reminds me of Dick Foppen the way he runs the local network in Zwolle. But, that's enough. I've already said too much.' He stood up, a signal for Wouter to go. 'Tell Else I'll visit her one of these days. She's someone else who's doing a lot of good for the Jews.'

'Thank you for all you've told me.' Wouter pulled the *jenever* bottle from his pocket. 'For your troubles. Sorry it's not a full one.'

'Bols. I haven't seen one of these since before the war.' He took the brown stone bottle in his calloused hands and held it up to the light so he could read the lettering.

Wouter smiled, turning to leave.

'Wait. I'm sorry I can't help you find this girl of yours. She may still be in Zwolle, but nowhere's safe and they move them quickly through the network.'

'And your brother? Could he help?' ventured Wouter.

'I'm sorry. I can't give you his details,' the man said with a guarded expression. 'You understand, don't you?'

TWENTY

WOUTER

As soon as he arrived back at Else's, he set about writing to Laura. At last there was hope she'd managed to escape unscathed, though he worried there'd been no definite sighting of her. The lack of address didn't bother him as he was confident that someone in Else's network would be able to get the letter to her. He just needed to find the right words. Settling down, it took him several attempts and several wasted sheets of paper before he managed to get something down he was happy with.

Lieve Laura,

As I sit writing this letter to you I imagine the smile on your face when you read it. There's a chance you'll decide to throw it away unread but I won't allow myself to think of that. Today I met a farmer who thinks he remembers helping you though he was a bit vague. It gave me hope that you've managed to find somewhere safe. But where are you? Are you with people who are nice to you? Do you ever think of me? I constantly ask myself these questions. Sometimes I'm close to giving up hope, but I'll keep trying as I have to believe we'll be together again soon.

I don't want to dwell on what happened. Was it my fault? I really don't know anymore. I just hope one day soon I'll be able to explain to you and you'll forgive me.

Please reply. Please tell me you're safe and well. Please tell me you forgive me.

Your true friend,

Wouter

It would have to do, he thought with a sigh, as he slid the single sheet into an envelope and sealed it. He looked up at the sound of Else's step on the stairs and she expressed surprise that he was up so early. He told her of his visit to the farmer and the sliver of hope that he'd seen Laura. 'The first thing I did when I returned was to write this letter. You will help me get it to her?' His hand shook a little as he held it out.

'Of course, but you must be patient.'

In the following weeks, Wouter hardly had a chance to brood on the lack of response from Laura. Else had passed his letter on to Gerrit, a loyal man who had worked with her right from when Berkenhout became a reality. Gerrit accepted the task without question and could be relied upon to work with contacts stretching across the country. Someone would know about Laura's whereabouts, he said, but it could be months for Wouter's letter to arrive, if it ever did. All Wouter could do was wait.

More and more people were pouring in from the west and Else needed all the help she could muster to distribute food to the growing number of families sheltering *onderduikers*. From early morning till late, Wouter and Klaus were busy making deliveries all over the Veluwe and became adept at dodging the Germans. They used Else's network of contacts to alert them to any danger as they drove between addresses. Instrumental in helping them was Jan, the boy who had inadvertently precipitated the ambush and demise of Berkenhout when the Germans had spotted him nearby, shooting him in the foot. He'd been out of action for months but now that his foot had healed he was determined to 'get back at the *moffen*', as he put it. Together with his friend Nico, they devised an effective system of communication, helping Wouter and Klaus keep one step ahead of any potential danger.

One morning, Else began clearing the breakfast plates almost as soon as Wouter and Klaus had finished eating. 'I've got a new assignment for you both,' she said, smiling at Wouter. 'There's a group of people who need our help but they live quite a way from here. It's really a favour for an old friend of mine who heard about our work and decided to do her bit too. She lives in a huge house with a spacious attic, cellar and garden. I said I'd try to get supplies over to her. I don't know much about her *onderduikers*, except they haven't managed to find anywhere to stay for more than a few days, so no doubt they're pleased to have somewhere more permanent. Oh, and Dick's managed to get hold of some petrol, so the van should make it to Zwolle. Is that all right with you?' She watched Wouter for his reaction.

'Why, of course,' he said, a knot forming in his stomach. But would he have time to go searching for Laura as well as carry out the delivery?

'My friend has offered for you to stay over if it gets late,' said Else, as if she'd read his mind.

'That's very...' began Wouter before Klaus interrupted him.

'No need, I've got a cousin in Zwolle. I haven't seen her in ages and I'm sure we can stay with her,' said Klaus, winking at Wouter.

Wouter hardly dared believe this turn of events, but how could he be optimistic of finding Laura? Zwolle was a large place and the chances of finding anyone with news of her were slim. He'd become even more worried for her safety after reading in Else's copy of *Vrij Nederland* that refugees were streaming into Zwolle daily, scattering across the town into every available hiding place. This coincided with a concerted effort by the Nazis to flush out Jews for arrest and deportation to death camps in Eastern Europe. Death camps. Those two words sent an ice-cold shiver down Wouter's spine. He was thankful he wouldn't be making the trip on his own.

'We'll drive via my cousin and she'll be able to make enquiries while we deliver to Else's friend. Then we can begin our search.' Klaus clapped Wouter on the shoulder after he slammed the back door of the van shut. 'So you see, it's going to work out after all.'

Wouter was grateful for Klaus's encouragement, but couldn't imagine they'd actually find Laura on the basis of one enquiry. Having Klaus with him certainly made it easier. If it didn't work out, at least he wouldn't have to deal with the disappointment on his own.

Klaus' upbeat conversation, though irritating at times, kept them going on the tedious journey through rural countryside, small towns and villages. While Wouter kept alert for any signs they might be pulled over and searched, Klaus chatted about his cousin, Eva, who had been a singer in a Berlin nightclub before the war.

'A talent scout spotted her when she was performing in a musical in Amsterdam. It didn't surprise me as she's got a powerful voice and was always being picked out for leading roles. But a Berlin nightclub?' Klaus shook his head. 'If you ask me, she had a thing going with the talent scout. But it didn't last. These things never do with her. She took fright when the nightclub was stormed one night by Nazis looking for homos. She left the next day and returned to her parents' house near Zwolle. They knew nothing about her decadent life in Berlin,' said Klaus with a strident laugh. 'My uncle and aunt are very straight-laced and would be appalled to hear the things their only daughter got up to.'

'She must find Zwolle very dull after Berlin,' said Wouter.

Klaus laughed again. 'Eva? Not her. She couldn't stand it at home, so moved into a house with five others, all actors or performers of some kind. Eva has a habit of making her own entertainment wherever she goes. Like throwing parties after curfew for the neighbours and anyone else who wants a bit of fun. Germans too.' He raised his eyebrows at Wouter who threw him a surprised glance.

'Sounds dangerous,' said Wouter, returning his attention to the road ahead. They were approaching the outskirts of Zwolle. Groups of Nazis swarmed by the side of the road but none took any interest in their beaten-up van, which mingled in with the rest of the traffic. Maybe they had other things on their mind.

'Maybe, but life has to go on. Sometimes it's better to get them on your side and they might do you favours in return.'

It was the first time Wouter had heard Klaus speak like this. Klaus had always had such a black-and-white view of the Germans and this hadn't changed as a result of the soldiers he'd encountered. Single-minded brutes intent on carrying out orders and who were insensitive to the distress of people no different to themselves. The ones he'd come across were cold, calculating bastards. 'How can you say that?' he said, shooting Klaus a dark look.

'Because we're all in it together, whatever you might think. Just look around you. Most of them are no more than kids.

They've been told what to do and daren't protest in case of reprisals. So they toe the line and try to look aggressive but if you look them in the eye you can see their fear. There, look at that one.' Klaus briefly caught the attention of a young soldier, who happened to stare straight at him as they slowed down to pass a parked car. He was standing slightly apart from his unit of six or seven men, all barely out of their teens. Ramrod straight, he stood with his razored fair hair neatly away from his high forehead, his pale eyes staring directly at Klaus. He lifted his arm and shouted out, causing the group to look round.

'Turn next left,' urged Klaus, leaning forward in his seat. 'Now. Then right.'

Swearing profusely, Wouter swung the van past the car and down the road Klaus indicated.

'Sorry. Thought it best we got out of there. I didn't like the look of that lot,' said Klaus, allowing himself a sigh once they were well away from the main road. 'That's the problem. Get a group of them and they start behaving like thugs. Did you see how many there were? There must be something going on. Keep on down this street and you'll see the church up on the right. We'd better park behind the church and walk back through the side streets. Eva doesn't live far from here.'

Eva's house was squeezed between two taller ones along a narrow cobbled street. The once-white paint was peeling from the door. It was opened by a lanky young man with floppy black hair that he kept sweeping off his face. He was wearing a paint-splattered smock and held a brush in his hand. They had obviously disturbed him at his work, but he didn't seem to mind as he welcomed them in, even before they were able to say they were there to see Eva.

The hallway was cluttered with rusty implements, a stack of metal pails and piles of battered-looking shoes, many with the soles hanging off. In one corner, a large heap of yellowing newspapers threatened to spill all over the dark red tiles. A female voice called out from the kitchen asking who the visitors were.

'Friends for you,' the young man called back before disappearing into a door on the right.

A petite woman appeared in the doorway and took a long drag from her black cigarette holder before speaking. Her appearance was striking. Messy blonde curls held back with tortoiseshell clips on either side of her head. Bright red lipstick slightly escaped the curve of her lips. She wore a floral gown pinched in at the waist, emphasising her full figure.

'Klaus, *schatje*!' she cried in a deep voice. 'What a surprise! And you've brought a friend too. Come in and have a glass of wine.'

The kitchen was marginally less messy than the hallway, though from the number of unwashed glasses it was obvious that there must have been many occupants in the house.

'We can't stay long as we're making a delivery in town. I'm working for the underground now,' said Klaus, pulling himself tall as he spoke.

'Oh, how exciting!' said Eva, clapping a hand over her mouth. 'You must tell me all about it. But first, a drink.' She selected three glasses, then swirled them under the tap before filling with red wine and a splash of water. 'Sorry, but this will have to do. It's not so easy to get hold of supplies anymore,' she said with a shrug. 'Let me find something to go with this. I know there's bread somewhere.' With a shriek, she unearthed a complete loaf, not minding the greenish tinge along one side, which she sliced off. All the while she kept up her chatter, pausing every so often to pull on her cigarette holder, which she laid elegantly across a mother-of-pearl ashtray.

'Now tell me what you get up to with your "underground",' she said, narrowing her eyes as she sat down. 'It can be terribly dangerous. And unlucky. I had a friend who got arrested right at the start of all this and was sent to Kamp Amersfoort where he's been ever since. All he did was to arrange travel documents for a Jewish couple he'd met through the theatre. The problem was that they were both men. Someone somewhere in that group can't have liked what was going on and sneaked on him. You don't do that kind of thing, do you?' She frowned, her eyes darting from one to the other, then sniggered. 'I mean, help Jews escape.'

'Not yet,' said Klaus, joining in her laughter. 'But since you mention it, we have a request to make. Wouter's looking for a Jewish friend he's been told is somewhere here in Zwolle.'

The smile disappeared from Eva's face. 'Why do you think I can help? I don't like to get caught up in that kind of thing.'

'We're not asking you to get involved,' said Klaus. 'Just if you might have heard of any newcomers to the area. A lot have been hiding in the woods near Kampenveld, but it's no longer safe for them there.'

'And your friend?' said Eva, addressing Wouter. 'Was she hiding in the woods?' Eva's hands trembled as she took another cigarette and tried to fit it into her holder.

'We both were,' said Wouter, 'until the Germans found the camp. Berkenhout? No, you probably haven't heard of it,' he said, watching Eva shake her head. 'Berkenhout was so well hidden that almost no one knew about it. Well, someone did and must have passed on information. I was the first to hear the *moffen* approach and got out as fast as I could, but Laura... I don't know what happened to her. I want to find out if she made it.'

'So you are Jewish.'

'No, I'm not. I went into hiding when it looked like I'd be sent to Germany. There's no way I was prepared to go and do their dirty work.'

'Or me,' said Klaus. 'It's how we met. Hiding out in the woods.'

'Oh, Klaus! Why didn't you say?' Eva stood up and clutched the end of the table. 'Does anyone know you're here?'

Klaus went and put an arm round her and she sobbed against his shoulder. 'You don't realise, I'm safe here. They don't bother us. I can't go through all that again.'

Klaus raised his eyebrows at Wouter. 'Eva, listen. The last thing I want to do is upset you and really there's nothing to worry about. We're just two acquaintances visiting some friends we haven't seen in a while.'

Eva lifted her head. Her eyes were wet with tears that spilled down her cheeks in dark smudges. 'I'm sorry. I had a bad experience when I was living in Berlin. Did Klaus tell you?' She spoke to Wouter, who nodded.

Her artist friend popped his head round the door to ask if everything was all right. Eva waved him in and slopped some wine into a glass for him. She seemed much calmer now, introducing her cousin and Wouter, as if she'd known him for years.

'We're having a party after curfew tonight. There'll be singing and dancing and I've even managed to get hold of some rum to make punch. Do say you'll come.'

It was as if their earlier conversation hadn't occurred as she lifted her cigarette holder to her lips, pulled on it deeply and threw her head back theatrically to blow out the smoke.

TWENTY-ONE

WOUTER

'Well, that went well,' said Wouter sarcastically, once they were back in the van. 'And I really don't want to go to this party. I'm not in the mood and have no intention of dancing.' As the words came out, Wouter knew he sounded like a truculent child, but it was the way he felt. Eva and her friends just weren't his type and her phony behaviour made him uncomfortable.

'Come on, it'll be fun. We both need a bit of cheering up and who knows who we'll meet.' Klaus relaxed into his seat with his hands clasped behind his head.

'I'm not sure I trust her. All that talk about not wanting to get caught up in the Resistance,' said Wouter. 'I wouldn't be surprised if something's going on that she doesn't want to talk to us about. She's happy enough to throw parties and invite any old person along and then makes out she can't possibly make any enquiries on our behalf.'

'Just give her time. She has a tendency to overdramatise stuff. When she was a girl she was always having tantrums, which she'd forget about five minutes later. But she's got a heart of gold and I'm sure she'll come round. With all the people she knows there's bound to be someone who can help.'

Wouter grumbled under his breath, putting an end to the conversation.

It was late afternoon when they arrived at the house of Else's friend. Set back from the road with its own driveway lined with well-tended rhododendron bushes, the sprawling house looked like a former school. Wouter rang on the bell, tapping out the first few notes of Beethoven's 5th as Else had instructed. They were kept waiting a couple of minutes before a querulous voice came from within, asking who was there.

'Hello, I'm Wouter and this is Klaus. We're Else's... friends,' said Wouter.

The door was opened by a woman with grey-flecked dark hair and a face with deeply etched lines that gave her a worried look.

'I'm Truus. Else didn't say who would be coming. But I'm pleased to meet you.' She glanced quickly at the van parked in full view of the road, then spoke more urgently. 'Bring it round to the back, will you? There's a shed where you can put the supplies – it's unlocked – then knock on the kitchen door to be let in.' With a quick glance towards the road, she shut the door on them.

Wouter was surprised to find a crowd of people sitting around the kitchen table. One of them looked familiar, though he couldn't quite place him. He was engaging the others, a young couple and a woman about his age, in a game of bridge.

'Why, hello. Wouter, isn't it?' said the man cheerfully, and held out his hand.

'Do you know each other?' said Truus.

'*Schat*, we were both in Berkenhout about a year ago. I was helping Dick Foppen out at the time, so wasn't an *onderduiker* in the true sense.' The man laughed as he placed an arm round her shoulders. For a moment, her face softened into a smile and her cheeks took on a hint of colour.

'Now you say it, I do remember you,' said Wouter. 'You were there when I first arrived, weren't you? Sorry, I don't remember your name.'

'Niels,' he said, beaming.

It all came back to him. Wouter had arrived with a dozen or more and it had all been a bit of a muddle. People were milling about and because it was dark it was impossible to get the hang of the place. At first, Wouter couldn't see any huts at all, but of course that was the point. The branches and leaves covering the roofs did a pretty good job of concealing the huts and with no artificial light it was impossible to find the entrance. It was unnerving. All the newcomers were anxious about living in such close quarters in the woods among strangers, but Niels had seemed quite relaxed in all the chaos. He'd made them stand in a semicircle so he could tell each of them which huts they'd be sharing. Wouter hadn't been too pleased but from the murmurings among the group, he'd known he wasn't the only one unhappy with the allocation.

'I hadn't been there long myself,' said Niels. 'I thought it ridiculous that Dick put me in charge of new arrivals. I cracked a few jokes, though no one seemed to laugh.'

Wouter remembered being unimpressed by Niels's attempts to cheer them up. After a two-hour trek on foot with a bunch of people he didn't know, he'd been in no mood for jokes.

Those early weeks were chaotic. So many people coming and going while the camp settled into some kind of order. Wouter had kept himself apart, despite Niels's attempts to make everyone get to know each other. Then, one day, he was gone. Like so many, his stay was short, making way for others in urgent need of concealment. By then, Wouter was the one in nominal charge, a position he never imagined he'd hold for more than a few weeks. But as the pressure on places eased, the atmosphere in the camp became calm and Dick told Wouter he was pleased about the continuity he represented. Now here was Niels, back again, and Wouter was in no mood to be friendly.

'We're about to have our evening meal. Will you join us?' said Truus, who was stirring a pot of soup on the stove. Niels was already moving chairs around to make space round the table.

The offer of a meal was too good to turn down. As he gulped down the first few spoonfuls of the thick brown bean soup, Wouter realised how tense he'd been all day. Still there was the prospect of returning to Eva's later on. Maybe he would let Klaus go back on his own, he thought, stifling a yawn. He was placed next to Truus, who told him that her local group had been sending more and more people her way after she agreed to give shelter to *onderduikers*. Speaking in a low voice, she recounted how twice in the last week more newcomers had turned up on the doorstep, looking so forlorn and frightened that of course she couldn't turn them away. Others might have, but she thought it morally wrong, living on her own in such a large house. So, with help from volunteers, she had the top floor converted into a living space with its own kitchen and bathroom. Concealed, of course, behind a false door in a large wardrobe.

'Aren't you worried you'll be found out?' Wouter spoke quietly. He needn't have kept his voice down, as Niels was in the midst of telling one of his stories, interspersed with loud chortling.

'Yes, constantly. But the underground have been marvellous the way they organise everything and keep me informed of any unusual activity that might lead to a raid. I've stood aside for too long when I should have done more. Like so many, I didn't want to get involved in case I got found out and arrested. Then Niels turned up one day, one of Else's refugees.' She smiled. 'He told me all about Berkenhout and his work with refugees and somehow convinced me I could help too. Besides, I've been alone for too long after my parents died. You can see what a big house this is, so it's only right that I do my bit for others in need. Do you understand?'

Wouter nodded as an image of himself fleeing from Berkenhout leaving Laura behind rushed into his head. He coughed into his hand to cover up the emotion that threatened to overwhelm him. He coughed again. 'Not everyone who escaped from Berkenhout is accounted for,' he said. 'I'm looking for a young woman, Laura Wechsler. Is the name familiar?'

Truus furrowed her brow, though he wasn't sure if this was in concentration or her natural expression carved through years of worry. 'I think so,' she began, and Wouter's spirits began to soar before she slowly moved her head from side to side. 'I don't know. There was a girl, but she was about twelve and moved from place to place with her parents. They must have stayed for a couple of nights. I remember her eyes, big and dark and she scarcely said a word. The family kept themselves to themselves. After they left, they were meant to be heading for the coast and were hoping to get over on a boat to England. That's all I know. But it doesn't sound as if it could be her.'

Confused, Wouter shook his head. Her description fitted, but it didn't seem possible. Yet another false lead. 'No, the Laura I know was on her own. And your description is of a child. Laura's a young woman.' He sighed, not entirely convinced. Then again, maybe it had been Laura. 'I can't think why she'd want to go to England. You will let me know if you hear anything?'

Truus smiled. 'Of course. I can tell she means a lot to you. I'll have a word with Niels. He's bound to find out something. Why don't you come back tomorrow?'

TWENTY-TWO

WOUTER

The dark streets were quite deserted with only the occasional German vehicle crawling by, ready for the church clock to strike eight and ready to pounce on anyone who dared venture out of doors. At Klaus's suggestion, Wouter parked the van in a different place to the side of the church. Being spotted twice in one day would be hard to explain.

They set off at a brisk pace, making sure they kept well hidden in the shadows and away from the kerb. As they turned into Eva's street, they found themselves following a tall man wearing a long dark coat with the collar turned up. He seemed in a great hurry. Klaus held on to Wouter's sleeve and gave him a warning look. They fell back as the man drew level with Eva's front door, knocking twice before it opened. He slipped inside and the door closed behind him.

'Probably just one of Eva's party guests, but it might be best to wait a while before we go in,' said Klaus in a whisper.

'That man was a *mof*. You can tell by his coat. There's something very odd going on. Don't you think that's why Eva got so upset when we told her what we're up to?'

Klaus stuffed his hands into his pockets and fixed his eyes

on the ground. 'Look, it's probably not as bad as you think and he certainly doesn't look as if he's going in to raid the place.'

Wouter turned away, furious he'd been dragged into this. All he wanted was to find Laura and there was no chance of that now. Already on edge, he turned round at the sound of the click clack of hurrying footsteps coming towards them. He shrank into a doorway and watched as a woman, head down, passed by in high heels. He caught the trail of her perfume, a sweet muskiness mixed with a trace of tobacco. Instantly, he was transported back to when he was a child at bedtime, his mother leaning down to tuck him up and kiss him goodnight. It was all he could do to prevent himself from running after the woman so he could hold on to the feeling.

'Good evening,' said Klaus, touching the peak of his cap, just as the church clock began to chime.

The woman caught his eye and nodded briefly, pulling the tips of her collar tight as she hurried past. She also rang on Eva's door and, with a quick backward glance, disappeared inside.

'Come on, I'm going in,' said Klaus as if pulled towards the party by a magnetic force.

'Wait for me,' said Wouter, intrigued to discover more.

'Eva invited us,' said Klaus to the lanky man wearing a scarlet silk scarf and matching red lips who let them into the dark hallway. He nodded and led the way down a corridor to a room humming with laughter and chatter. There must have been at least twenty people crowded in the large room with Eva at the centre, holding her cigarette holder aloft in one hand and a long-stemmed glass in the other. Spying Klaus and Wouter, she shimmied over, kissing them each three times, while calling over her shoulder for drinks to be brought.

'I'm so excited you could make it and you're just in time for the entertainment. It's not much tonight, just some singing round the piano and dancing for those in the mood. Here, drink up,' she said as the lanky man handed them each a glass of punch. Greetings over, she wafted back to her friends who parted to allow her into their group.

Klaus drained his glass, declared it good and went in search of a top-up.

No sooner had he gone than the woman who'd passed them in the street tapped Wouter on the shoulder.

'Hello, I'm Dita. I'm Eva's neighbour. Didn't I see you earlier?' She tipped her head to one side as she appraised him.

Wouter caught another trace of her perfume as he introduced himself. He was struck by the mass of dark chestnut curls that framed her delicate features, giving her a fleeting resemblance to Laura.

'Yes, that was me. My friend and I held back when we saw a couple of people arrive. We didn't want to make it obvious there was something going on in here.'

'I wouldn't worry about that. Everyone knows about the parties Eva throws and if they don't come, they turn a blind eye.'

'Do you often come to her parties?' said Wouter, eyeing the guests who all seemed to know each other.

'Of course,' she said. 'It's the only fun anyone can get round here and the whole street comes. And it's an excuse for Eva and her actor friends to put on a show. So how do you know Eva?'

'She's my friend's cousin. We were running an errand in the area and decided to pay her a visit.'

'And she invited you to stay. How charming! Here, *proost!*' With an amused look in her eye, she lifted her glass against Wouter's, holding his gaze for a long moment.

From the corner of the room, the tinkling of a piano started amid much clapping and cheering, before developing into a raucous number. Through the crowd, Wouter could see the pianist was the man who'd let them in. He sat hunched forward, a cigarette in his mouth, pounding on the keyboard. Eva stood beside him, tapping out the rhythm with her hand until he calmed down his playing almost to a whisper. The room fell quiet as she began to sing, her voice deep and smoky. It was a French love song and several guests joined in the chorus.

'Doesn't she sing beautifully?' Dita sighed, slotting her arm through Wouter's. He glanced at her with a smile, enjoying her warmth against him as they swayed in time to the music. When the song ended to much applause and whistling, they chinked glasses again and drained them. The lanky man appeared at Wouter's elbow and before he knew it, he'd drunk several more glasses of punch, when the pianist ramped up the tempo again and several couples took to the floor dancing a fast version of the jitterbug.

'Dita, my darling.'

Wouter recognised Eva's artist friend, who appeared at Dita's side, speaking in a slurred voice as he kissed her noisily on the cheek. 'Won't you dance with me?' he said, grabbing her round the waist and making her squeal. They whirled off towards the other dancers, narrowly missing a couple who were flailing their arms not exactly in time to the music. It was Klaus and a very red-faced woman whose long auburn hair flew out around her. Wouter, feeling tipsy, laughed at the spectacle and clapped his hands. At the end of the dance Dita was returned to him, pink-faced and giggling, and he caught her in his arms to steady her.

'My turn now,' he said, and headed back into the throng, just as the pianist slowed his playing and Eva's sultry voice rose up above the din. It was just couples now dancing in hold. Wouter pressed himself close against Dita, breathing in her scent. Closing his eyes, he felt himself sway with the drink, as he imagined it was Laura in his arms and he wished it would never end. He wasn't concentrating on the music when he realised there were now two voices, a deeper male voice accompanying Eva's. He lifted his head to see who it was when Dita whispered in his ear. 'It's Emil. He always joins in at some point.' She pulled Wouter towards her again.

'Who?' said Wouter, coming to his senses.

'It's fine. He's fine,' said Dita.

Standing beside Eva with a hand on her shoulder was the man they'd seen arriving earlier. He had a young kindly face but there was no mistaking he was German from his buttoned-up grey jacket and the metal spread-winged eagle insignia above his chest pocket. Seeing them sing together as they gazed into each other's eyes, Wouter had to admit they were the perfect duo.

'But he's German,' Wouter whispered urgently against Dita's hair. 'I need to get some air.' He slipped his hand into Dita's and led her, resisting, out of the room, past an embracing couple and towards the kitchen. He shut the door behind them.

'What's up with you?' Dita yanked her hand from Wouter's and folded her arms.

'Can't you see? That *mof* standing in the middle of the party and acting as if nothing's unusual.'

Dita relented and lifted a finger to his lips. Speaking in a low voice she said, 'Emil's Eva's friend. They were both singers in Berlin and by coincidence he ended up in Zwolle. Now, please.' She leant in close and kissed him. In the dim light, he was unable to see her face, just the outline of her dark hair. He wanted to resist, but kept imagining she was Laura melting into his arms and it was an intense feeling. Time stood still. The strains of the two voices from next door no longer bothered him. It was just Laura and him, the two of them, entwined in an embrace that he never wanted to end.

TWENTY-THREE

WOUTER

A chink of light escaped from the edge of the blackout curtain onto his face, bringing him to. He was lying in a double bed with the sheets rucked up to his left. He stared up at the unfamiliar ceiling, which had a brown stain at its centre. Where was he? Groaning, he reached out with his arm. It came down flat and he breathed out. Had Dita been with him? He was sure he'd been on his own at the end of the evening. Or had he? He groaned again, hoping fervently it wasn't the case.

The door opened and Klaus came in holding two cups of ersatz coffee.

'Ah, you're awake at last. Bit too much to drink, *heh?*' he said with a grin. 'We were wondering when you were going to wake up.'

Wouter propped himself on one elbow and blinked, still trying to recall the events of the previous night. He did remember that Dita had said she'd felt a headache coming on and wanted to go home. Concerned for her wellbeing, he'd agreed to walk her the short distance back to her front door. He'd wanted to go in with her to make sure she was all right, but she'd insisted that she was fine and just needed to lie down.

He'd retraced his steps to Eva's, still feeling more than a little tipsy.

The party was winding down and most of the guests had left. Only the pianist remained, playing a soulful tune that reflected Wouter's feelings.

'Where did you learn to play so well?' Wouter took up a position next to the piano. He envied the man's ease at switching between different styles of playing, all without looking at a musical score. As if in a trance, the pianist slowly turned his head towards Wouter, then returned to his playing. Wouter sighed and went in search of Klaus and Eva.

'Wouter! There you are! Come and join us,' called Eva, holding on to the door frame. Seated at the table was Klaus, laughing and giggling with the flame-haired girl who was on his lap with both arms draped round his neck. Eva walked unsteadily to the counter and slopped the remains of the rum punch into a glass, handing it to Wouter. 'Are you all right?' she said, holding the back of a chair for support.

'Yes, fine.' Wouter coughed as the strong liquor caught the back of his throat.

She laughed. 'Now tell Eva everything.' She pulled the chair sideways and fell heavily onto it.

What had he told her that caused her to keep topping up his glass with neat rum? After a bit, nothing seemed to matter: Klaus and the girl giggling, the pianist's moody melodies from across the corridor, Eva's concerned face as she leant forward. The images merged and washed over him, drowning out his own voice droning on and on. Later, much later, he had a vague recollection of Klaus and the girl, each on either side of him, helping him up the stairs.

·   ·   ·

'Did you... were you here?' Confused, Wouter looked from Klaus to the bed.

Klaus chortled as he handed Wouter his coffee. 'Where else do you think I was? This place isn't a hotel.' He sat down on Wouter's side of the bed.

'And the girl you were with? What happened to her?' Wouter's mind refused to work. The idea of a threesome appalled him so he tried to obliterate it with a long gulp of the lukewarm liquid. He felt slightly better.

'Sandra? Oh, she's around here somewhere.' Klaus made a show of darting his eyes around the bedroom as if he expected to find her. There was no mistaking the amused expression on his face. 'But not *here*. She might have gone home. Anyway, what does it matter? It was a bit of fun, that's all. And you were quite amusing yourself, you know.'

Wouter groaned again. He rubbed his eyes as if that would help. When he opened them, Klaus was still there, grinning.

'Wait. That German, the one who was singing with Eva. What happened to him?'

'I can't say I took much notice of him. But now you mention it... he must have left early. He certainly wasn't around at the end. Why don't you ask Eva?'

Eva looked as bad as Wouter felt; she had dark smudges under her eyes and all her lipstick had rubbed off. She sat hunched over a cup of ersatz coffee with a cigarette in one hand. The holder was nowhere in sight.

'Help yourself,' she said, waving to the kettle that was simmering on the stove.

'Thanks. Klaus brought me one already,' said Wouter, positioning himself opposite her.

'I can tell Dita likes you,' said Eva, coming to with a broad smile. 'She's a good girl. You won't break her heart, will you?'

Wouter shook his head. 'I don't think that's likely to happen. I hardly know her. Anyway, I have my own problems if you remember. My Laura.' He took in a deep breath. 'It's as if she's disappeared off the face of the earth. The last I heard was that she was here in Zwolle, but no one I've spoken to is sure what's happened to her.'

'Emil, he might have some news.' She laughed throatily.

'That German is your friend?' said Wouter in disbelief.

'Look, Emil's not what you might think.'

'He's German, he's a *mof* and he knows exactly what goes on in here. Isn't that a bit strange?'

'No, not if you know what he's been through. Please, don't look like that and listen to what I have to say.' Eva took a long drag from her cigarette and let out the smoke in a long sigh. 'Yes, he's in the SS, but not by choice. After I fled Berlin, he heard they were recruiting, so he joined up. He didn't know what else to do. It's not ideal that he's a member of the Gestapo as we can't be open about seeing one another but it's a reason why I hold these private soirées. A wonderful excuse to sing together again.' She looked wistful.

'But can you trust him?' asked Wouter.

'I do because he's my best friend and he would do anything for me. But I do worry about the life he's chosen. He'd come off far worse than any of us if we got raided. Can you imagine, a German officer caught colluding with the enemy?'

'So why run the risk with these parties? Anyone can wander in, just like we did. Word gets round. I'm surprised you haven't been found out sooner.'

'You have a lot to learn,' said Eva, through half-closed eyes.

TWENTY-FOUR

LAURA

I jump awake at the sound of boots thumping across the floor above us. It's pitch black but I daren't switch on the light.

'Do you hear that?' Bets whispers urgently, tugging at my sleeve in the darkness.

'Shh. Don't make a sound. It's got to be a raid.' I grab her hand for comfort, then climb in beside her. We cling to each other and I sense the trembling of her body. We both stiffen at the scraping of furniture above us and raised male voices. Then comes the higher-pitched voice of Liv, indignant and confrontational as ever. I will her not to goad them as they'll be only more determined to turn the place upside down till they find what they are looking for. She carries on and I catch odd words, but none of them make any sense. The German voices cut across her – are there two, three of them? The confusion carries on until the door slams. We flinch. Then silence.

I rush to the window and tentatively push aside a corner of the curtain. I make out several pairs of boots, their metal tips glinting in the pale light of dawn. I quickly drop the curtain in shock.

'They've definitely gone, have they?' Bets is over by the

steps leading out of our jail and is straining to hear anything at all. This happens minutes after the clip of boots have died away. As there's been no sign of Liv leaving, I have to believe she's still in the house.

'Liv, Liv?' Are you there?' Bets calls, first in a tentative voice, just in case Liv is not alone, then becoming more panicky. No answer. 'She can't have abandoned us? Can she?'

I don't want to believe it either. 'She's up there, I'm sure of it.' I try to steady my voice but it cracks, betraying my fear. I eye the trapdoor, our only means of escape.

Together we stand on a stair halfway up and heave our shoulders against the trapdoor. One, two, three attempts, but it won't budge. We both shout hoarsely, despairingly.

We flinch at the sound of a door thudding shut. I run to the window to see the back of Liv's darned stocking legs as she disappears down the path.

Can you imagine what's going through our minds? How she'd persuaded the Germans to leave who had no idea we were inches away from them. And now no one knows we're locked away down below. Our terror intensifies at this realisation.

Exhausted, I slide down onto the floor and hold my head in my hands. This is worse than the terror I'd experienced when the shots rang out signalling the end of Berkenhout. I hadn't realised how lucky I'd been simply to run. Here, I'm losing my mind, imagining the walls and low ceiling crowding in on me, sucking out what little air there is. Is this some obscure punishment meted out by Liv because she hates us?

Hours pass. I become aware that Bets has come to sit on the floor next to me, her body pressed right up close against mine. 'Talk to me, Laura. I can't bear it when you're silent.' I lift my head at this, but can't think of words that have any meaning. 'Remember when we first met and our first night in the church? You were telling me about Berkenhout, but you didn't say anything about the friends you made. Tell me about them.'

I begin with Sofie, how she became my best friend after we shared our stories and the way we learnt to cook thanks to Corrie, and the discovery that we both loved teaching children. Bets listens while I carry on describing the kindness so many people have shown us, each going out of their way to make life not just comfortable, but full of little pleasures. I am, of course, thinking about the weekly visits from Else, Liesbeth and Dick, bringing coffee, cake and gossip, and how Jan used to make us laugh with his escapades in the woods.

'But there was someone else, wasn't there?' Bets nudges me and I realise I must have gone silent. It's the first time I allow the tears to fall, releasing all the pent-up emotion I've been carrying since my terrifying escape from Berkenhout.

'I don't think I'll ever see him again,' I say through sobs.

'What was his name?'

'Wouter. He made me feel special, but I doubted him and by the time I realised my mistake it was too late.'

Again, Bets listens patiently, letting me talk on about Wouter and it calms me down to do so.

'So you've had no news. But that doesn't mean he's lost to you. I wouldn't be surprised if he's out there searching for you right now.'

I turn my head to look at her and smile through my tears. I'm grateful she's given me a reason to carry on.

We both make more attempts to shift the trapdoor, but each time are defeated. I don't know why I hadn't thought of it before, but it's only when a sliver of sunlight lands on my arm that I know what I have to do.

Naturally, the window is locked but after rattling the handle back and forth a few times, I'm able to push it open. I shout in surprise as a blast of cold air hits my face but I don't care who hears me, even if there's a passing German. But my

elation turns quickly to despair on realising the window has a
metal bar running right down the centre. We don't have a hope
of getting out. Our only chance, surely, is to take it in turns to
stand watch for signs that anyone might be walking past. It's our
only hope.

Finally, we hear footsteps in the street beyond the hedge
and we freeze. Neither of us has the nerve to call out in case it's
the Germans come back to get us. And if it's not them, what if a
sympathiser were to walk past?

'The next time I'll call out for help. We have to,' I say, trying
to summon as much courage as I can muster. She nods
uncertainly.

From down the street, we can hear a couple approach who
are in conversation – she's teasing him and he laughs in reply.
As they draw level, Bets and I nod to each other and I cry out,
'Help! Please help! We're trapped down here. Please... can you
come and help?'

The voices fall silent. Whoever is there doesn't reply nor do
they come to investigate. We can't even hear their footsteps and
I'm convinced they're tiptoeing away, so keen are they to get
away unnoticed. It's a blow. What kind of people refuse to get
involved? Why? To protect themselves? Don't they have a
conscience?

'What do we do now?' asks Bets, who is sobbing.

'We keep going till some kind person is prepared to help,' I
say more ferociously. There has to be someone.

We're beside ourselves when the end finally comes. Hours must
have passed without the slightest sound from above. When it
happens, it's not as we expect. The gate squeaks open and Bets
grabs my hand so hard I have to suppress a cry. We're so
surprised that we nearly forget to call out till she's halfway
along the path with a man walking alongside her.

We both bellow at the same time.

'Liv! You're back!'

'Let us out! Let us out!'

At the sound of the muffled scrape of the chest being moved away from our trapdoor, we hug each other in relief.

TWENTY-FIVE

WOUTER

The cold air on his face was a welcome relief after the stuffiness of Eva's kitchen. He needed to start thinking clearly and the revelation about Emil did nothing to reassure him. It seemed unlikely that Emil, an SS officer, would be on the side of the Jews. Everything Wouter had heard about the Germans suggested that he'd be searching for Jews, not helping them. But he was Eva's friend... no, the last thing Wouter should do now was to put Laura in any danger. Full of resolve, he decided to retrace his steps to Truus.

He was only a little way up the street when Klaus came rushing after him, calling that he wanted to come too, but this was a visit Wouter needed to make on his own. He kept walking without looking back. 'Don't be long, we need to get going,' Klaus shouted after him, but Wouter wasn't listening. He was too preoccupied with thoughts of Laura as he hurried away.

Plunging his hands into his coat pockets, he walked briskly to Truus's house, a good mile away. Avoiding the centre, he almost got lost in the side streets. He came upon a small square with a fountain and sat on the stone ledge for a moment while he got his bearings. Somewhere from behind him came the clatter of clogs or boots on cobblestones. Not waiting to see who it was, he darted down an alleyway leading back where he'd come from. A young woman was sweeping the flagstone outside her house and looked up as he approached her.

'Which way to the *Kalverlaan*?' he said.

'You're miles away,' said the girl with a quizzical look, but she gave him directions. 'You won't want to go through the centre today. There are loads of *moffen* about and they're stopping people at random.'

Wouter thanked her and hurried on his way, concerned by what she'd told him. If this stranger thought he looked like the sort to be stopped and searched, he knew it must be true.

Truus was on her knees scrubbing the hallway. 'I wondered if I'd see you,' she said, her cheeks red from her exertions. 'Come in and let's see if Niels has left some coffee for us. You may have to wait for him. He's only just left.'

After the chaos at Eva's, this kitchen was a picture of neatness. Wouter took a seat at the table noticing the surface was damp and there was a faint scent of disinfectant. Truus fetched two cups from a cupboard and shook the coffee pot left simmering on the stove. There was only enough for one cup and a splash more. She shrugged and gave Wouter the full cup. 'I insist,' she said before he could object. It tasted of real coffee. Sniffing deeply before taking a sip, he nodded.

'Don't ask. No one round here asks.' Truus laughed.

'Where is everyone?' asked Wouter.

'They've finished their chores and are up in their rooms reading or writing or whatever it is they get up to. In return, they get a bed and I feed them. It's a little like a hotel except the guests help out and can't move around as they wish,' she said through pursed lips.

If Laura were here, she'd pull her weight – Wouter was

certain of that. He could see her putting her back into any chore without complaint. She'd offer to give lessons to the young ones, prepare the vegetables for the evening meal, ever helpful, ever willing. He caught his breath. He knew this was the Laura of his imagination. Truus's words suggested the reality of hiding Jews was quite different.

'Don't get me wrong,' continued Truus. 'I'm grateful for the help, but one or two are quite demanding.' She lowered her voice. 'The young married couple who arrived two days ago insisted on having their own room. Imagine it! There are seven of them up there in the attic with a partition kindly rigged up by Niels. Bless him, it was his idea to install a small kitchen and bathroom up there to give them privacy.'

Both Wouter and Truus's gaze shot up to the ceiling at the sound of a muffled thump. Truus shook her head. 'See? They behave as if they own the place. The number of times I've told them to keep down the noise. Just imagine if a collaborator happens to be passing.' She sucked up the remaining drops of coffee and put her cup down with a clatter. 'I'm sorry. It gets to me sometimes.'

Her mood lifted when Niels walked back in the door. He was carrying two bulging bags, which he dumped onto the table. 'Apples and more apples.' He laughed, rolling a few out and handing one each to Truus and Wouter. 'There are more where these come from.' He winked at Truus, making her giggle.

'Come and sit down and tell us what you've found out,' she said, crunching into an apple and patting the seat beside her.

'Something and nothing,' said Niels, winking once more in Truus's direction.

Wouter's stomach flipped at the prospect of definite news. He disliked the way he came on to Truus, making a show of lifting a tendril of her hair and looping it behind her ear while whispering to her. He knew full well why Wouter was there and seemed to enjoy withholding what news he might have.

Truus came to Wouter's rescue. She gave a quick slap to Niels's wrist. 'Well then? What do you have for Wouter?'

Niels turned serious as he looked at Wouter. 'Hans showed me a list of all the refugees he's helped pass through Zwolle and Laura's name is on it. She came on the final trip his brother made before the Germans caught wind of what was happening. So that was good.' He gave Wouter a quick smile. 'He also told me he'd placed her with a woman living next to the Grote Kerk. Unfortunately, it didn't last.' He paused.

'What do you mean? Are you saying she's no longer there?' said Wouter, feeling increasingly agitated.

'I'll tell you if you let me finish,' said Niels curtly. 'The woman got cold feet. Not long after the placement, the town filled up with soldiers. You probably saw clumps of them standing around near the Town Hall when you drove in. A friend of the woman was raided and they found five *onderduiker*s hiding in the cellar. A van took them away and the friend was treated roughly. I don't have any more details, but I'm sure you can see how dangerous it is for all of us who try to help.' He glanced at Truus who nodded.

'Even more dangerous for the people herded off to some godawful camp,' said Wouter.

'Of course. But there's no evidence that's what happened to Laura. Hans only dealt with the original placements. He wasn't able to tell me any more,' said Niels with a serious expression.

Wouter let out a long sigh, part relief, part frustration at another dead end. He wouldn't have been surprised if Niels knew more than he was letting on and was enjoying Wouter's discomfort.

'But he did tell me he thought she was no longer in Zwolle.'

'No longer in Zwolle? Is she or isn't she? Niels, is there something else you're not telling me?'

Niels gave an embarrassed cough. 'No, of course not. Hans isn't happy that I pass on information to strangers.'

'I'm hardly a stranger...'

'All right. But Hans is wary, especially with all the rumours circulating about the Berkenhout raid. Look, I have to be careful what I say...' His voice drifted off as he held Wouter's gaze. He lifted his shoulders in a shrug. 'If you'd taken charge,' he said in a quiet voice.

It was as if he'd punched Wouter in the chest.

So that's what it was all about. It was common knowledge that Wouter couldn't be trusted because he'd messed up. Let everyone down. Let people die when he should have been standing up to the *moffen*. Maybe Niels thought, heaven forbid, that he was colluding with them. Was that a smile on his face?

'What do you know?' Wouter burst out. 'You conveniently left. You've no idea what it was like to be faced with a load of *moffen* ambushing us, shooting their pistols. It was terrifying. We had to get out as fast as we could. The escape routes were useless.' Wouter wanted to say more but stopped at the look of disbelief on Niels's face.

'I wish I could be of more help, but I can't go against Hans,' said Niels. 'He's become extra cautious about passing on information in case of reprisals.'

Wouter gave a short snort and stood up to go. 'I'd better be off,' he said, swallowing his anger. But first he went over to Truus, who looked embarrassed at their altercation.

'I'm sorry,' she said, slightly despairingly.

'It's fine. I'll work something out. Now, look after yourself, won't you?' He lifted her chin and held her gaze for a moment before leaving.

TWENTY-SIX

WOUTER

As he turned into Eva's street he became aware of a commotion. A crowd of people were milling around outside her house. A hum of voices, some raised, filled the air. He noticed the wide-open door and could see several people crouching over something bulky on the ground. Wouter stopped dead. His initial thought was that Eva had been raided, but if that was true where were the Germans ordering people about? With a feeling of dread, he approached the scene.

He couldn't see the face of the woman bent over the body, but realised it must be Klaus's girl from the party from the way her auburn hair fell in waves down her back. Next to her stood Dita, a hand over her mouth as if she were about to be sick. Bending over the inert shape was Eva, sobbing loudly.

Wouter rushed forward and fell to his knees beside Eva. 'It can't be,' he gasped.

Klaus lay face downwards, his leg at an awkward angle. His face, twisted to one side, had a smudge of blood stretching from his brow to his neck. His jacket, a dark stain right in the centre. It didn't look as if anyone had tried to move him.

'Shot in the back. He didn't stand a chance,' said a voice next to him. It was Eva's artist friend who was at his shoulder. He spread a thin blanket over the body.

'Did you see who did it?' Wouter spoke in a shaky voice.

Eva sat back on her heels. He hardly recognised her pale face streaked with mascara, her lips bare and trembling.

'I was about to shut the front door when a gun went off,' said Eva's friend. 'It gave me such a shock. I slammed the door shut and tried to see who it was through the peephole. But when I opened the door again, he'd gone and Klaus was on the ground.'

'It must have been a *mof*,' said Wouter grimly.

'No, it wasn't. That much I know. I did catch a glimpse of the man and he wasn't in uniform. Maybe he was expecting someone else and Klaus walked out at that moment. I think he was just plain unlucky.'

'A collaborator, if you ask me,' said a sharp-nosed woman in curlers who pushed forward to listen. 'They're sly, they are. Pretending to be one of us, but doing the dirty work of those bastards. Ever since that lot have come pouring into town, there've been stories of our men jumping over onto their side.' She sniffed loudly.

That was when the trembling started. Was she referring to the person who'd shot Klaus? Or Klaus himself? Wouter stared at the body of his friend, unable to grasp how quickly it had all happened. How could a life be terminated so rapidly and for no reason? Less than an hour ago, he'd stood in the kitchen, his mind on Laura. He'd been so intent on getting away that he'd hardly heard Klaus's perfectly reasonable request to head back home. If only he'd had his wits about him and asked Klaus to come along with him, they'd be chatting and ribbing each other as normal.

'It's not your fault.' Dita slipped her arm through his.

Wouter couldn't stop the tremor that had started in his hands and now spread throughout his whole body.

Two uniformed policemen arrived and roughly pushed people aside. Those standing toward the back, the ones craning to see, melted away. Wouter had a feeling of dread. Everyone knew the police were not to be trusted. Too many stories had emerged about their ill treatment of Jews, making them no better than the Germans. How could you trust anybody when it was impossible to know where people's loyalties lay?

Wouter watched helplessly as the men in uniform tugged at Klaus's jacket, causing him to roll onto his back. A gasp went up as his twisted face became visible. It was the first time Wouter had seen a dead man. The fact it was Klaus made it all the more shocking.

'Here. I've got it,' crowed one of the policemen, extracting papers from the inside pocket of Klaus's jacket. He handed it to the other man who examined them, grim-faced.

'As I thought,' he said, lifting his head to smile at his colleague.

Wouter couldn't stand watching these liars any longer. 'What are you saying? He hasn't done anything wrong.' He snatched the documents from the policeman who grabbed his wrist in a painful grip. He just had time to catch sight of the ID card with Klaus's name and photograph. All in order, as well he knew. Before he knew it, he was ordered to show his own documents, which he kept in his shirt pocket.

'Take this one to the station,' ordered the first policeman. 'I'll get the body moved.'

Wouter flinched as the policeman roughly grabbed him by the arms. He twisted round to see he was the only one left at the scene. Everyone, even Dita and Eva, had vanished.

. . .

Wouter stared up at the tiny window high up on the wall of the interrogation room. It afforded very little light and was the type that couldn't be opened. It was stuffy and the thick air was making him drowsy. How long he'd been kept waiting he had no idea, but he needed to steady his thoughts as he tried to make sense of it all. No doubt the delay was a ploy to make him angry so they could force him into saying what they wanted to hear.

He turned his head at the sound of a key grating open the lock. A young man walked in, his uniform hanging off him, making him look younger than he probably was. He had an armful of folders, which he locked inside a small metal filing cabinet. Wouter half stood, but the young man gestured to him to stay put, saying his boss would be along shortly. He left and the door clunked shut.

Wouter sighed out a breath. The glass of water he'd been given was now empty and he wished he'd asked the young man for another. There was nothing to do but wait. And think.

Could Klaus have been a collaborator? Could the policeman have known something that Wouter hadn't or even been a collaborator himself? Wouter tried to think back to conversations he'd had with Klaus but all Klaus had ever said was that he wanted to escape the Germans. He was just another man on the run, aware of the dangers, but not enthused enough to want to fight. Probably a bit scared, despite his bravado. A bit like himself. Then another thought occurred to him. Maybe they believed Wouter was a collaborator too and were taking so long because they were gathering evidence against him. Those files, the ones in the filing cabinet, could they be full of incriminating evidence?

After another interminable wait, the door opened. The policeman who had grabbed Klaus's ID walked in with a slight nod of his head. He scraped the metal chair back and sat opposite Wouter, grunting under his breath. He looked as tired as

Wouter felt. Wouter thought better of speaking first so kept looking down at the table between them.

'Your name?' said the man without any preamble. His pen hovered over a form in front of him.

'Wouter Brand.'

'Address.'

A tiny pause while Wouter decided to give his parents' address. He didn't want to deviate from any of the information they might have on him.

When he was satisfied that everything Wouter said tallied with his form, he laid down his pen. 'What were you doing with Klaas...'

'Klaus...' Wouter corrected him. 'I... we were visiting his cousin, Eva, who lives at 24 Kerkstraat.' He watched as the man put a question mark next to Klaus's name.

'It's quite a way to come from Kampenveld. Why were you with him?'

'We came in my van. Klaus doesn't... didn't drive,' said Wouter, swallowing hard.

The policeman dipped his chin as he moved to another document. 'Why did you call him Klaus?'

'Because that's his name.' *Why did you call him Klaas?* he wanted to ask, but decided against it.

'Have you ever worked with any organisation associated with the Resistance?' The policeman lifted his head to stare at Wouter.

'No, I haven't.' Wouter thought of his time at Berkenhout and the deliveries he'd made for Else, knowing this to be an act of resistance. His eyes darted to the sheet of paper covered in small writing but he didn't dare peer any more closely. He hoped the information he gave couldn't be traced back to Else in some way.

'Did your friend tell you what he was involved in, that he was a member of the NSB?'

'You must be mistaken. He certainly never told me anything about that.'

'But that was where you met him, wasn't it? At a meeting of the NSB where you also signed up?'

'Absolutely not!' Wouter half shouted. 'I know nothing about such things and have no desire to either.'

'Hmm,' said the policeman as he deliberated his next line of questioning.

'You were a postman, it says here. But you're not anymore, are you?'

Wouter felt his stomach tighten. How did he have this information? His mind spun as he thought of a plausible explanation.

'No, I left to look after my mother who was ill. And when she recovered, my job had been given to someone else. You know how it is, these days.' He gave an apologetic smile, but the policeman didn't respond.

'Your aggressive behaviour toward a member of the police force,' he said eventually. 'In normal times, it would earn you an arrest.' He paused. 'But I'm prepared to overlook it this time.' He extracted another form from his pile of papers and scribbled on it. 'On this occasion, you will be required to pay a fine.'

Wouter took a long silent breath in, relieved his interrogation appeared to be at an end. He handed over a note from his wallet. Without a word, the policeman took it and bent over the form to make further notes.

'Any further misbehaviour will be brought to our attention and the punishment will be much harsher next time,' he said at last.

Wouter nodded, trying hard to look remorseful. He put his hands on the table in readiness to stand up, but the frown on the policeman's face made him keep put.

'I'm letting you go for now, but you may be called in for further questioning. We will need to investigate the discrepancies between the information we've received and your statement.'

'But I've told you everything I know. He was just an acquaintance, no more,' said Wouter, his heart pounding.

'Like I said, we will need to investigate this further. Now, do you want to leave or not?' For the first time, the policeman grinned but Wouter knew for certain he was not being friendly.

TWENTY-SEVEN

LAURA

The steps lead to freedom, but my legs are shaking so much. Two strong hands reach down and hoist me out onto the cold flagstones. I'm incapable of moving but find myself being gently lifted aside so Bets can be pulled out too.

'You're safe now.'

I focus on the red-cheeked face smiling down at me and am struck by the blueness of his eyes. The accent isn't strong, but it's unmistakable. Emil is his name. What is going on? Nothing made sense just five minutes ago and it makes even less sense now. I slide my eyes onto Liv who is standing right behind him. Bets is sobbing with relief, but my eyes are hot with anger. I stare at Liv. What can she have been thinking?

'Why did you leave us on our own?' I try to raise my voice, but it's still hoarse from the hours of crying out for help.

'You don't understand, it wasn't like that. I left you for your own safety.' Her eyes seem to plead with me and she's trying to look remorseful. I want to believe her but brush the thought away. I can't let her get away with it that easily.

'You left us deliberately, didn't you? Do you have any idea

what it was like to be trapped down there? We thought we were going to die.'

She doesn't answer but goes over to the larder and brings out the remains of a joint of meat and some cold potatoes. I can feel my anger dissolve at the sight of this food, the first we've seen in what seems like days. Bets stops crying and even manages to force a smile. No one says another word as we sit at the table and devour the fatty meat and cold potatoes as if we've been served up a feast. Liv and Emil partake of it too. I keep my eyes on my plate to avoid any conversation or confrontation. I'm aware of the irony of this quiet domestic scene, but I can do or say no more till I regain my strength. I expect Liv to break the silence to let us in on what she's been up to and why this Emil is here, sitting at her table. But it's Emil who clears his throat and speaks.

'I can only imagine what you must be thinking when you hear me speak. When I tell you that I'm a member of the Waffen SS, you mustn't be alarmed.' He lays his hands flat on the table as if that will somehow calm us. I don't know what I feel right now, but I do want to hear more. 'I was living in Berlin as an actor, but it was too dangerous to continue working there. A friend suggested I became a soldier, even though I knew I wasn't cut out to be one. It was a choice I made because I didn't believe I had an alternative. Within days of moving to my barracks, I was horrified to learn of the extensive movement of Jews on cattle trucks to German and Polish camps. Not to work, as most believe, but to die. Yes, die.' He says it more forcefully as we look on in shock. Then he seems to pull himself together. 'I was expected to condone it, but how could I? Stand by and just let it happen? My mother's best friend is Jewish and I used to play with her son till we went to separate schools. They were lucky. His father had the foresight to get the whole family out to Switzerland at the first stirrings of war, but I never knew why. The thought that these kind, friendly people who would do anything for us could have been removed from everything they have ever loved or known to be sent to their deaths.' He pauses to take a deep, hesitant breath. He looks up from Bets to me and something like despair is written on his face. I want to trust this man, but is it safe to do so?

'I realise that I must continue to serve in the SS for now, despite my serious misgivings. To challenge their authority would be disastrous for me. But I can't stand by in silence. It means taking risks so, in my own small way, I devote myself to helping Jews escape while it's still possible.'

I nod, still not understanding.

'You're here to help us?' says Bets, and she leans forward.

Emil glances over at Liv, but she keeps her expressionless eyes fixed on her lap. I could throttle her the way she's leaving it all to Emil. But I force myself to listen to him. Liv – she can't be trusted.

'It will mean changing your names and losing your Jewish identity,' I hear him say quietly.

Have I missed something he said? I let the enormity of his words sink in as Bets asks him where we're to go.

'First to the safe house of a friend of mine who lives close by. After that, I don't know. Zwolle's too dangerous, so it'll have to be somewhere you won't be found.'

Emil's words turn over and over in my head as I try to process what this latest terrible development means. If I heard him right, then Laura Wechsler will cease to exist. I will be forced to live as someone who isn't me and remain in denial about my past, possibly for the rest of my life. But do I have any choice in the matter?

I realise, to my horror, that everything that has happened since I left the safety of Berkenhout has been an utter waste of time. Panic grips me as another thought strikes me that I won't ever see my darling Wouter ever again. But it's worse than that:

the idea I have to move to some place where he won't be able to find me is more terrifying than even losing my identify.

I stare at Emil, hoping it's all a big mistake, but his face is blank. Of course he knows that Bets and I have no power to make him change his mind. Shuddering inwardly, I keep staring at Emil, unable to express what I'm thinking, but I know I must resign myself to an uncertain future.

TWENTY-EIGHT

LAURA

Bets and I aren't much good for one another right now. She's as anxious as me. We're free of our prison, a new hiding place found for us, but neither of us are able to blank out the horror of being locked up and abandoned. Our constant questions only serve to wind each other up.

'What if Emil hadn't walked her back home?'

'But he's German, a *mof...*'

'And if he hadn't come up the path and seen us at the window?'

'He might have left her at the gate and gone away.'

'And she would have ignored our cries for help...'

'And left us to rot.'

I would never have believed that the only person I could put my trust in would be a German soldier in the Waffen SS. But without Emil, we'd be at the mercy of Liv who, I'm convinced, is losing her mind.

Emil tells us it was entirely by chance that he met Liv. He was calling in on a friend and stepped out into the street when Liv appeared running towards him in a state of obvious distress.

He brought her into the friend's house, promising to help her. At first, nothing she said made any sense, so they made her drink some brandy to try to calm her. It had more than the desired effect and she passed out on the sofa till morning. Emil had to go back to his barracks but was able to return after making some excuse to his superior. When Liv set eyes on Emil, she flew into a panic, saying she must go home as she'd forgotten something, but she couldn't remember what it was. That something was us. It chills me to the bone to think that, if Emil hadn't been with her, we'd still be locked up in that horrific dungeon.

Thanks to Emil, we've escaped our hellhole.

'It'll just be for a day or two till I can arrange somewhere more suitable,' he tells us. Frankly, I don't care where we go as long as it's far away from Liv. I'm sure the feeling is mutual. You should see the look of relief on her face as we gather our meagre belongings and depart without uttering a word. She never wanted us staying and only took us in to please Hans, her lover. Fat lot of good that did her as he's never been back.

We hurry along beside Emil with scarves pulled up round our faces against the biting cold. There are few people out in this weather and no one takes any notice of us. It's not far to his friend's house, the one he took Liv to. The friend is away for a few days, he tells us, but the man she shares with will look after us.

We slip in through a back door into a large warm kitchen. It's chaotic in here, but immediately I feel myself relax among the stacks of dirty plates and cups, piles of newspapers and, look, there's a tabby cat curled up in a basket next to the *kachel*. A lanky man with floppy hair is lounging, legs up, on a dark-green sofa, reading a book. Bets and I exchange a smile.

'Meet Lars,' says Emil.

'*Hoi!*' says Lars, looking up briefly before returning to his book.

'This is Laura and Bets,' says Emil, raising his eyebrows at us.

'Oh, hello. Welcome.' Lars stands up and I'm struck by how tall he is. 'Excuse the mess, but Eva's had to go away for a few days. There's been a bit of a to-do here. A death in the family. So as long as you don't mind, you can stay as long as you like.'

'It's good of you to help out,' says Emil. I'm surprised to hear him say this. Shouldn't we be the ones thanking Lars? Then I remember how much Emil's done to help us and it gives me a warm feeling. But straightaway he goes and spoils it by saying he won't be able to come back for a while as he's being sent away for training. To see if he's suitable officer material. As he says the words I'm gripped by a coldness that prickles my scalp and invades my stomach. I want to stop him from leaving and am overcome by a desire to hold on to him. 'I thought you hated the Nazis. Can't you refuse?' I plead, panicking that we're about to be abandoned once more.

'What will happen to us?' Bets whispers. She's biting on her lip.

Emil lets out a long-suffering sigh. At least it sounds like one. 'I know. It's a shock to me too. I only found out this morning. These things happen fast and if I don't comply, it'll only arouse suspicion. Look, it won't be for long and you'll be safe here, I'm sure of it.'

Lars is nodding, though slowly, as if he's only just comprehending what Emil is suggesting.

'I have to go.' Emil smiles his boyish smile and I wish I didn't feel so strongly about him leaving. We all stand awkwardly, before Bets rushes forward and throws her arms around Emil's waist.

'Don't become one of them – you mustn't. And come back soon,' she says. I turn away at the sound of her voice breaking. I simply can't bring myself to hug him in the same way.

'Take care, both of you now,' says Emil, reaching for my shoulder and giving it a squeeze. His face has gone quite red.

The door sticks as he pulls it to and he has to wrench it into place. The finality of the gesture makes me sure we won't be seeing him again.

TWENTY-NINE

LAURA

Lars does his best to make us feel at home. He doesn't seem to have any idea about hiding places and says it'll be fine for us to sleep in a bedroom on the first floor. Bets and I have to share, but don't care as it's the first proper bed we've slept in in ages.

It's past nine when I wake up and I go to open the curtain. I hadn't realised how close the houses are across the street as we can look straight into their large bedroom windows. I quickly draw the curtain shut before anyone can see me staring out.

'Wake up. It's morning.' I sit on Bets' side of the bed and shake her awake. Her body jerks and she lets out a cry. 'Sorry, I didn't mean to scare you. Just don't go opening the curtain in case we're seen.'

She gets up on one elbow and rubs her eyes. 'Who can see us?'

'No one. I'm just being careful.'

Lars is in the kitchen frying eggs. They smell good and my stomach growls, a sign that my nerves are finally calming down.

'Can I?' I hold out my hand and he gives me the spatula so I can fry eggs for Bets and me. Bets cuts three slices from the loaf of bread and Lars spoons coffee into the pot. The water in the kettle comes to the boil and makes a rattling sound.

'This is a huge house,' I say, by way of conversation. 'Who does it belong to?'

Lars shrugs. 'We rent it but the landlord never bothers us. Ideal, really, as we're always having visitors.'

The eggs are ready to slide onto the plates. Lars fills the cups with steaming coffee and we sit at the table.

'What do you do for a living?' I ask, through a mouthful of egg and bread.

'Me?' Lars looks surprised. 'I'm an actor. Like Eva and Emil, when he's not playing at being a soldier. At least he's got some income, but there's barely any work for the rest of us. I work in a bar in the centre two nights a week, but I wouldn't say it's a living.' He lights a cigarette and pushes the packet towards us. I haven't seen Bets smoke before, but she takes one and leans forward so he can light it.

'So what plans do you have?' he asks Bets, who gives a dry laugh.

'Short or long term?' She blows smoke towards him. He laughs too and I'm sure I see something pass between them.

'Future plans. After the war and all that,' he says, tapping the ash of his cigarette into his saucer.

'I'll go abroad. Maybe become an actress. I've done a bit of acting at school, you know.'

My mind starts to drift as they continue to laugh together. I'm reminded of the first time Wouter took notice of me. There'd been rumours the Germans were closing in and we had to clear out of Berkenhout. It was a squash in Henk's van and I was pressed up against Wouter. In the darkness, he took my hand and laced his fingers into mine. Never before had I experienced such an intense feeling of happiness, which lingered long after we were separated. But I knew then it was only the start and that we would be together again once we returned to the hidden village.

I glance at Bets and see that same happiness radiating across her face.

I don't want to look. A sharp pang reminds me that I'm losing touch with everything that made me happy.

I'm at the sink scrubbing at the encrusted egg pan when a woman's voice calls out from the hallway. Instinct makes me drop the brush and pan with a clatter and head for the stairs. Bets clearly hasn't registered what is happening and gawps at me with her mouth open.

'Bets, come on!' I'm annoyed with her now.

Lars stands up and laughs. 'Calm down, it's only Eva.'

Feeling slightly foolish, I return to the kitchen as Eva wafts in on a cloud of perfume and cigarette smoke, holding her slender black holder aloft. She's wearing a gorgeous red satin gown with a Japanese print and I realise it reminds me of my mother's favourite outfit she wears for the theatre. Tears prick my eyes and I catch my breath. But Eva isn't looking at me; her mascara-smudged eyes are gazing into the middle distance.

'Lars, darling, please fetch me a drink,' she says, before sinking onto the saggy sofa with a sigh. 'Now, do tell me what's going on.'

Lars runs after her like a puppy, supplying her with a glass of *jenever* (it's still only ten o'clock) and a clean saucer for her cigarette ash. I'm mesmerised by her and can only assume she must be a proper actress.

'Don't tell me, you came with Emil. I keep telling him I'm not running a hotel but he never listens. Another of his good deeds, I fear. Any idea where he is?' She squints through a cloud of smoke at Lars who helps himself to a cigarette from her packet.

'Back to barracks for now, but he said something about going on officer training.'

Eva snorts out a plume of smoke in surprise. 'What, Emil? Oh God, it sounds as if he's been forced into it. But it's probably for the best if he disappears for a while.' She swings her head round to look at me appraisingly. I feel awkward in my shabby brown dress and my hair is a mess. But I don't think she's even noticed as she carries on. 'We've had such a to-do here and I blame myself for it. It was just another of my soirées and we were having such a lot of fun. Emil came of course, but I'm sure he had nothing to do with it.' She pauses. I'm sure she's waiting for me to ask her why.

'To do with what?' I say, and her chest begins to heave.

'Darling Klaus, my dear cousin. Shot dead. Just outside here.' Her voice gets higher and higher. 'My first thought was the Germans had done it, but none were in the area that day. The police believe that Klaus was a collaborator but it can't be true. I'm sure they won't find anything on him. He was just another young man who didn't want to go to Germany.' She fishes in her pocket for a handkerchief for her nose and eventually calms down. 'It was such bad luck. He'd only come to Zwolle to help out a friend with a delivery and dropped in as we hadn't seen each other in ages. The stories he told, you should have heard them. Hiding out in the Veluwe woods for weeks on end. It's where he met Wijnand. I think that's his name.' She pauses. She's back pulling on her cigarette holder, then waves it in the air to make a point. 'The friend he brought with him. It was when Wijnand started on about some girl who'd gone missing and asked if I could help. But what could I do? He looked so downcast that I asked them to my party. I thought it would cheer them both up. Next day, they...' She stops to stare into space. 'I thought they had gone back to Kampenveld. It's all such a mess.'

'Did he say anything about Berkenhout? The village hidden in the Veluwe woods?' I ask.

Eva looks vague as she takes another drag on her cigarette holder, leaving dark-red lipstick on the end. 'He might have. I don't recall. Lars, I'm sure there was a crate of *jenever* left over from the party. Have you seen it?'

Wijnand. Can she have meant Wouter? But that's impossible. There must be dozens of young men hiding out in the Veluwe, so the chances it was him must be slight. But what in the world would Wouter be doing here in Zwolle looking for me? Unlikely, as the last time I saw him he'd been so moody that we'd hardly exchanged two words. I'd been so upset with him, but knew him well enough not to show it. I'd thought if I let him sleep on it, it would all blow over in the morning. What a mistake.

I try to ignore the wave of sadness washing over me. I must stop hanging on to these dreams.

THIRTY

LAURA

We're relaxing round the kitchen table after our meal when a loud bang on the door jolts us to our senses. It's unmistakable. And it's what Eva has been fearing ever since we arrived. Terror is etched on her face as she flaps her hand, gesturing for us to disappear. We don't need any encouragement to rush up the stairs to the top of the house. Surely no one will come searching up here. We head for a closed door and I try to shove it open, but there's something stopping it. I squeeze through, but it's only a pile of chairs that have fallen against the door. It's a spare room of sorts with all kinds of junk piled high – ideal for hiding. We crawl under a table, pull a large cardboard box in front of us and wait.

After a few minutes Bets heaves a sigh and says, 'I don't think I can do this anymore. I'd rather take the risk and return home.'

'I know, that's what I want too,' I say in a fierce whisper, furious at the injustice of it all. We're being passed around like some unwanted baggage and no one knows what to do with us. It's pretty obvious we've become a burden, even to Emil who was so keen to help us. I'm close to tears as I think back to all those people who were prepared to put themselves out to save us from the Germans. Tante Else, Dick, Henk... they never gave a thought to their own safety, only ours. How were they to know that sending me away from Kampenveld would put me at even greater risk? They must have believed there'd be people who would have my best interests at heart.

'The problem is Zwolle, I'm convinced of it,' I say. 'It's become too dangerous. The Germans must know what happened to Klaus, even if they had nothing to do with his death. I reckon Kampenveld sounds a lot safer and I think we should go back.'

Bets doesn't say anything at first, but then grips my arm. 'Why would Kampenveld be any different? No, I can't keep this up, this terror every night. The only solution is to get over the border, away from Holland, away from this.'

It's gone quiet downstairs, but still we sit under this table, digesting the enormity of Bets' suggestion. She's right, of course. We need to get away, but where to? There's nothing that anyone here can do for us anymore, even if the war were to end tomorrow. It's time we stood on our own two feet.

Eventually, I say, 'Emil, he has to help us. He said he would.' I can't see her face, but am sure she's nodding in agreement.

It wasn't a raid, just one of Eva's actor friends dropping by for some evening entertainment. Apparently it happens often. No one thought to tell us there was no cause for alarm, so we were kept up there needlessly. Eventually, after an hour at least, Lars's voice floated up the stairs telling us the coast was clear and we could return downstairs.

We come down to a jolly scene. Eva in her element, drinking red wine and smoking one of her long cigarettes while holding forth to Lars and her friend. All of them are laughing.

'Laura, Bets, all is well. Come and have a glass of wine,' says Eva, catching sight of us hesitating at the foot of the stairs. She makes a swirling gesture with her cigarette holder, before returning to her story.

Why not?

The wine is sharp and catches at the back of my throat. But after a couple more sips, it doesn't seem so bad. Eva's stories start to be amusing and Bets and I join in the laughter. She's flirting with Lars again but I hardly notice as he fills up my glass. The lights are low and it's hard to make out anyone's faces, so I switch off from the murmur of conversation till I become aware that Eva is humming a tune. She breaks into a soulful song and I'm spellbound. It's only when Lars and the friend join in that I catch on to the words. Lost love, longing, loneliness. My throat tightens and my eyes prick, but I'm determined not to let it show. I close my eyes and lower my head, hoping that no one is looking in my direction. By the time I'm back in control, I look up but no one has noticed. And why would they? They're only interested in themselves.

THIRTY-ONE

WOUTER

After his release, Wouter had wasted no time in driving back to Kampenveld, the empty seat beside him a stark reminder of how precarious his own situation had become. Every vehicle driving up behind him or approaching made him anxious, so convinced was he that he was about to be rearrested for something he knew nothing about. The journey took less than an hour, but each minute felt like an eternity. The whole time he sat forward in his seat, gripping the steering wheel tightly. By the time he arrived back in Kampenveld, he'd convinced himself it was imperative that he got away before he put himself or anyone else at risk.

When he walked through the door, Else rushed towards him and threw herself round his neck. She knew all about Klaus's death and Wouter's arrest. 'I should have known the dangers of getting into trouble were so much higher in Zwolle. I wish I'd never sent you there.'

Wouter felt himself go cold. 'Who told you this?'

'Sit down,' she said, pulling him by the hand. 'I received the news this morning from a colleague of Gerrit who works for the police...'

'The police?' he gasped.

'I know,' she said with a deep sigh, 'but it's not what it seems. Thijs knows he's in a dangerous position when he passes on information to the Resistance, but he's always careful to cover his tracks.'

'But who... what does he look like?' Wouter tried to remember who he met other than the man who interrogated him.

'I can't say. I haven't met him. But Gerrit said he doesn't look old enough to be a policeman. Do you think you might have seen him?'

Of course. The young man who came in to deposit those papers in the filing cabinet. 'Yes, I think I did, but only briefly. I can't see how he can have known about me.'

Else leant over and patted his arm. 'It's best not to dwell on it. Just count yourself lucky that he happened to be there at the right time. Now, I have something that might cheer you up. It's a letter. Let me find it.'

Humming to herself, she went in search of the letter and pulled out several from the overstuffed drawers. Wouter allowed himself a few moments to imagine it was from Laura, but Else would have said right away, wouldn't she?

'Here we go. Ah, I need my glasses. I'm sure they were here.' She patted a pile of papers before rummaging again in the drawer. 'I don't want to get your hopes up, but I think that Oscar's girlfriend has seen Laura.' Glasses found, she was able to focus on the letter, which she scanned till she found what she was looking for. 'Ah, here we are. This is what Kiki writes.' She cleared her throat and read: '*It's a struggle to find anyone willing to take in Jews now the risks of being found out are so much greater. There are just so many of them arriving all the time, all desperate to avoid being sent to the camps. So I was particularly pleased about two young girls I helped move from Zwolle to a village not far from Maassluis. It's quite remote and*

with new identities I'm confident they won't be discovered. I
thought you'd like to know one of the girls was at Berkenhout.'
Else paused and smiled broadly at Wouter. 'Kiki has to be
careful not to divulge the girl's name, but it could be Laura,
couldn't it?'

'Does she describe her or say anything else?' Wouter held
his breath.

'No, sorry. That's it. But I'd say that's a strong enough lead
for you to go to Utrecht and find out more. And I'm in desperate
need of food and clothing coupons. Money too, if Oscar is up to
producing it. You can collect the documents at the same time.'

But first, Wouter needed to speak to Dick Foppen and fill him
in on all that happened when he was in Zwolle. Dick took the
news calmly but expressed his concern that Klaus had been
concealing his activities. Had Klaus told Wouter anything to
suggest he was collaborating with the Germans? Wouter
thought back over their conversations but everything Klaus had
ever said pointed to the contrary. He'd been convinced that
Klaus was an *onderduiker*, just like himself. But then he
remembered.

'There were a couple of instances when I doubted him. We
were arriving at his cousin Eva's party when I spotted a man in
a long coat knocking on her door. I held back and warned Klaus
that he looked like a *mof*, but he didn't seem in the least
concerned. I forgot about the man till later when he began to
sing a duet with Eva at the piano. I remember noticing the
insignia on his lapel, proof enough he was in the SS. Then
everyone was cheering and clapping and weren't in the least bit
perturbed that there was a *mof* in their midst. I couldn't believe
I was the only one unnerved by him.'

Wouter paused as he recalled Klaus's behaviour that day.
'Ah yes, there was something else Klaus said to me. We were

driving into Zwolle and there were all these Germans lining the street. Klaus was staring at them as we drove past and came out with something I thought odd. He said that sometimes it's better to get them on your side in return for favours. At the time, I dismissed his comment as the kind of thing Klaus was liable to say without really meaning it. But I wonder if he was trying to tell me he was involved in some way.'

Dick rubbed his chin thoughtfully. 'Or maybe he was just thinking about it. Nothing's come to light about him, but it's not always obvious who's a collaborator and who isn't. People can be very secretive in their dealings with the Germans. Did he ever say anything else to give you cause for concern?'

'I don't think so, but I was never looking for it. Now I wish I had.' Wouter slowly shook his head.

'It may be harsh to say it,' said Dick, 'but now that Klaus is dead it doesn't worry me what they find out about him. However, the police clearly suspect your involvement. It's no longer safe for you to stay in Kampenveld.'

'I know. I've come to the same conclusion,' said Wouter with a heavy sigh. 'Though it feels as if I'm always running away. I wish I could have done more.'

Dick was shaking his head. 'Now, listen. You've done more than most and should remember that. Not many would willingly go and live in a dugout so they can help a load of strangers. It didn't work out the way you or anyone hoped, but I valued your support, and still do.'

'Thank you,' said Wouter, attempting a smile. 'For being so good to me.'

Dick took Wouter's hand and shook it vigorously. 'Think nothing of it. Go and find your Laura. She deserves you.'

The night before his departure, Else invited Liesbeth and Griet to join them for a meal. Liesbeth was no longer living with Else since she'd landed a job as a doctor's assistant in the next village, but she was a frequent visitor and still helped out with the occasional delivery when Else asked her. Griet arrived with her little boy, who charmed everyone by hiding in his mother's skirts and peeking out with a cheeky grin. Griet seemed happier than the last time Wouter had seen her and appeared to have forgotten about the incident when she'd thrown Wouter out of her house.

'Sit down, everyone, and I'll serve up,' said Else, heaving the big black pan that had been simmering on the stove onto the table. She lifted the lid and the room filled with a delicious aroma. Instead of the usual beans and potatoes, she'd cooked up a stew with pork she'd managed to obtain from one of her contacts. None of them had tasted anything that good for years and they all ate in silence, savouring each mouthful as if it were the best restaurant food.

'You've been so kind, Else, I don't know how to thank you enough,' said Wouter as he laid his knife and fork down on his empty plate. Liesbeth and Griet offered their thanks too and Bertje whispered a tiny *dank je wel*.

'*Goed zo*, Bertje,' said Else, leaning over to stroke his cheek and he looked up at her through his lashes. Griet lifted Bertje onto the floor so he could play with his wooden cars. Else moved over to the cupboard for a bottle of *jenever* and four glasses.

'Another bottle? I thought you didn't drink,' said Wouter with a wry smile.

'You know I don't usually, but I haven't the heart to tell Henk.' Else handed round four glasses and poured out the fiery liquid. 'But let's not talk about Henk tonight. Griet, you have some good news, I think?'

Griet reddened as she told them she'd heard that Bram had been released from a detention centre near Amersfoort. It had been Dick Foppen's doing. He'd used his underground contacts to persuade the Germans that Bram was innocent of the charges of assisting the Resistance. 'But he can't come home, so will have to go into hiding with friends who live over forty miles away.' A shadow crossed Griet's face as she spoke in a low voice so Bertje could not hear. 'It's best we stay with my parents till it blows over.'

It was a familiar story: people's desperate need to evade the Germans, regardless of whether they were involved in the Resistance or were Jewish. Each person around the table had suffered their own traumas and would doubtless experience more, but for now they were united by their willingness to help one another with a determination never to give in.

Wouter had one more visit to make to his parents. Only a few weeks had passed since he'd seen them and the strain was clearly visible on their faces. They'd had no further raids, but the threat was always lurking in the background, causing his mother, in particular, unnecessary anxiety. He decided to spare them details of why he needed to move away by telling them he was going to Utrecht to work with a Resistance group who'd had success in supporting Jews. He wasn't being entirely untruthful, as he'd be staying with Oscar and his girlfriend, both active members in the production of forged documents for people needing to disappear in a hurry.

'Well, son, I'm delighted to hear you're finally going to do something useful.' His father had shaken his hand vigorously, but his mother began to weep.

'Must you go? Why Utrecht? It's such a big place and there'll be ten times the number of Germans on the street. Wouter, I know it's been difficult for you here, but I'm sure we can help you if you stay. Can't we, Len?' She spoke in a whine, which seemed to annoy him.

'No, we must let the boy go. It'll be safer for him away from Kampenveld,' he said, grim-faced.

Wouter had been dreading this moment. On a whim, he decided to tell them the real reason for his departure, though he gave only a sketchy account of Klaus's death. As soon as the words were out, he regretted them. To see his mother's face crumple and hear her weep again filled him with despair. 'Ma, you have nothing to worry about,' he said, trying to reassure her in a soothing voice. 'You know I'd never work for the Germans. And it's highly unlikely that the police will come looking for me as there's absolutely no evidence of me collaborating.'

But his attempt at being encouraging failed to lighten the mood between them and he was left with the feeling that he was letting them both down.

THIRTY-TWO

LAURA

We leave at dawn before anyone is up. Emil has instructed us to wait by the back door, which we mustn't open till we hear six raps. The wait is agonising. What's the hold-up? Has his contact decided it's too dangerous to take us after all? I wish he'd stayed to explain. Bets keeps sighing and checking the contents of her bag but I daren't say anything in case it stirs up her old anxiety. I can't have her causing a scene right now. But when the knock comes, even though we're expecting it, it gives us both a shock. Bets grabs my arm in a painful grasp. Shaking her off, I open the door a crack and am surprised to see a woman dressed in a long black coat and a navy hat jammed down on her head. I'm about to close it, when she whispers it's fine. 'Come quickly and I'll tell you on the way.' She doesn't wait and hurries along the path to the back gate.

Hers is the only car on the dark street and she's already in the driving seat with the engine running. I climb into the front beside her and Bets gets in the back. Without a word, the woman pulls away. Peering forward, she almost mounts the kerb as she steers the car around the corner. I can hear Bets catch her breath but we both remain silent until we reach the suburbs. By now, it's starting to get light.

'Sorry, I needed to concentrate. It's a nightmare driving without lights, but we'll be fine now. By the way, I'm Julia.' She beams across at me and I feel myself relax. 'Paul normally drives but was in such a hurry shifting boxes for the new arrivals that he's hurt his back. There simply aren't enough of us to do it all. It's been hard to recruit enough people.'

It's quiet in the back and I crane my neck to see Bets has fallen asleep.

'Why are you involved?' I ask quietly.

She assesses me with a quick look before carrying on. 'I live a few streets away from a Jewish neighbourhood and I've seen terrible things. One day, the chemist my family has been to all my life disappeared, just like that. He was an old man, no family, but always had time to discuss any worries or ailments we had. I remember, as a child, him coming to the house once with a special tincture he'd prepared for my cough. He was so good to us; my mother even called him her friend. The night they came, they broke down his door and wrecked the shop before hauling him away. There were shattered bottles everywhere and the pungent smell of spilled medicines hung around in the street for weeks. Every time I walked past it was a horrible reminder of what these monsters are capable of. He was the first, but every few days there'd be news of more families we knew who'd been driven from their homes and forced to board those trains to Westerbork. Paul and I couldn't just stand by and watch our neighbours treated in this way. So we joined a small underground group that coordinates help for *onderduikers*. We're now part of a bigger one called the LO. Have you heard of it?'

'I think so. The name is familiar, but we don't get told much.' I want to ask her more, but up ahead the cars are slowing and Julia suddenly brakes and I push my hands forward to stop myself falling. Bets cries out from the back.

'*Verdomme!* It's a road block.' Julia swings the car off the main road into a side street, but it peters out. She struggles with the gear stick and it makes a fearful grinding sound as she manoeuvres the car round and heads back towards the road we were on. As she pulls out, we almost collide with a car hooting its horn.

'Duck down!' she cries. 'Make sure you can't be seen.'

I crouch with my head on my knees, hardly daring to breathe. From the roar of the engine I sense she's driving fast and pray she knows what she's doing. She pulls the car up short, swears, then off we go again. I want to look up but am too scared of what or who I'll see. The Germans must surely have seen us and that's got to be why she's racing to get away. After a bit she stops swearing and the jerky movements of the car have ceased.

'Is it safe to sit up?' comes a voice from the back.

'Sorry, of course. I was miles away.' She lets out a long sigh. 'Are you two all right?'

I turn to look at Bets, who nods weakly. 'I suppose so,' I answer for us both.

'It's guesswork where they'll set up the next roadblock, but I'm getting used to them. Though it might not seem like it.' Julia's back to being chatty. 'The trick is to take evasive action before they spot you. That one was a bit close.'

'Have you ever been stopped?' I ask.

'God no, but Paul has. He was lucky he didn't have anyone in the car with him at the time. Just had to explain why he had crates full of food. The Germans took them off him, of course, and wrote down his details. Next time he'll be arrested.' She speaks the words calmly and I can't detect any emotion on her face. Is that her way of coping?

We reach the outskirts of Utrecht where she will hand us over to another woman, whose name is Kiki. She will take us to a safe house where we'll be given our new papers. Then what? Is it really necessary for them to be quite so secretive? Every time we make these changeovers I'm filled with dread that something will go wrong, but I have no choice but to put my trust in strangers sent to help us.

THIRTY-THREE

LAURA

'That's her.'

Julia pulls up and keeps the engine running. On the opposite side of the road stands a tall woman with her back to us. She's gazing into the window of a bookshop and doesn't turn round.

'You know what to do. Now take care.' Julia pats my hand and smiles at us both.

A few people are walking along the street. Normal people. Bets and I get out of the car and link arms. We've been told to walk towards the church two streets away. When Julia drives away we know to keep our eyes straight ahead.

'Nearly there,' I whisper.

'Shh. Don't look,' mouths Bets.

From behind, we hear the growl of a motorbike slowing as it comes alongside us. I'm determined not to stop. Out of the corner of my eye, I glimpse a uniform. The engine idles as the motorbike keeps pace alongside us. We keep walking, arms locked and I'm praying that he won't accost us. Too late. As the German stops the engine and levers the bike onto its stand, he shouts out, '*Halt!* Move aside, will you?'

We have no choice but to stop. I dare not look him in the eye, so stare at a spot on the ground in front of me. Bets grips harder on my arm. There's a sound of footsteps, and a man in a raincoat with a hat pulled over his eyes is hurrying towards us oblivious to the danger he's running into. The German positions himself in his path with his hand raised. So it's not us he's after but we can't afford to draw attention to ourselves. We sidestep them both and hurry into a side street where we break into a run till we reach the church up ahead. Out of breath, we check there's no one behind us, then enter through a side door.

The only other person is a figure lighting a candle. Her head is covered with a black scarf. At the sound of the door clicking shut, she turns and it's the woman we saw looking in the bookshop. She takes a step forward and introduces herself as Kiki. I can't believe she can be much older than me, but seems so self-assured as she tucks a stray auburn curl under her scarf. Shaking us each by the hand she says, 'You must be Laura. Bets. Well done for getting past that *mof*. I was convinced he was after you.'

'You were there? I didn't see you go past,' I gasp in surprise.

'I know their tricks, but they don't know the shortcuts I do. Best not to take any chances, so let's not hang around here.' She pulls out two patterned scarves, one navy blue, the other green, from her coat pocket and instructs us to cover our hair.

'It'll do for now,' she says, after tucking away any strands of hair that escape from mine.

Out on the street it's quiet. Kiki leads us along a series of alleys and narrow streets to a square where two children are kicking a ball back and forth. An old woman is sweeping the cobbles outside her door and looks up. '*Goedendag*,' says Kiki cheerfully. The woman's eyes flick from me to Bets before she returns to her sweeping. I'm sure I can hear her muttering and can't help thinking this isn't the first time Kiki has brought strangers to these parts.

Several doors along, Kiki puts a key in the lock and ushers us in. The small house has a musty smell, but looks lived in, two dirty cups on a low table, a newspaper folded on a chair, though there's nobody around.

'Emil tells me you've had a tough time these past few weeks,' she says, 'but I want you to know you'll be quite safe here. The house belongs to a good friend of mine who's away a lot. He doesn't mind if people stay over from time to time.'

Her smile is kind. In other circumstances, I think we could even be friends. But for now, she gets down to the serious business of handing over our new identities. Everything remotely Jewish must be erased from our names, family history, even to the way we look.

'Bets, we managed to find you a good match.' Kiki lays down a worn yellowing card. The picture is of a young woman with wavy fair hair framing a slim face. Bets is delighted and practises her new name – Margriet van Ommen. 'My passport to my new life,' she laughs, but I remain silent as I watch Kiki lay my new identity on the table.

'Don't worry about the picture. There's nothing we can't fix.'

I stare at the picture in disbelief. No one would ever believe the likeness – the fair hair, high forehead, dimple, the steel-rimmed glasses. 'But it doesn't even begin to look like me. How can I possibly get away with it?'

Kiki merely shakes her head and reaches into her bag for a dark red scarf, which she unfolds. Inside is a blonde hairpiece tacked along the outer edge. The idea is so ridiculous it makes me laugh. The others laugh too, not realising my laugh is because I'm horrified. Kiki smooths the false fringe straight and places the thing on my head, tying the ends around the back.

'Not bad at all,' she says, leading me to a small mirror that hangs on the wall. The girl who stares back is me wearing a hairpiece. I still don't look like the one in the picture.

'Here, once you put on these no one will be able to tell,' says Kiki, gazing at my reflection from behind. She hands me a pair of glasses, almost identical to the ones worn by the Laura in the photo. They help to hide my dark eyes and when I tilt my head so that my left ear is showing, I can see that maybe Kiki has a point. She's gone to a lot of effort, but there's no way I'll wear that ridiculous hairpiece.

Still, my new name is Anne-Marie Schipper and I'd better get used to it. I keep repeating it to myself but it's hard to accept as my own. It's a good Dutch name and I imagine Anne-Marie Schipper to be long-limbed with curly blond hair and wide blue eyes. The hair I know I can fix under a scarf, but I can't get away from the fact that I look like my mother, who was often called 'exotic' by her wealthy friends.

Kiki has another trick up her sleeve and rummages in her bag again. 'Try this. It'll make you look a bit older.' She holds up a crimson lipstick and removes the cap with a click. 'Would you like me to show you?' I nod, though I know exactly how it's done. How often I used to watch, transfixed, as my mother applied her lipstick, powder and rouge before guests arrived for dinner. I loved the way the glossy red lipstick transformed her from my mother into this glamorous creature who always attracted admiring glances from her guests.

Kiki holds my face steady with one hand while she draws a line across my top and bottom lips and tells me to press them together. She applies another layer and leans back. 'Beautiful,' she says. 'Take a look at yourself.'

I turn my head again towards the mirror and see my mother gaze back at me. I let out a gasp and can feel tears prick in my eyes. Will I ever see her or my father again?

'Here, take it,' Kiki presses the lipstick in my hand and closes my fingers around it. 'It'll make you feel confident when you need it. Make sure you're wearing it at times when someone might ask for your ID.'

THIRTY-FOUR

LAURA

Kiki still hasn't told us where we're going next. She's had to leave to attend to an urgent job, though she didn't tell us what. Only that she'd be back within two days and that she's left enough food for us. 'Don't answer the door to anyone and under no circumstances go outside' was her parting shot. As if we'd dare to, after everything we've been through. Besides, I don't trust that old woman who was sweeping her step when we arrived. What if she's a sympathiser or reports us to someone who is? Every little sound we hear through the thin walls puts us on edge and makes us more fearful.

It's late afternoon on the second day and Kiki should be back any time, when Bets grabs my arm. 'Did you hear that?' she says urgently, her eyes darting to the wall that separates us from the neighbour. Since we came here, there have been lots of soft thumps and the sound of footsteps on bare floorboards, but this is different. 'Someone's knocking,' I whisper. The unmistakable sound is of knuckles rapping on the dividing wall. After a pause, comes a sharp tapping and the mirror on our side comes crashing to the floor. We both gasp at the noise, then laugh as we realise that someone is knocking in a nail, probably to hang up a picture.

'This isn't much use anymore,' I say, going over to the mirror and picking it up. It has a jagged crack right down the centre and when I look in it my face is horribly distorted. I quickly turn it over and place it on the small table by the door. Isn't a cracked mirror meant to bring seven years' bad luck? I shudder and push the thought quickly out of my mind.

Kiki arrives in a rush, bringing a blast of cold air through the front door. 'I'm sorry I'm late,' she says breezily, closing the door quickly behind her and undoing the scarf tied under her chin. We must look as if we've seen a ghost, for she asks if anything is the matter.

'No, nothing. Just some banging next door,' I say, and show her the broken mirror. 'We thought someone might be trying to get our attention.'

Kiki frowns and ushers us into the small kitchen at the back. 'Look, we can't take anything for granted so we'll leave the back way. Can you gather your things together quickly? We must hurry.'

I shoot Bets a glance and she's looking as worried as I feel. We don't argue and it doesn't take more than a few minutes to throw our few belongings into our bags while Kiki sits at the kitchen table and shuffles through some papers she's brought.

It's getting dark as we slip out of the back door that opens onto an even darker alleyway running along behind the houses. Kiki has obviously done this before as she leads us out into a narrow street where a car is parked beneath an unlit lamppost. We don't need to be told to get in and she gives us a blanket to put over ourselves in case we need to duck down out of sight. She pulls away and I realise our escape has taken no more than a couple of minutes.

Kiki seems lost in thought as she drives through the back

streets and out towards the countryside. For a while, there's still a little light in the sky and the dark shapes of tall trees lining the road are visible. As it gets darker, though, it's hard to see the way ahead, but the lack of headlights doesn't bother her and I wonder if she often drives at night.

'We've got about another hour's journey, I'd say,' she calls over her shoulder. 'Are you both all right back there?'

'Fine. But where exactly are you taking us?' I ask, giving Bets's hand a little squeeze.

'I should have told you, but I needed to concentrate on getting well away from Utrecht. The next bit's going to be a bit tricky but if you follow my instructions I'm sure everything will work out.'

Bets squeezes my hand now and keeps hold of it. We whisper between ourselves, promising to stay together whatever comes next. Kiki seems to have forgotten to speak to us as she concentrates on taking a series of turnings along narrow roads.

'I'm taking you to Maassluis where you'll stay overnight with an old friend of mine. Henny will take you down to the river tomorrow early where you'll catch a boat over to Rozenburg. From there, I'll give you instructions on how to reach the village where my mother's friend, Mevrouw Teuling, lives on a farm. She's expecting you.'

'So, you won't be coming with us?' I squint over at Bets to see her expression, but it's too dark.

'Oh no, I'm expected back in Utrecht, but you shouldn't have any problems. I'm confident you'll be quite safe there until all of this is over. Mevrouw Teuling's husband died last year and her son recently left to work in Germany, so she needs all the help she can get.'

We remain silent in the back as we mull over what she's just told us. It's the most dangerous thing we've ever had to do and she's expecting us to do it alone?

'Don't worry, you have your new identities, so even if you're accosted everything is in order. The story is that you're going to help out a family friend who's sick. I've managed to get hold of a couple of boxes of aspirin and a bottle of cough tincture. Play your part well and you'll be fine.'

THIRTY-FIVE

LAURA

]Henny wakes us before dawn and apologises for the watery porridge and weak tea she serves us. We sit close to the barely warm *kachel*, which she keeps going with a few sticks she's gathered from nearby fields. We may be out in the cold for a long time, she tells us, so we should try to stoke ourselves up. She's already been so kind, putting us up at short notice and providing us with a meal of sorts last night. Her rations hardly stretch to enough for herself, just a few cabbage leaves, a turnip and some hard black bread, but she's just about surviving thanks to Kiki, who provides her with a few basics in exchange for helping people like us. It doesn't seem fair payment given the risks she's prepared to take, but these are desperate times. People go to virtually any lengths for the promise of food, however little.

'I'll walk with you as far as the road leading to the dock but it's best I'm not seen with you. It'll only raise unnecessary questions,' she says, before we leave the house.

I'm surprised there are so many people out early on a dark and bitterly cold winter's morning and they all seem to be heading in the same direction as we are. It dawns on me that they are also wanting to catch the one ferry crossing of the day.

'It's always busy, but if you keep together and push your way to the front you'll get on,' Henny says encouragingly. 'I'd best say goodbye to you here.' She wishes us luck and gives us each a hug. We thank her for helping us and she waves her hand in parting as if it's nothing.

'Let's go.' I slot my arm through Bets's and we take care not to slip on the cobblestones that lead down towards the crowded dock. It's total chaos as people jostle and shove each other to get to the front. We hustle as far forward as we dare without drawing attention to ourselves, not that anyone is looking. We all face the ancient rowing boat where six men are waiting, oars at the ready, to row us across.

'I had no idea,' I whisper to Bets, whose face has turned white.

'Isn't there meant to be a ferry?' she says, and her voice comes out louder than she intended. A woman in a checked headscarf turns to us and laughs. 'Ferry? There hasn't been one since the Germans requisitioned it. That's all that runs these days and you'll be lucky to get on first time.' She muscles forward with the smug look of someone who's done this before.

An unshaven man in a shabby grey coat and with a grim expression is shouting something I don't catch. I think he's the one in charge. The crowd surges forward. There must be sixty, maybe seventy of us. 'Stay close,' I urge Bets, who's in danger of being lost in the swirl of people. The man lets people on one by one, counting under his breath. The boat fills up quickly and I can't see any available seats, but still he lets on more.

It's now our turn and he looks me in the eye. I smile, glad I remembered to apply my lipstick before we left, and, with a leer, he lets me step aboard. I'm just relieved to have made it, but the feeling is short-lived. To my horror, I realise he's barred Bets from boarding.

'My friend. She's with me. Please let her on.' I desperately clutch at his sleeve but he shrugs me off.

'Full up. She'll have to wait with the rest of them.' He bends down to untie the rope attached to a metal ring on the dock and pushes the boat away with a shove.

'I'll wait for you,' I call out to Bets, but I don't think she hears. She's surrounded by others shouting furiously at the man for leaving them behind.

'Sit down,' barks the man, and two young women smile sympathetically and make space on the packed bench for me. I'm nearly in tears as I try to get a glimpse of Bets, but we're already heading out into the channel and I can't make her out. What will I do? The next boat won't go till tomorrow morning and I can't hang around for her. Miserably, I sink into my seat and clutch my bag to me for warmth as a cold easterly wind blows across, making my nose run. I close my eyes and listen to the rhythmical splash of the oars, willing the journey to be over. After about half an hour, we reach the shore, but it seems much longer.

I'm glad to be on solid ground again and waste no time hurrying away from the crowds milling around on this side of the river. I'll work something out with Mevrouw Teuling and hope we can come back and meet Bets tomorrow. But the walk along the side of the road between the fields takes far longer than I anticipated. I pass one or two people hurrying along, faces pinched with the cold and hunger. No one is any mood for greetings.

I've been walking for hours and need to take a rest when I notice a huddle of farm buildings up ahead. Perhaps someone there might let me stop a while and even give me a drink. My feet are numb and my fingers are beginning to throb.

I knock on the door of the farmhouse and immediately a dog starts barking from within. I consider retreating onto the road when the door opens a chink and a small grey-haired woman eyes me suspiciously as she holds on to the brown and white mongrel by the scruff of the neck.

'Mevrouw, I'm so sorry to bother you. Could I please come in out of the cold, just for a few minutes?'

'You're not a Jew, are you?' she says, and I see her look at my dark hair escaping from the scarf I'm wearing and I wish I hadn't been so stubborn about wearing the hairpiece. Her dog begins to growl.

'No. No, of course not. My name's Anne-Marie Schipper,' I say feebly, as if that explains my non-Jewishness. 'My mother's Italian.'

"Hmmph,' she says. 'You can come in, but only for a few minutes, mind.'

I'm so relieved to step inside out of the cold that I can forgive her for her churlishness. If I wasn't so cold, I'd have turned on my heel and looked elsewhere for a more friendly welcome.

'There are Jews looking to hide round here and I don't want anything to do with it. Now, if you're sure you're not one of them.' She peers at me and I hope she can't see my cheeks turn red. But she shakes her head and shuffles off to the kitchen and gestures for me to sit on an upright wicker-based chair.

'So, what made you come knocking?' Her tone isn't aggressive and she does place a cup of milk and a slice of bread in front of me. Anyway, I'm ready with my story, which Kiki has practised with me and Bets. I think of Bets with a jolt, and hate to think of her having to wait to cross that beastly river.

'I'm visiting my aunt who's been unwell and finding it hard to fend for herself.'

The woman suddenly looks interested. 'Does she live near here?'

I realise I've made an error in saying she's my aunt, but I have to keep on with my story so tell her the name of the village.

She shakes her head and says she doesn't know anyone from there.

'I've walked from the harbour, but it's a lot farther than I thought,' I say.

The woman makes a loud snorting sound and the dog, now lying with its head in its paws, jolts awake in fright and scrambles to its feet. 'You've got a good couple of hours on foot. Here.' She cuts another thick slice from the loaf and spreads it with something that resembles butter, but I can see it isn't. She wraps it in some brown paper and thrusts it towards me.

'Thank you so much,' I smile. I'm grateful all the same for her kindness, despite her earlier unfriendliness.

'And be careful, Anne-Marie. With your looks, you can easily be mistaken for a Jew,' she says as she ushers me to the door and closes it behind me.

THIRTY-SIX

LAURA

The sun is setting over the polders: low lying fields that stretch away into the distance on my left. The streaky orange and pinks are a beautiful sight and give me something to think about other than the cold. I'm wondering how long it actually takes for the light to fade from the sky when a motorbike draws up alongside me. I kick myself for not watching out as I'm about to be accosted by this man in German uniform. Instinctively, I pull my scarf over my forehead and hope he doesn't notice my features.

'What is a pretty girl like you walking out so late?' He tilts his head to stare at me. He's quite handsome and has smiling blue eyes. He doesn't look dangerous, but I've learned to take nothing for granted.

'I'm taking medicine to a family friend who's unwell,' I say in German, trying not to look him in the eye.

'You are? Show me.' He switches off his engine and heaves the bike up onto the stand. I'm surprised at how tall he is, but maybe it's the big heels on his black shiny boots that make him look tall. Silently, I thank Kiki for having the foresight to give me the medicines. I open my bag and show him the two boxes of aspirin and a bottle of cough medicine.

'And where does your friend live?' He tips his head down to look me in the face. He doesn't seem threatening and I'm confused. I think I'd better tell him.

'That's quite some way from here. If you walk, you'll find yourself out after curfew. That won't do, will it?' His expression suggests he finds it all amusing.

I shake my head and wait for him to speak, but am shocked by what he suggests. He wants to give me a lift on his motorbike. The idea frightens me but how can I refuse?

As he helps me onto the back of his bike, he tells me his name is Friedrich and asks me mine. 'You have the same name as my little sister,' he says. 'I missed her birthday; it was on Sunday. She's fourteen.' I nod and smile. I don't want to encourage any more conversation than is necessary, but get the feeling he's missing his family. Somehow, that makes this acceptable.

We set off down the road and I'm sure he wants me to put my arms round him, but I keep hold of his coat with my bag on my lap between us. He shouts above the noise of the engine and tells me he's only recently moved to this area after being stationed at Zwolle. I wonder if he knows Emil, then I wonder if he's like Emil and isn't that bad a Nazi, but I say nothing, just the occasional murmur to show I'm listening. Besides, my mind is on what is going to happen next. I've never met Mevrouw Teuling and he's about to find out that she isn't ill at all.

He slows the bike to turn down a track that leads to a house with a deep roof that comes almost down to the ground.

'Thank you very much. Here will be fine,' I say, relieved, as I clamber off the back. Of course he's not about to just leave me and go. My mind races ahead and I know I'm for it now. But instead, he stands beside his bike and looks at the ground for a moment. Can he be nervous, shy even?

'Anne-Marie, I would like to see you again. Maybe tomorrow I will come to you if I'm not needed at headquarters. Hmm?'

I can't quite believe what he's saying, but am so relieved he's not interrogating me further or wanting to come in that I blurt out, 'Yes.'

His whole face lights up. 'That is good. *Auf wiedersehen!*' He jumps back onto his bike and I watch as he rumbles away into the dusk.

THIRTY-SEVEN

LAURA

The front door opens to reveal a tall woman with curly brown hair and ruddy cheeks. I'm relieved Friedrich didn't hang around to see how well this woman looks.

'Hello, I'm Anne-Marie. You must be... Mevrouw Teuling?'

She nods briefly. 'I was out at the back and heard the sound of a motorbike. Is that how you came here?'

'A German on a motorbike turned up as I was walking here and offered to give me a lift. I couldn't really refuse.'

She clicks her tongue and I feel foolish, aware I've done something wrong. 'And where is the other girl? Kiki told me there'd be two of you.'

'We got separated when we were boarding the boat.'

'Well, you'd better come in out of the cold, and you can tell me everything,' she says, and I'm grateful to be led through into the warm kitchen. In one corner, a *kachel* radiates heat and a pot of something is simmering on the stove. She sits me down and serves us both a bowl of the cabbage and turnip soup with some hard biscuits. It's not much but is enough to revive me.

'Well, it sounds as if you've had quite a day,' says Mevrouw Teuling, pushing her bowl aside and looking at me expectantly.

I smile nervously and confess I don't know where to start, so she prompts me by asking how I met Kiki. She's easy to talk to and I end up pouring out everything about my escape from Berkenhout and the kindness of so many people in keeping me hidden from the Germans. And how I'm having to get used to my new name and identity, which has been already been put to the test. I make sure I fill her in on the story Kiki fabricated about my visit to help a sick friend. She laughs when I show her the medicines, saying they are bound to come in useful.

We sit long into the evening, exchanging stories and sipping hot tea made from herbs she grows in between the cabbage rows and dries to use over winter. It's the most normal I've felt in months.

It appears Kiki is the daughter of Mevrouw Teuling's best friend whom she met when their children were at kindergarten. They've been friends ever since, though they haven't seen one another for months as Kiki's mother lives in Hilversum, too far to make the trip since the war's been on. Mevrouw Teuling has been getting by, but it's been tough for her since her husband died of a heart attack months before the occupation began. She managed to keep the farm going with her son, Noah, until he received the order, only last month, to go to work in a factory in Germany, leaving her to cope on her own.

'He's worked all his life on the farm and isn't cut out for life in the city. I worry about him and hope it won't be for long. It can't go on for much longer, can it?'

I shake my head. In truth, I've long since given up thinking about life afterwards. I don't even know where home would be. There's no point allowing myself to imagine being reunited with Mama and Papa, let alone Wouter. No, it's best I concentrate on getting by day by day.

'And your friend, Bets? Do you think she'll be able to find her way here?'

'I didn't realise it was so far to walk. I thought I could go back and meet her, but now I don't even know if she'll manage to get the next boat over.'

'There's nothing you can do but wait. It's too risky to walk back now that German knows where you are. What did you tell him?'

'As little as possible. Just that I was visiting with some medicines for you. He seemed more interested in me than what I was doing.' I'm bracing myself to tell her he intends turning up tomorrow, but don't want to spoil the evening.

'What do you mean?' says Mevrouw Teuling, looking concerned.

'I did nothing to encourage him but he said he'll be back to see me. He wasn't threatening or anything,' I say feebly. 'I'm sorry, but how could I refuse?'

'And then he turns up and isn't the friendly *mof* you thought he was?' She shakes her head and sighs deeply. 'But it's too late now, so our stories will have to agree. I suppose I'd better act ill.'

THIRTY-EIGHT

LAURA

The rumble of the motorbike announces his arrival. Mevrouw Teuling nods at me and disappears upstairs. I wring out the floorcloth and lay it on the side of the pail before retying my scarf, making sure that my hair is well hidden. A pointless exercise, I know, as he has already seen my dark hair. No doubt he's come to his own conclusions about me. His knock on the door is tentative.

'Anne-Marie. How nice to see you.' I'm struck by how handsome he looks in his uniform, but quickly push the thought away. I notice he's carrying a bundle tied up with string.

'Friedrich. Please come in.' I explain that Mevrouw Teuling is still unwell and in bed, but he doesn't seem to be listening as he places his bundle on the kitchen table and proceeds to untie it.

'Look what I've brought for you to cook us.' I stare as he brings out potatoes, leeks, carrots and then, with a flourish, he unwraps a large lump of pork. I stop myself from gasping. Is this a test because he's guessed I'm Jewish? Maybe the thought hasn't occurred to him as he places a bottle of red wine on the table and says, 'I think we need a bit of cheering up, don't you?'

My mind races. I've no idea how to cook a piece of meat like this, not because it's pork, but because we had a housekeeper at home who made us the most delicious meals, which always appeared like magic. Of course, she never served up pork, though occasionally my father used to bring home a piece of smoked sausage, which he'd slice thinly and share in secret with me, making me promise not to tell my mother. 'Things that are forbidden are the best,' he used to say, with a finger to his lips.

'Why, thank you. Do you want me to prepare it now?' I ask, hoping he'll decide to come back later while I get Mevrouw Teuling to do something with it.

As he sits down, he laughs and makes himself comfortable by stretching out his long legs. 'Now would be nice. First, bring me two glasses so we can have some wine.'

I'm not sure if Mevrouw Teuling even has wine glasses as I search through the crockery cupboard. My fingers fumble and I almost drop a patterned china cup. I find two mismatched glasses. They'll have to do.

'Come and sit with me and we can have a little talk before you prepare the meal.' He seems friendly, though I know I shouldn't trust anything he says. I'm aware I'm sitting across the table from a Nazi, however honourable his intentions appear to be. 'Tell me everything about yourself, Anne-Marie. Where you come from, your family, how long you intend to stay here.' He leans forward and fixes his blue eyes on me. I quickly look away as panic grips me and I try to run through my story in my head before speaking. These questions, are they his way of getting me to confess I'm a Jew?

'My family... they live in Maassluis. My father had a green-grocer's shop for years, though he was forced to close it last week as there's nothing for him to sell anymore. The people, they have nothing to eat, nowhere to buy food now. It's desperate.' I'm making it up as I go along and hope it'll deflect him away from asking too much about me. He frowns a look of concern, but it could be annoyance and I wonder if I've said too much. When he speaks, it's in a low voice and I have to strain to hear.

'My family are also suffering. So many shortages and we're a big family, six children. I'm the eldest. My mother's very sick and they can't get the medicines for her. I'm stuck here and there's nothing I can do to help them. My unit's always on the move and I've been relocated four times in six months, but never back to my home town. I really hope that this war is over soon so we can all get back to behaving normally.' He runs his hands across the blond stubble covering his scalp.

It's not what I expect to hear and as I listen, he seems to change before my eyes. I see a young man, nineteen, maybe twenty, not that confident. He's fighting for his country, but not because he wants to. What atrocities has he seen, I wonder, or even been a part of? If he was stationed in Zwolle he will almost certainly have been on the lookout for Jews. The thought we might have met under such different circumstances makes me shudder. He mustn't know I'm Jewish. I take a sip of wine for courage.

'After the war, my mother talks of taking me to Italy where she has family I've never met. They live on a small island called Ischia, which she makes sound so beautiful and peaceful. I wonder if I'll ever have the chance to see it.' I make a show of sighing and look up to see if I've managed to convince him of my lie.

'Italy.' He pauses. 'So is it from your mother that you get your dark looks?' He looks pensive and I'm beginning to wish I hadn't elaborated this lie.

'People say I look just like her, especially in photos when she was a young woman.' I smile and wish we could talk about something else, but his cool blue stare suggests he's not finished yet.

'With your looks, you should be careful you don't get mistaken for a Jew.'

My stomach lurches as I laugh a little too loudly. 'That's why I always make sure I carry my ID with me.' I pat the pocket of my skirt.

The sound of footsteps on the staircase make us both look up. Mevrouw Teuling makes a show of hanging on to the bannister as she shuffles down and I notice she's messed up her hair. If she isn't unwell, she's certainly good at pretending. She even manages a croaky voice as she introduces herself. Friedrich doesn't look pleased. He was probably hoping to have a dinner with me alone, but that's too bad. This is Mevrouw Teuling's house so he can't complain.

'Anne-Marie tells me you've been ill. Is it serious?' He takes a step back from her. I can tell he's worried she might be infectious.

'The fever has gone, but I still have the rash across my back. Would you like to see?' She makes a show of fiddling with the back of her blouse, while pretending to have a coughing fit.

'No! Please don't. There's no need for that. I think you should go back upstairs.' He makes a shooing gesture at her, but she stands stock-still and purses her lips.

'I will do as I please in my own house, so if you don't like it, you can leave.'

My heart begins to pound as I watch the two of them. I notice how young he looks, so unsure of himself, but I mustn't let that sway what I think of him.

'Anne-Marie, you will come with me,' he says suddenly, his eyes pleading. He grabs my arm and marches me to the door before I have a chance to protest. I shoot a desperate glance back at Mevrouw Teuling who whispers, 'I'm sorry.'

Outside, it's a bitterly cold night and all I can think is that I should have grabbed my coat and gloves. He's still holding on to my arm as he steers me towards his motorbike parked a little way down the track. Then, without a word, he takes hold of my other arm and pulls me to him and kisses me hard on the mouth. His breath smells of the wine and I try to wriggle free but his arms are holding me against him.

'I must go back inside,' I manage to gasp, but he's not listening.

'No, Anne-Marie, stay with me. Can't you see that I want you?'

His breath is hot on my neck and I feel his hand fumbling at the waistline of my skirt. I grow rigid with fear.

'No! Please, not here.' I wrench his hand away and it seems to make him come to his senses as he covers his face with his hands and takes a shuddery breath.

'I'm going back inside now and we will forget this happened,' I say in as firm a voice as I dare.

I dread that he'll try it on again, but he merely whispers, 'I'm sorry. I did not mean to upset you.' I give him a curt nod and walk shakily back to the house, praying he won't follow me. Relief pours over me as I hear him start up his engine and drive away.

Mevrouw Teuling is waiting by the door. Her face is so drawn I wonder if she might be ill after all. She hurries me in and closes the door on the dark night, then draws me into a tight hug. In silence, we return to the kitchen and take in the food on the table waiting to be cooked. We glance at each other and our faces break into smiles, knowing we're about to prepare the best meal either of us has enjoyed in years.

THIRTY-NINE

WOUTER

No one took any notice of the figure hurrying along in the shadow of the enormous Dom church tower as it boomed out twelve noon. The few people out on the streets were more concerned with trying to keep out of the biting wind that had swept in from the east overnight.

He stopped under an arch and tried to rub the feeling back into his hands. Looking around, he noted he was opposite a café whose name was only just discernible from the peeling sign over the door. Café Annelise was correct, but he couldn't work out why a woman was watching him so intently from inside the window. She was dressed in a dark trench coat with a navy scarf over her hair. Surely that wasn't right. He was expecting a young man with blondish hair and a ruddy complexion. A moment of fear gripped him as he saw her rise from the table and move towards the door. As he turned away to disappear down a side street, he caught sight of her hurrying out of the café towards him.

'Wouter?' she said, narrowing her eyes against the bright sunshine.

He nodded and she laughed, saying he had nothing to

worry about. 'I'm Kiki. Oscar wasn't able to come so he told me who to look out for. His description wasn't too helpful. Look out for a tall man with short dark hair, but he might have grown it. Thick eyebrows. He got that bit right.' Her laugh was infectious and Wouter smiled in relief, grateful for her efforts to put him at his ease. He raised his eyebrows and she laughed even more.

'We shouldn't hang around here. Let's go.'

The last occasion he'd met Oscar had been when he'd come to visit Sofie at Berkenhout. He'd been aware that they were boyfriend and girlfriend, but the young man, barely sixteen and slightly gauche, had made little impression on Wouter. Oscar had come across as polite but shy, and he remembered how flushed his cheeks looked whenever they exchanged a few words. When Oscar had stopped his visits, Wouter had hardly noticed, only understanding why after observing Sofie's growing friendship with Karl.

It took a moment for Wouter to realise that the broad-shouldered fair-haired man who strode towards them down the long corridor was Oscar.

'Kiki, *schat*, you found him despite my woeful instructions. I was wondering who you might end up bringing back,' said Oscar, kissing her noisily on the cheek.

'There weren't any other men lurking in doorways so it was a bit of a giveaway.' Kiki shook back her auburn curls and lifted her face for a proper kiss. 'Now, let me go and put on the coffee while you two have a good chat.' She unbuttoned her coat and tossed it over the back of a chair before disappearing towards the rear of the house.

'So, welcome,' said Oscar, stretching out his palms with a sweep of the room. 'Not bad, is it? And we've got the whole place to ourselves.' He walked around the spacious living room as if to demonstrate his point. It was shabby, with brown paint flaking off the walls and ill-matched furniture not quite hiding the bald patches on the faded carpet. There was an assortment of sofas and armchairs arranged haphazardly around a large coffee table covered in newspapers, letters and other papers. Over in one corner, an antique clock chimed the hour. A dark mahogany dresser dominated one side of the room. Both reminded Wouter of his parents' house, but this room was a lot bigger.

'Impressive. Do you mind me asking how you came by this place?'

'It's our headquarters and we get to live here too,' said Oscar with a broad smile. 'I'm in charge of the "procurement of documents". We can produce anything from birth certificates, marriage licences, work permits to school diplomas. But most of our forgeries are personal IDs.' A loud clatter from the kitchen made him wince.

'Is it just you and Kiki here?'

'Just me and Kiki. Do you like her?' He frowned as if Wouter's answer were important to him.

'She seems very nice. Where did you meet?'

'We're members of the same party and met at one of the meetings. In fact, it was the one where I got my promotion.' He ushered Wouter to take a seat on one of the chairs without papers strewn all over it. 'So, Else told me you're here to pick up some new IDs for people back in Kampenveld. She also said you needed to get away for a while. Why's that?'

Wouter sighed deeply as he began to recount the events leading to Klaus's death and his own arrest. 'The police turned up, insisting Klaus was a member of the NSB. I'm sure they were looking for a scapegoat as they ended up arresting me and tried to accuse me of being a collaborator too. They let me off but I'm now on their records.'

Oscar sucked in his breath. 'Silly question, but do they know you've come here?'

'Course not. As far as I know, they have no idea I work for Else. But it worries me how much information they have on me.' Wouter frowned as he ran a hand through his hair.

'I'm sure you'll be fine. They'll only be interested in what's happening locally. Unless you've done something terrible, you'll be off their radar in a few days.' He leant forward and spoke in a low voice. 'Have you heard how Sofie's doing? The whole Berkenhout raid and her attack – God, it was a terrible shock. I wrote to her, of course, and should have gone to visit her, but I've had no time off since I've taken on all the extra work. I still feel responsible and wish I could have done something to help,' he said ruefully.

'If it's any consolation, I haven't seen her either, not since Berkenhout,' said Wouter, warming to him. 'There's been such pressure on hiding places and she's had to move around. Fortunately, Liesbeth's been a fantastic support to her.'

'I'm glad,' said Oscar with a sharp exhalation. 'And I've also been worried about my family. Especially Jan. You haven't heard from him, have you?'

Wouter's face broke into a smile at the mention of Oscar's younger brother. Jan had always been around the camp, delivering supplies and gossip. Everyone cheered up when Jan arrived, bringing a gust of normality they all craved. 'You can be sure Jan is fine. His foot's healed and he still has a limp but that hasn't stopped him getting back into his clandestine work. He's proving to be very effective at keeping a watch out for any unusual activity and reporting back to Else and Dick. He's even pre-empted several raids.'

Kiki came back into the room carrying the coffee tray. 'I hope you don't mind, but we've run out of sugar.'

'Don't worry about that,' said Oscar with a wave of the hand. 'An order came in this morning to run off some blocks of coupons. A few extra will cover it.'

'Is it that easy?' said Wouter in astonishment.

'Only if you know what you're doing,' said Oscar, his mouth twitching into a smile.

'And Oscar is the only one round here who does.' Kiki laughed, snuggling up to him and draping an arm around his neck.

FORTY

WOUTER

The two flights of narrow stairs creaked with every step. Oscar led the way past three bedrooms and up an L-shaped staircase to the second floor. The musty smell grew stronger the higher they climbed, signifying that this part of the house hadn't been inhabited for years.

'Wait a sec,' instructed Oscar. He disappeared into a darkened room and Wouter could hear the squeak of a door being opened and the scrape of something being dragged across the floor.

'You can come up now,' came a muffled voice.

In the semi-darkness, Wouter almost tripped over the step ladder positioned directly below the square hatch. Blinking, he gazed up to assess how he was to climb up when the beam of a torch caught him in the eye. 'You need to put your hands here and haul yourself up,' instructed Oscar from above.

The attic was spacious, tall enough to stand up in and stretching from one side of the house to the other. The windows at either end were covered in a thick blackout material. Pools of light from the lamps rigged up on side tables gave the room a homely feel. Oscar went over to a long low table, which had a printing press on it and removed the cover. The shelves above contained rows of what looked like ration books alongside stacks of blank paper and a clutch of ink bottles.

'I said I'd get some documents done for a young Jewish couple looking to get over to Switzerland where her parents now live. It'll take me a bit of time to complete. Do you want to watch?'

The documents were fake birth certificates. The copper script made them look exactly like the real thing. Oscar unscrewed a pot of ink and dipped in his pen, before scratching it onto a piece of scrap paper to ensure the flow was even.

'Here goes,' he said, briefly looking up at Wouter. With a sharp intake of breath, he pressed the pen lightly on the form and began to make quick brushstrokes. It took him a quarter of an hour to complete all the sections. Then, with a flourish, he swept his hand across the bottom of the form, producing a flowery signature worthy of a pompous Town Hall official.

'Don't touch,' cried Oscar as Wouter leant in for a closer look. Oscar took a piece of blotting paper cut to the correct size and pressed it carefully over his masterpiece.

'Where did you learn to do this?' asked Wouter, intrigued.

'From someone I met in Hilversum who specialised in calligraphy. She showed me how to perfect the script and I found it came naturally to me. I was already turning out personal documents but I was getting bored. Once I'd mastered the loops and curlicues of Meneer Rupert Hillegom's signature I was let loose on all of these.'

'Do you charge?' asked Wouter.

'What do you think?' said Oscar with a wink. 'We have to keep the organisation afloat somehow. Thankfully, there's no shortage of work, as you can see.' He tipped his chin towards the shelves.

While he carried on with the second certificate, Wouter took a look round. He was particularly taken with the printing press, and poked at various levers and rollers to see how it worked. When he'd been a boy, he'd once visited his uncle who'd worked the printing press at a local newspaper. He shivered at the sweet memory of wet ink laid down onto the pristine news sheets rolling off the press.

Oscar glanced up from his work. 'We were so lucky to be given that press by a Jewish journalist who'd purloined it from his employers. Just before the company was shut down by the Germans. He got out in the nick of time, taking the press with him. Luckily it comes apart and he was able to hide parts in his trousers and the rest in a small bag. He then nonchalantly carried it out of the building.'

After swirling out his fake signature, Oscar announced he had finished. He leant back in his chair and stretched. 'I could do with a drink,' he said, going over to a low cupboard for a bottle of brandy and two glasses. 'Now, tell me. Why have you really come?' he asked, handing a glass to Wouter. 'I mean, you say you're here to pick up a batch of IDs for Else, but I could've had those sent on through the network.' He settled into the cushions of an armchair and placed his glass on the small table next to him.

'I've lost touch with a girl I knew at Berkenhout. Laura Wechsler.' Wouter gazed at the liquid as he swirled it round his glass.

'The name's familiar. Wasn't she friends with Sofie?' Oscar frowned as he tried to recall. 'But I don't think I ever met her. What happened to her?'

Wouter pursed his lips together. 'I wish I knew.'

'But she must have been with you at the time of the ambush.'

Wouter drained his glass in one gulp. 'That's when it all went wrong. Foppen meticulously planned all the escape routes. We'd all gone over it again and again. God knows why he put me in charge. I used to lie awake running through all the scenarios but nothing prepared us – me – for when it happened for real. You have no idea. They burst in so fast. The shots ripped through the village and I had just one thought, to get out. Ever since that day, I can't stop thinking about the consequences of what I did. I left her behind. And now she's gone.' Closing his eyes, he let out a long breath.

'God, it must have been terrifying, but you can't go blaming yourself for what happened.'

'Who else, then?' Wouter shot him a dark look from under his eyebrows, then continued in a mocking voice: '"Wouter, I see you have leadership qualities and am putting you in charge of the escape in the event of a raid." Couldn't be clearer than that, could it?'

'You're far too hard on yourself. Neither Else nor Foppen has ever said a bad word against you.'

'Probably to spare my feelings.' Wouter sat slumped in his chair, feeling sorry for himself. Why would he believe anything Oscar or anyone else said when he knew he'd failed the simplest of tasks?

'Let's look at the facts. Surely everyone was accounted for after the raid, so Dick Foppen must have some record of Laura.'

'Nothing. There have been rumours and false trails but all came to nothing. It was Else's idea I come here. She thought you might have prepared papers to help her escape.' Wouter looked up, his eyes full of hope.

'Laura Wechsler,' said Oscar, as if trying the words out for the first time. 'Let's go down and ask Kiki. She might remember the name.'

FORTY-ONE

WOUTER

Kiki stood in the kitchen mashing potatoes, carrots and onion for *hutspot*. Her cheeks were flushed with the exertion and the steam that rose from the black pan. Oscar walked over, dipped in a finger and winked at her before declaring the dish to be delicious. She slapped his hand playfully as he went in for more.

Wouter watched the scene with envy before turning away. He found it hard to imagine himself and Laura in such a domestic scene, sharing jokes, being so relaxed in each other's company. Even if they were to be reunited, how could he be sure she'd even want to be with him after all they'd been through?

'Leave that a moment,' said Oscar, appearing to notice his discomfort. 'Wouter has something to ask you. About someone he knew at Berkenhout he thinks you may have helped escape.'

'Ah yes. There have been a few. Who was it?' Kiki placed her masher down and found a lid for the pan.

Wouter hesitated before saying Laura's name out loud as if doing so was tempting fate. What if Kiki had never met Laura?

That would be the end of his search. And if she had met her? Heart thumping, he had to push on and find out. 'Laura Wechsler,' he said with a catch in his voice.

'Ah, Laura. Of course. And Bets. I took them to Maassluis only a week or two ago. They're staying with a friend of my mother's. She has a small farm across the river and needed help after her husband died and her son was forced to work for the Germans. It's quite remote, so they'll be safe there.' Kiki gave a reassuring smile.

Wouter let out a long breath, relief washing over him. 'That's... very good news. But have you heard from them since?'

Kiki laid a hand on Wouter's arm. 'Sorry, no. But that doesn't mean bad news. Letters can take weeks to come through.'

Wouter nodded as he tried to imagine where Laura must be. He'd never been to Maassluis but knew all about the hardship people were enduring. News was coming through about people having next to no food with many dying from starvation. Rations counted for nothing as shops had nothing on the shelves. The rivers and canals were frozen solid, making it impossible for supplies to get through, and what little did, the Germans were taking for themselves. It worried him that Laura was facing this new danger but he tried to push the thought from his mind as he asked who Bets was.

'A friend she met when escaping from Kampenveld and they've been together ever since. It's been tough for them, never staying anywhere more than a few days, moving from place to place. The worst of it was when they were in Zwolle...'

'Zwolle? So it's true. In the letter you wrote to Else you mentioned helping a girl from Berkenhout. I must have been in Zwolle at the same time, but no one knew of her. Please, tell me more.'

Kiki spoke quietly as she explained their ordeal at the hands of Liv, only escaping from their cell thanks to Laura's nerve and quick-wittedness. It was bittersweet news, but the main thing was that she was alive.

'And you knew nothing of this?' said Kiki.

'No. Not a thing. The last time I saw her was when we were both in Berkenhout. Before the ambush.'

'So you won't know that an SSer helped them escape? A nice friendly one, though, who didn't really want to work for the Germans.'

Something rang a bell. Surely it couldn't be. 'He wasn't called Emil by any chance?' he ventured.

Kiki laughed out loud. 'You know Emil?'

Wouter shook his head in disbelief. 'No, not exactly. I came across him at a party. He wasn't in uniform but as soon as I clapped eyes on him I could tell he was a *mof*. Everyone seemed to know he wasn't a threat and seemed pretty relaxed around him, particularly when he started singing a duet with Eva. I suppose it's starting to make sense.'

'Eva was one of the others who gave them shelter thanks to Emil.'

'Really?' said Wouter. So Eva was a good sort after all, despite her misgivings about getting involved. Perhaps it was the circumstances of Klaus's shocking death that had changed her. The most important thing was that she'd helped Laura. His Laura.

'If it hadn't been for Emil,' Kiki continued, 'I dread to think what might have happened to Laura and Bets, and countless others. They were the lucky ones. And now Emil's been moved away for officer training and hasn't been in touch. I just hope his commanding officer didn't catch wind of the work he was doing to help Jews. He was well intentioned but his superiors wouldn't see it like that.'

Kiki continued to describe Laura and Bets' escape and her

own involvement in escorting them to safe houses. Like Wouter, she'd been nervous of Emil's motives, but said she'd learned to trust him after hearing of the dozens of Jews he'd helped slip through the Germans' hands. Emil had brought Laura and Bets to her after hearing of her work with the Resistance.

At this point, she draped an arm round Oscar's neck and leant in towards him. "But it was thanks to Oscar I was able to provide them with new ID cards and travel documents.'

Oscar butted in, slightly sheepish at not realising one of these was Laura. 'Kiki hands me the information and I just get on with faking the documents. Sometimes I have twenty or thirty a day, so I don't take much notice of the details. But Laura's name definitely should have rung a bell.'

'That's because I didn't hand you her real details. It would be far too dangerous for a Jew trying to escape Holland. So I came up with the name Anne-Marie Schipper and gave her a disguise.'

'Anne-Marie Schipper,' said Wouter, sounding out her new name. Of course a Jewish name like Laura Wechsler would have aroused suspicion, but so too would her appearance.

'What was her disguise?'

'It was simple really. Don't laugh. I rigged up a scarf with a blonde fringe and a pair of spectacles. It was quite convincing, especially when I had the idea of getting her to wear red lipstick. It made all the difference and she looked about ten years older.'

Wouter did laugh then and blew out his cheeks, failing to imagine what she must have looked like. How could such a disguise mask her distinctive dark features and eyes? He couldn't imagine she'd be prepared to go through with it, but worse, she must have been terrified. The relief knowing she'd managed to get away and was safe flooded him with warmth, as if he were close to her again.

'Well, I think this is a cause for celebration,' said Oscar, fetching a bottle and three small glasses from a cabinet and placing them on the kitchen table.

'*Proost*! To Laura!' they cried in unison as they chinked glasses.

The three of them talked and laughed long into the night, fuelled up by Kiki's *hutspot* and numerous refills. They avoided any more talk of the war, but instead shared plans for the future. With his newfound skills as a printmaker, Oscar was harbouring an ambition to run his own printing firm, while Kiki talked about reviving her family business manufacturing furniture. Wouter, who had only been able to think of the immediate future and finding Laura, listened as she described the beautiful inlaid cupboards her grandfather used to make and sell to rich clients. All at once, the memory of something stirred inside him, of a yearning he had experienced when whittling bowls, ladles, toys and even stools for people in Berkenhout. At the time, he'd dismissed Petr's comments about how good his woodworking skills were, but what if he were to train to become a proper craftsman?

Before he had the chance to say anything about such a dream, Oscar, more than a little drunk, staggered to his feet, fumbled in his pocket and brought out a small brass curtain ring. 'Darling Kiki,' he began, making her giggle. 'Seriously, I know it's not much but when this is all over, will you marry me?'

'Ask me again when you're sober.' She laughed, taking the curtain ring from him and trying it on several fingers before finding one that fitted. 'But for tonight, I'll say yes.' She wrapped her arms round Oscar's neck and gave him a lingering kiss.

Wouter clapped his hands in approval, imagining himself proposing to Laura. *Maybe, just maybe*, he thought. As if reading his mind, Oscar broke off from his embrace with Kiki to slap Wouter on the back. 'And you,' he began, slurring from drink and happiness, 'must return with Laura for a proper celebration.'

'Yes,' he said. 'We would love to.'

FORTY-TWO

WOUTER

The next morning someone knocked at the door, tapping out the opening bars of Beethoven's 5th, signifying the caller could be trusted. Kiki let in an unshaven man with a shock of greying hair, carrying a shabby briefcase.

'Willem. Another assignment?' she yawned as she covered her mouth. It had been a late night and she was the only one up.

'Urgent new intelligence that must go out tonight. I trust you'll be all right with that?' He didn't wait for her to reply as he tugged open the straps of his battered leather bag and extracted a typewritten sheet of paper from a concealed compartment in the base. 'I know it's short notice but I need one hundred copies and they must all be distributed to...' He paused as he looked up the street name.

'By tonight?' Kiki was wide awake as she mulled over the implications of his request.

'By ten p.m. That's the instruction. I'm sorry.' The man brushed back a lock of lank hair as he looked up from the untidy sheaf of papers he was holding.

'Leave it with me,' said Kiki, suppressing a sigh.

'Good. I'm not expecting any more assignments this week.'

'I should hope not.' Kiki went over to the door and waited for the man to jam the remaining papers back into the concealed compartment of his case and leave.

She sat down on the sofa and read the lines written on the paper she'd been given. She didn't expect to make sense of the message, a statement about a man called Piet taking his dog for a walk along the beach at Scheveningen.

'Who was that?' said Oscar, descending the stairs in bare feet, his fair hair sticking up from sleep.

With a sniff, Kiki threw the piece of paper down. 'Willem. He needs a hundred copies distributed tonight.'

With a frown, Oscar scanned the sheet. 'Let's hope the intended recipient knows what this is about.'

Wouter appeared shortly after, rubbing his stubbly chin and looking slightly worse for wear. Last night's celebrations, though enjoyable, had taken their toll and he had a raging thirst. "Can I help?'

'Thanks,' said Oscar, 'but two of us working the press won't get them printed any faster. It'll take most of the day to turn this into a hundred copies. Perhaps you can help Kiki distribute them tonight.'

'That's a good idea,' said Kiki with a bright smile. 'One of us can push them through letterboxes while the other keeps an eye out for anything untoward. Don't look so alarmed. I've done it dozens of times and never been spotted.'

Wouter took in a deep breath as he thought about it. 'Are you sure I should come along? I wouldn't want to endanger the work you're doing. You do know I'm already known to the police.'

'Look, I won't pretend it's not risky, but this piece of paper could just save someone's life.'

.   .   .

Wouter wore Oscar's black trousers, raincoat and hat to help him merge into the darkness. Kiki had studied the route on a map and ascertained that it would take them no more than an hour to complete their mission. She explained how it was common practice among Resistance workers to deliver leaflets to dozens of houses, even though the message was intended for just one person. It was an effective way of throwing the *moffen* off the scent as they simply didn't have the resources to go questioning so many households.

Apart from one or two cars it was eerily quiet as they set off across town to their designated address. They divided the leaflets between them, twenty-five in each of their pockets. It was a little before curfew, and they looked like any couple in a hurry to get home.

'We're here,' whispered Kiki as they turned the corner onto a wide street with rows of tall houses on either side. 'Not ideal,' she said, as two cars, a motorbike and a van drove past in quick succession. 'Follow me,' she said, and she strode towards an alleyway Wouter hadn't noticed. She walked the length of it and back, before decreeing that it was safe. 'Wait here and keep an eye out, while I do the first batch. If anyone comes along, anyone at all, step out and walk towards me and I'll catch you up.' She pulled her hat down over her forehead and headed across the road towards the first house. It all went like clockwork and she was back within a few minutes having got rid of her load.

'Your turn now,' she said, with an encouraging slap on his shoulder. 'Start on this side and make sure you don't miss any out.'

Wouter gave her a quick nod and stepped out of the alleyway, keeping close to the houses on his right. He worked fast, taking little heed of the snapping sound that the letterboxes made as he hurried to push the material through, until a man's voice called out from inside one of the houses. He rushed on, annoyed at his mistake. *Twenty, twenty-one, twenty-two*, he counted silently. One more to go. At number twenty-three he pushed open the gate, which made a slight squeak. He glanced quickly behind him, but the street was empty. He was reaching his hand out to post the leaflet through the narrow slit, when the door swung open to reveal the bulky frame of a man slipping on his jacket. He hadn't noticed Wouter, as he turned to say goodbye to a woman standing behind him.

'Be careful, Fritz, *schat*, and make sure you're not seen.'

Wouter shrank into the shadow of a bush and held his breath. He could see the woman was wearing a silk blue dressing gown, which she held tight against the cold night air. The man mumbled a few words Wouter couldn't catch, before kissing the woman on her lips and neck, then disappearing down the path. She giggled and gave a little wave at the retreating German officer and closed the door with a soft click. Wouter stood with the leaflet in his hand, now crumpled, which he returned to his pocket. Breathing heavily, he waited a moment before venturing back to the alleyway where Kiki was waiting anxiously.

'What took you so long?' she hissed.

'Slight problem,' said Wouter with a nervous laugh. 'I came upon a German officer visiting his lover. I thought it best not to hand him the leaflet.'

'You're joking! Did he see you?'

'Luckily, no. I hope you don't mind but I didn't get to deliver that one.'

Kiki was not amused. 'And what if that's the house we needed to get the message to?'

'Are you kidding? She certainly didn't give the impression she was working against the Germans,' said Wouter with a snort.

'Don't believe everything you see. Go back and deliver the leaflet and we'll finish the rest of the job together.'

Kiki stood on guard by the gate as Wouter crept up the path again and carefully inserted the leaflet. As he retreated down the path he was sure he heard the letterbox click as the message was retrieved.

FORTY-THREE

WOUTER

Wouter soon became adept at using the printing press, turning out material for Resistance groups in Amsterdam, Utrecht and Apeldoorn. He was pleased to be of help and often worked with Oscar late into the night, stopping now and then for a *jenever* to fortify themselves. Hidden away day after day, they waded through the never-ending pile of coupons, IDs and anti-Nazi leaflets. Kiki was often away, returning to pick up bundles of freshly printed pamphlets before setting out on another assignment. He often wondered exactly where she went, but she was always vague on the details. If Oscar knew, he didn't let on, saying that all that mattered was they were thwarting the Germans from achieving their evil aims. Wouter was secretly relieved to be let off delivering leaflets; having almost made a mess of it last time, he wasn't likely to be given a second chance.

It was late afternoon and Wouter was nearing the end of a particularly large order for leaflets to be distributed to the south of Amsterdam. He had the house to himself – Oscar was away in Kampenveld visiting his mother and Jan; Kiki had been out since morning and wasn't due back for a few hours. The press had been playing up today, depositing splodges of ink onto every few sheets. His fingers were stained black from repeated attempts to retrieve the damp sheets from between the rollers. He knew it needed to be fixed, but that would have to wait, such was the urgency of the assignment. Wouter knew better than to argue with Kiki.

'Wouter? Can you come down?' Her voice floated from below. Wouter cocked his ear, surprised to hear her back so soon. She sounded anxious and he wondered what could be the matter. Then at that moment, the press jammed with a harsh grating sound. 'Just give me a minute while I finish off,' he called out, trying not to make things worse by attempting to extract the sheet stuck fast.

'I've received a letter with news about Laura. She's not at all well.'

Wouter's heart leapt in his chest. All this time that he'd been carrying out essential work for the Resistance he'd consoled himself knowing she was safe; he never considered for one moment she might fall ill. It must be serious for Kiki to come home specially to tell him. Needing no further persuasion, he flung a thick blanket over the press before hurrying over to the hatch and lowering himself onto the threadbare rug below.

Kiki was frowning as she read the letter in her hand, but smiled when he appeared. He knew he must look a sight with his unkempt hair flying round his face and smudges of ink where he'd pushed his hair back in exasperation. He hastily wiped his cheek with the back of his hand. 'What's the matter with Laura? Is it serious?'

She nodded, saying she was sorry to be the bearer of bad news. 'Apparently, she's been ill with a high fever for some days and isn't getting any better. Mevrouw Teuling was able to fetch a doctor who managed to stabilise her condition till her temperature went up again. She thinks it's the lack of nutritious food that is making her weak.' Frowning, she folded the letter. 'I knew it was a risk sending the girls to that part of Holland, but I had no idea how grave the situation was with regard to food.'

Wouter couldn't bear to hear any more. Why had he allowed Oscar to persuade him to stay on and help him, when he should have gone straight to Laura as soon as he'd heard she was safe? He snatched the letter and saw it was dated over a week ago. It would take him another two days, at least, to get over there. Would it be too late? His voice shook as he spoke. 'I should have gone weeks ago. I only stayed because I saw how much you and Oscar needed my help.'

Kiki laid hand on his arm consolingly. 'You did what you thought best. The documents you've helped produced will have saved dozens of lives. You mustn't blame yourself.'

Wouter gave a desperate sigh as he thrust his hand through his hair. 'Kiki, please, can you help me get to her?'

Kiki's face softened and she hugged him tight, telling him she'd do all she could, that he would leave the next day, taking medicines and as much food as he could carry. As she stroked his head, his eyes welled up and, for the first time since his escape from Berkenhout, he wept.

FORTY-FOUR

LAURA

For days, there'd been the threat of snow under a leaden yellow sky. And still there's no sign of Bets. Did she ever make it across on the ferry, or maybe she changed her mind? I hope not. She's now my only friend and I can't bear to lose her too. I often look out for her, hoping to see her trudging along the long road to farm, but I hardly see a soul. In some ways, it's a relief, because I'm still fearful that Friedrich will return.

Before, Mevrouw Teuling would have been worried about being cut off, but we both know the likelihood is that Friedrich won't be coming back. However, we're grateful for all the food he's left, which we've managed to eke out in soups and stews. Up to now, I don't suppose I appreciated quite how low our own food supplies were. Apart from a few miserly handfuls of dried beans and the discovery of some ancient jars of *applemoes* in the cellar, we have nothing, and as long as the field behind the house lies under a thick frozen crust it's almost impossible to dig out the last of the potatoes. The hunger never goes away; it's a wretched hollow feeling, often accompanied by painful cramps. How I long for a piece of meat, however small, to make a proper meal of, instead of the watery soup we fashion from one small potato and a quarter of a turnip. Then there's the problem of fuel. There's barely enough wood to cook with, let alone heat the kitchen, so we sit wrapped up in our coats next to the cold *kachel* trying to conserve our energy. After the snow, we keep telling ourselves, we'll go in search of food and fuel.

The coughing begins one evening after a spoonful of soup goes down the wrong way. I think nothing of it, but I keep coughing and a rawness starts in my chest. Mevrouw Teuling prepares me a cup of hot water, adding a drop of her precious brandy and a few crystals of honey she's managed to scrape from the bottom of an old jar. It tastes good and revives me for a while. When the coughing starts up again, she tells me I should go to bed and finds me an extra blanket. But I don't sleep at all well and in the morning my cheeks are on fire. As I try to stand up, I feel dizzy and have to hold on to the bedpost for support.

The last thing I remember clearly is Mevrouw Teuling fussing over me, telling me to rest and placing a cool flannel on my forehead. I'm too weak to make sense of her disjointed words as I drift in and out of consciousness.

FORTY-FIVE

WOUTER

It took him almost a week to reach Laura. Kiki was too busy to take him, but had arranged it all, including the river crossing with a reliable fisherman she knew, but she warned Wouter to make the journey under cover of darkness to avoid detection. By day, he hid wherever he could find shelter. After his first night spent trudging along frozen dykes and deserted country roads, he came across an empty farm building. It had only one door that hung off and banged at each cold gust of wind, but he was grateful, at least, for a roof over his head. The following day, he had no such luck and was forced to snatch a few moments' rest behind a large oak tree at one end of a bare field. By the time he reached the fisherman's hut on a secluded section of the river, he was almost delirious from lack of sleep and the cold.

The old fisherman was waiting for him, a stocky man in voluminous dark trousers and collarless jacket, a small flat cap perched on the back of his head and an unlit pipe he kept clenched between his teeth. He spoke in a dialect Wouter found hard to follow, but few words were needed as Wouter handed over the thirty guilders, a small fortune, into his outstretched hand. He was too weary to worry whether the old man was even capable of rowing them across as he stepped into the rocking boat and tried to ignore the puddle of water sloshing around his feet. Grinning his yellow teeth at Wouter, the old man grunted a few words of encouragement and pushed the boat off into the inky darkness.

Wouter was thankful not to have to keep up a conversation. The soft rhythmical swishing of the oars made him drowsy. Even the feeling of seeping, cold damp up his trouser legs didn't bother him. The fisherman steered towards a tiny light that flickered, on off, on off, from the far shore. As they drew near, Wouter spotted a dark figure, the man's son, who lifted a hand in greeting. A muscular man with a shock of pale-gold hair, he hauled the boat to shore and tied the chain to a wooden stump.

'My father says you'll join us for supper and stay till morning.' He spoke good Dutch and had a kindly smile.

The relief Wouter felt at this invitation was overwhelming. In the cramped cottage, some yards up from the shoreline, Wouter was welcomed by the man's wife who had prepared a fish stew, and later provided a pile of blankets so he could sleep between the nets stacked up in the outhouse. It was the warmest he'd felt in days. The next morning before light, he was on his way, armed with food for the journey and directions on how to reach the village where Mevrouw Teuling lived.

The girl who eventually let him in hadn't exactly been unfriendly, just cautious and probably a little frightened to be faced with this dishevelled stranger who'd arrived in the half dark. Reluctantly, she let him into the kitchen, closing the door behind him firmly, before introducing herself as the neighbour's daughter who was helping look after the patient. With that, she told him to wait in the kitchen and disappeared upstairs. Wouter had to suppress the urge to run after her. He paced up and down, imagining Laura lying above him, too sick to speak.

The click of the front door announced Mevrouw Teuling's return. Wouter braced himself as he waited for her to find him in her kitchen. The girl came flying down the stairs and out into the scullery where he could hear the murmur of their low voices.

The door opened and Mevrouw Teuling entered, appraising him with a frown. Hesitating, Wouter took a step forward. 'I'm very sorry for the intrusion, but I was hoping that Kiki had let you know I was coming. I've brought some food and medicines.' He looked down at the two parcels he was holding, looking somewhat crumpled after the journey. 'My name is Wouter, a close friend of Laura,' he explained.

An anxious expression flitted across the woman's face as she turned abruptly to speak to Mieke. 'You'd better go home now. And thank you for staying.' She handed over a few coins and the girl's face lit up.

'Thank you, *mevrouw*. Would you like me to come tomorrow?'

'No, that won't be necessary. I'll let your mother know if I need any help.' Taut-faced, she walked Mieke to the door. The girl turned to throw Wouter an anxious glance.

'I didn't mean to cause any problems,' said Wouter when Mevrouw Teuling returned. 'When you weren't here, I admit I was rather insistent she let me in. You shouldn't be too hard on her.'

Mevrouw Teuling let out a sigh. 'We've had some trouble here recently and I don't want Mieke running back home and spreading rumours. A stranger round these parts is bound to set tongues wagging and when you mentioned Laura, I thought it best she leave before you said too much else. You see, Anne-Marie' – she emphasised the words – 'is the young woman Mieke has been looking after.'

'Ah yes,' said Wouter, closing his eyes at his error.

'Never mind. It's done now. There's nothing to prove Laura

isn't Anne-Marie Schipper, so if Mieke tells anyone we'll simply deny it.'

Wouter opened his mouth to speak and was silenced by the sound of a voice crying out. It wasn't one he recognised but it had to be Laura. He could hear unintelligible, breathy words that tailed off into a rasping cough. 'Is she in pain?' he asked, his heart thumping uncomfortably.

'She does this whenever she's having a nightmare. It's the fever. The doctor says it's nothing to be alarmed about, but it is distressing all the same. Come and see her, but don't be alarmed by her appearance. She's actually improved a lot, but she's still not fully conscious.'

Wouter followed Mevrouw Teuling up the stairs, but hung back in the doorway as she bent over the bed. He was unsure what to do or say. From where he was standing, he could see the shape of Laura and her dark halo of hair against the pillow.

'Come on over and hold her hand. Talk to her.' Mevrouw Teuling pulled up a chair and gestured for him to sit. He stared down at Laura's gaunt pale face. There were inky shadows beneath her closed eyes and she resembled no one he knew. She looked so fragile, so different, and it scared him.

'Go on. Take her hand.' Mevrouw Teuling spoke gently.

He reached for her hand and was surprised to find it felt warm against his own. For a short moment Laura's eyes flickered open and he was sure she recognised him. Encouraged, he leant close to her ear to whisper a few words but her eyes closed again. Disappointed, he looked up at Mevrouw Teuling, who merely shook her head. 'Keep talking to her. I'm sure she can hear you. I'll be downstairs. Stay as long as you like.' The warmth of her hand on his shoulder was a comfort and he wished she'd stay. He'd never nursed a sick person before. What if she stopped breathing?

Once alone, he calmed down and found it surprisingly easy to talk while keeping an eye on the bedclothes gently rising and falling with the rhythm of her breath. 'I want to tell you what happened that day. Why I didn't come to get you. I meant to, really I did, but I panicked and ran for my life when I should have been looking out for you. It was a selfish and cowardly thing to do and I've never stopped regretting it. I want you to believe me when I say that from that moment on, I've been searching for you. Can you ever forgive me?' His voice was breaking and his cheeks wet, but he didn't expect a response as he gazed at her face, so peaceful in repose. 'I made a big mistake not coming to rescue you, but I never gave up hope. You see, every enquiry I made was a dead end and no one had any firm news. So I wrote you letters not really knowing if they'd reach you. I refused to believe you were dead, but it was almost as bad imagining you never wanted to see me again.' He gripped her hand again and as he did so became aware she was gripping his back. Her eyelids fluttered slightly, then opened. Holding his breath, Wouter waited for her to close them again but she kept gazing at him.

'Well, are you going to say hello?' His voice cracked as he spoke. He leant over and placed his lips on her cheek where he stayed for a long moment. He became aware of her hands reaching up to his neck and carefully he pulled her into an embrace. 'I thought I'd lost you,' he said, kissing her gently on the lips. When he pulled away he looked into her eyes, unsure just how much she was taking in. Then, as she began to smile, her eyes drooped shut.

Wouter decided to leave her to rest while he went to fetch her a drink. He was only gone a few minutes when that dreadful cry of hers started up again. He rushed back up the stairs, calling that he was coming.

She was awake again; she had tears in her eyes.

'I've brought you some tea. Do you think you can sit up?' He arranged the pillow behind her, hoisting her up as he laughed. 'See, you're as light as a feather.'

He sat down on the bed and handed her the cup, making sure she didn't spill any of the warm tea. She took a few sips in concentration before peering over the cup at him. Still she said nothing, but in that brief moment, he took pleasure in that they were together again.

FORTY-SIX

LAURA

There's a blackbird singing and it's taunting me. It's so loud, so shrill, I wish it would stop. If I could just open my eyes and shoo it away... but my eyes are stuck shut. I don't know how long they've been like this, but it's best they are. When I did open them a while ago, they hurt so much that I quickly closed them. I don't need to open them as I can see daylight through my lids. Strange, as it's normally so dark in here, even when it's bright sunshine outside. Perhaps I ought to get up and find Wouter. If it's morning, he'll be with Petr. I'm sure he said he was finishing off the wooden table and stools they were carving for the new hut. But that was before we had a row, I think. I know he's angry with me, but I can't remember why. Something about him wanting to leave Berkenhout ... but he wouldn't leave me, would he?

Perhaps I'll stay here a while. Thank goodness the singing has stopped. That bird must have flown off to pester someone else. At last I can get some peace. Sleep, that's all I want right now. Sleep.

. . .

Every time I try to swallow, my throat feels like sandpaper. Can't someone give me some water? I wrench open my eyes and I can see a glass of water on a table, but I'm too tired to reach it. Maybe if I call, someone will come and help me. I think about this for a long time, the cool sensation of water trickling down my throat. Why does no one come? I try out my voice but the only sound I make is a rasp. Oh, why is everything such an effort? Once I've had a sleep, I'll try again.

It's so peaceful in the woods today, though I know I mustn't take it for granted. At any moment, German soldiers could burst through the trees and gun us down, at least that's what we've been told. We must be vigilant at all times, especially during daylight hours. But nothing has happened yet, has it? I don't think they can be bothered looking for us anymore and must have gone elsewhere where they can be certain to find *onder-duikers*.

Surely a little excursion beyond the boundary can't hurt if I go down at dusk when there are definitely no *moffen* searching the woods. But wait, didn't I hear a loud noise a while ago, like gunshot? I start to shake my head but shaking makes it hurt, so I lie perfectly still.

I remember now. Wouter said he'd meet me at the boundary line at seven this evening. He has something important to say to me and doesn't want anyone to hear. Or was it that I have something important to say to him? I wish I could remember.

I'm sure I only closed my eyes for a moment, but he's standing above me stroking my hair. How can that be? I don't remember lying down, but then I don't remember walking down here either. It feels nice and there's no need for words. I don't want him to stop, but I hear his voice talking to someone else. I strain to hear what they're saying but it's all muffled and makes me even more tired. I'm just going to lie here and when I've had a rest, I'll ask what's going on.

The thud, thudding is getting louder and I know they're getting nearer, but I can't move. I try so hard to lift myself onto my elbows to get up, but it's as if I'm paralysed. They're coming to get me – I know it. I try to scream but nothing, nothing comes out. I feel as if my head will split with the pounding of those boots and now they're marching right over me. I screw my face up to force out a scream as a big black cloth is thrown over my head.

I hear soft voices and am aware of a shadowy shape moving to my left.

'I think she's waking up.'

Someone is bending over me and I can feel breath on my cheek. I hold my breath till they move away. Only then do I attempt to force open my eyes a crack. I'm in a room I don't recognise, a bedroom, and I'm lying in bed. I thought I heard two voices but there's now only one person standing at the window opening the curtains to let the daylight in.

'Where am I?' The words come out in a whisper and I see it's Mevrouw Teuling. She comes over and kneels down to take my weak hand in her two cool ones. She looks as if she's been crying. I make an effort to smile.

'Laura, you've been very ill for a while, so you mustn't exert yourself. How are you feeling?'

I don't know how to answer her, so close my eyes again. After a bit I ask her if she can bring me a cup of tea. She seems pleased with this idea and tells me to lie quietly and that she'll be back as soon as she can.

She leaves me alone and I start to doze until I'm wakened by the sweetest sound of a blackbird. I turn my head to look at it perched in the tree outside the window. When it strikes up its fluting song, its yellow beak quivers and I'm sure it's looking at me as it does so. It's a beautiful sound and I imagine it's singing just for me.

Someone is gently shaking my arm. I must have been asleep again and I flutter my eyes open. I'm about to ask for water when Wouter's face comes into focus. He looks tired and he pushes back his hair in a familiar gesture I'd forgotten. But it must be another of my mind's tricks, so I shut my eyes again. This time I don't go to sleep; instead I summon up the courage to open them again. When I do, I see he hasn't moved and his look of concern has been replaced by a smile.

'Well, are you going to say hello?' His voice sounds croaky. He doesn't wait for me to reply. Instead, he leans over and places his lips on my cheek where he stays for a long moment. It's an effort, but I manage to lift my arms and drape them round his neck so I can keep breathing him in. We stay like this until he draws back to gaze down at me. 'I thought I'd lost you,' he says, leaning down to kiss me gently on the lips. I close my eyes again, not quite believing this is real. For so long I've lain here with only my dreams for company. Horrible, strange, fearful dreams that end abruptly with me jerking awake, leaving me soaked in sweat with a pounding head. Occasionally, I'd see Wouter, but his features were always indistinct, just out of reach.

I wake with a shock. How can I have fallen asleep? He was here. He was kissing me. And now he's gone. I feel a sob start in my throat; the frustration at my inability to jump out of this bed and run to find him.

'I'm here, Laura. I'm here.'

Relief washes over me. He's standing at the door holding a cup of something.

'Do you think you can sit up?'

It still seems unreal, but I'm beginning to accept that this is happening and I must make sure I don't fall asleep again.

'See, you're as light as a feather.' Wouter laughs as he hoists me up onto the pillow he's plumped up. I don't feel it, though. I feel like an ungainly lump and wish he didn't have to see me like this. I must look a fright, but he doesn't seem to notice, or even care.

He sits on the bed and hands me the cup, looking intently at my hands so that I don't drop it. I take it obediently and concentrate on holding it to my lips. The liquid is sweet and warm as it slips down, soothing my parched throat. I exhale in happiness.

FORTY-SEVEN
LAURA

I'm sitting in the doorway of the kitchen catching the morning sun's rays, which are remarkably warm for the time of year. I'm listening to Mevrouw Teuling describe these events leading up to my illness and it's as if she's talking about someone that's not me. I'm astonished to hear just how ill I've been.

The aspirins I'd brought with me under the pretence they were for Mevrouw Teuling lasted only a couple of days. When my fever didn't subside, she called the doctor, but he was unable to do anything more than hand over more aspirin. In order to get well, he said, I would need plenty of liquid and nutritious food – but of course she was unable to provide it.

After some days, I was still semi-delirious and she knew she had to go in search of food. She arranged for Mieke, a neighbour's girl, to sit with me with instructions to cool my brow and help me drink water when I woke. The snow hadn't amounted to much but a bitterly cold wind still blew from the east as she trudged down the track and onto the deserted road towards the open fields. She'd had word that people were digging for carrots and beets. She hurried, as she knew that it wouldn't be long before the whole field would be stripped, that is if the Germans hadn't got there first and chased them all away. Walking with her head down, she kept her scarf pulled across her nose and mouth against the cold, so didn't notice when a voice called out to her. She turned to find it was Friedrich hurrying to catch up. Seeing him gave her a shock and her immediate thought was he'd want to come back to the house and find me, but he didn't seem to realise who she was. By the time he'd finished his questioning, it dawned on him who he was addressing. Fortunately, she had the sense to say I was no longer staying with her. She hoped he'd leave her on her way, but he turned friendly and insisted on walking alongside, chatting as if they were acquaintances. If it had been anyone else, she tells me, she'd have felt sorry for this young man, so obviously lonely and in need of company. But she remained silent while he chatted on as he bemoaned the fact he'd been unable to come back and that he'd missed me. He'd only ventured out because he could no longer stand being cooped up waiting for the snow to recede. Then he started on about the hunger they were all experiencing back at the barracks and Mevrouw Teuling had to force herself not to mention our dire plight. Nor did she want him to know she was out searching for food, so she stayed silent.

As they approached the scattering of houses on the edge of the village, Friedrich put a hand on her arm and said he needed to get back. He would try to get hold of some provisions for her when the weather improved. She deflected him with the lie that she was coping well enough. Her only thought was she didn't want him coming back to the farm and discovering I was still there.

The long trek out was only partially successful. She arrived to find the fields bare of any crop with only a few stragglers still poking at the iron soil with sticks. A young man, about to ride off on a bike with wooden tyres, took pity on her and advised her to keep on walking for another mile towards the bulb fields. They make a delicious stew, he called back to her as he rode off with a cheerful wave. Of course, she'd heard the rumours that people were reduced to digging up tulip bulbs for food, but she never imagined things would ever get that bad. Now, here she was, miles from home, desperately hungry and with an empty bag. She had no choice but to carry on.

Returning nearly four hours later and with only a handful of tulip bulbs, she was close to tears. She'd forgotten about poor Mieke and was about to send her home when the girl anxiously said there was a strange man waiting for her in the kitchen with a parcel of food. Her immediate thought was it must have been Friedrich, but Mieke's description didn't fit. The poor girl had been faced with the decision whether to send this stranger away, when he begged her to let him stay, saying he'd travelled halfway across Holland to reach this place. Reluctantly, Mieke told him he could wait in the kitchen, and that is where Mevrouw Teuling found Wouter. And I was lying upstairs, oblivious to it all.

FORTY-EIGHT

LAURA

The last few weeks have floated by like in a dream. A good one, where I'm free of pain and fear and where Wouter is my constant companion. Just occasionally when I'm about to fall asleep, I get that awful image of German boots marching over me and the sound of crunching between my ears. When I come to, sweating and exhausted, I force myself to accept that it's because my body isn't yet free of the illness. Yet, these nightmares continue to lurk at the edge of my consciousness, ready to overwhelm me again and again.

The doctor tells me I've had pneumonia and that it'll take some time to recover. Wouter says he'll stay as long as it takes, so I'm in no hurry. I worry that someone will discover his presence here and turn him in, but he says he knows enough about evading the *moffen* to stay safe. Besides, there are few of them left in the area but Friedrich could be one of them. He hasn't come visiting for a while, but I can't relax till I know he's gone. So I keep an eye on Wouter from the back door where he's out in the field behind the house. He forks over the earth and fills buckets with potatoes and turnips we had no idea were still buried when it was frozen. When he's dug it over he'll plant a new crop. He's sorted out suitable specimens of potato, cutting them in half so they go further and leaving them to dry out for a few days. It's remarkable to think these shrivelled brown lumps with their strange white protuberances will grow into vigorous green plants with a wealth of treasure hidden below the soil.

Mevrouw Teuling's husband used to have dozens of hens, supplying eggs to the local villages. The Germans put an end to that, the idiots. She's convinced that's what caused her husband's heart attack. The shock of eight men storming the henhouse and killing every single last hen. He tried so hard to prevent them, but they ignored his pleas as they booted, stamped on and shot those poor birds. Their squeals and shrieks were so heart-rending that Mr Teuling never recovered and died a month later. The tragedy was that it was so unnecessary. The *moffen* helped themselves to as many of the dead birds as they wanted, leaving the rest in a heap on the henhouse floor to rot. Had they no idea their value was in the eggs they laid?

All memory of what happened in there has been erased. Now, if you enter through the door, it's no more than a dark shed used for storage. At the back behind some sacking is another door you wouldn't know is there, leading to a room just big enough for a bed. That's where Wouter sleeps and where he hides whenever there's any possible threat.

From my position at the back door of the house, I keep watch for passers-by and listen carefully for the distant rumble of a motorbike.

However prepared you are, it's terrifying to experience a raid. I learnt that from the time we were evacuated from Berkenhout and six of us hid at Tante Else's house. She taught us the tricks of concealment, but she couldn't prepare us for the terror of German soldiers bursting in and ransacking the place. We knew we were safe in the summer house crouching beneath a false floor, but the dread of being discovered stayed with us long after they left.

. . .

It was eight o'clock and the three of us were playing a card game at the kitchen table when we were shaken to our feet by a pounding on the door. Wouter and I fled out through the back door and into the henhouse. He almost had to carry me as I was still too weak to run. When Mevrouw Teuling didn't come to retrieve us, we knew it must be serious, but had to stay put. Hours passed till we almost forgot why we were there. We couldn't be heard, so we talked in low voices, remembering our time in Berkenhout and turning over and over the terrible events that led to our separation. I wish I'd known it then, but Wouter had been wrestling with his conscience about whether he should really have been in the village. He thought he wasn't worthy of his place, which should have gone to someone in greater need. So what I interpreted as Wouter having regrets about me wasn't true at all. Had the ambush not happened, then he would have told me what he'd been going through. It saddens me that he hadn't felt he could discuss it with me earlier and could have saved us both a lot of heartache. But hearing his words was enough to believe he loves me.

It was the first time we'd spent so long alone together, pressed close against one another in that dark cramped space. There was no other way to lie, not that we minded, or cared; it was the safest I'd felt since that last evening with my parents, snuggled on my mother's lap like a small child, so blissfully unaware of what the future held. Then I felt Wouter's fingers feather-light on my cheeks, cupping my face and tracing my lips. His kiss was soft, soft, like sinking onto a deep pillow, but so much nicer. Unable to see each other in the velvety darkness, we melted into each other's embrace and I didn't want it to end.

At some point, we must have fallen asleep, for the next

thing I knew was the creak of the door and a draught of air blowing onto my face. Wouter had woken first for he was on his feet, tucking his shirt into his trousers, while I pulled the blanket up high in embarrassment. Not that Mevrouw Teuling noticed, so relieved was she to see the back of Friedrich. She somehow convinced him she was on her own again, but not before he insisted she cook him a meal with a piece of chicken he'd brought. The irony wasn't lost on her but he seemed unaware of the damage his compatriots had wrought on her farm the previous year. After the meal, he told her the reason for his visit: he'd come to say goodbye as his unit was moving on amid rumours they'd be returning to Germany. It was the first hint since fateful Dolle Dinsdag, the day when everyone had been duped into celebrating the defeat of the Germans, that the war was finally drawing to a close.

I've been wondering what's going to happen to us after the war ends. I'm sure Mevrouw Teuling would prefer us to stay on, and more than once she's said how indispensable we are to the running of the farm. I know she really means Wouter, who's done all the heavy work round here and has recently been spending days renovating the henhouse ready to turn it back to its original use.

Now I'm fully recovered, I can help Mevrouw Teuling around the house, but it's boring work and my mind has started to wander onto what I will do with my life. In Berkenhout, Sofie and I often used to talk about going to study in Ghent after the war, but that was when I believed I still had a family to return to. I have a vague hankering after teaching young children, but will need to finish my own education before I can even contemplate that. And where would I even go? I admit I did have a pang of jealousy when I received the letter from Kiki telling me that Bets had managed to get over the border to France. She'd looked so forlorn when I last saw her stranded on the quayside at Maassluis. But it didn't last long, Kiki said in her letter. She made it to Maassluis in a farmer's truck and was in a café drinking tea and wondering what to do next, when a man approached her and struck up a conversation. When it transpired he had links to a network of groups helping refugees escape Holland, she used her charms to persuade him to do the same for her. The months she'd spend in hiding and the stress every time she'd had to move had taken their toll and she saw her opportunity to get out. Of course I'm pleased for her, but after all we've been through together, it does make me sad to think I may never see her again.

Today is the first really warm day we've had this year and the haze in the sky makes me think of summer. I take a large basket of laundry outside and peg it onto the line at the back of the house. I walk over to where Wouter is sanding the door of the henhouse. He stops what he's doing and wipes the sweat from his brow before leaning in for a kiss.

'What will you do when you're finished?' I ask.

'What, this?' He frowns up at his handiwork. 'I hadn't really thought.'

'No, I mean after. We can't stay here forever. Will you return to Kampenveld?'

He doesn't answer, instead takes me by the hand and we walk over to where we can sit on the wooden bench with a view towards a cluster of tall trees. Inexplicably, I get a pang of nostalgia as I tell him it reminds me of being back in Berkenhout. He looks across at me and draws his dark brows together. 'It's time we talked about Berkenhout.' He draws in a deep breath. 'I wish I could explain why I didn't come to rescue you but I can't. The whole experience still haunts me.'

Closing my eyes, I lean into him with a sigh. It'll be easier for me talk like this. 'All this time I thought it was because of that silly argument we'd had. When the gunshots started, I knew I couldn't wait for you. Me and a load of others, we ran for our lives. It was so confusing, so much noise and chaos. I was so scared. I had no idea what had happened to you or anyone.' I shiver.

Wouter squeezes me to him and he kisses the side of my head before continuing. 'I should have come to find you. Only I was distracted by the bowl I was carving. I wanted to give it to you as a kind of peace offering and now it's gone.' His voice drops to a murmur. 'I should have had my wits about me and reacted when I heard the snap of twigs, but I was lost in concentration. I froze when they burst into the clearing, firing. I forgot everything Dick had taught me about responding to an attack and ran. I knew straightaway I'd lost you but how could I risk going back? It would have been suicide.'

I nod against his shoulder, listening.

'After days of sleeping out in the woods, I managed to get to Dick Foppen's place. So many had made it and when I saw you hadn't, I was convinced the Germans had got you.' Wouter's voice catches. 'Where did you go? Who helped you escape?'

'It was Henk. He helped me and others get out.' As I turn to Wouter I realise I've said the wrong thing. He buries his head in his hands and when he looks up his dark eyes are filled with something I find hard to read.

'God, what was I thinking? That should've been me. I was the one Dick put his trust in to lead you all to safety. What must you think of me?' He thrusts his hand through his hair in a gesture of frustration. Then he turns his blazing eyes onto me. 'But why Henk? What was he even doing over at Berkenhout?'

I shrug. It's something I've never questioned, but was it really so odd? Henk was always patrolling the woods or turning up with offers of help. Some had been wary of his motives, but, perhaps naively, I was grateful to have someone looking out for us. 'Does it even matter? The fact he turned up and managed to get us out is all I cared about. He looked after us and let us stay at his cottage until we could be moved to safety.'

Wouter is now staring at me, a deep frown on his face, and I'm not sure he believes me. 'I've always had my suspicions about Henk, but if he helped you, I suppose I must accept he did so in good faith. But you must understand there've been rumours about his dealings with the Germans, so it didn't occur to me to go and ask him what had happened to you.'

'Wouter, it's over. You can't blame yourself for what happened. Whatever Henk did or didn't do is in the past. Let's now talk about the future. Our future.'

SEPTEMBER 1945

FORTY-NINE

WOUTER

Wouter had a knot in his stomach. He leant towards the window, catching glimpses of familiar landmarks. They passed by deep-roofed farmhouses, great expanses of green fields, a stretch between magnificent beech trees in full leaf, and then the houses on the edge of the village lining the track came into view. There was the church tower just visible in the distance. It was all so familiar, but of course everything had changed.

He glanced across at Laura, who was leaning back with eyes closed. She no longer had that air of innocence he used to find so captivating, but she was no less beautiful. These days, she wore her shiny black hair longer and pinned away from her face. It made her look different, more self-assured and so removed from the frightened young girl he'd met on his arrival in Berkenhout. A lifetime ago, he thought.

As she opened her dark eyes, she smiled across at Wouter and squeezed his hand. 'What are you thinking?' she said.

'That you look beautiful when you're asleep,' he said.

'That's not all though, is it?' she said, her voice catching.

'You know me well,' said Wouter with a wry smile. 'I've

been thinking I'd like to go back and see what's become of Berkenhout. And that I'd like you to come with me.'

Laura turned her face to stare out at the trees rushing past the window. 'But we know there's nothing left, so what's the point?'

'I don't know. But I fled, not giving a thought to you or anyone else. I can't seem to let go of that. Going back with you would help me come to terms with it.'

'Don't look so sad.' She traced the set of his mouth with her finger. He focused his eyes on hers and smiled.

'I'm not sad. How can you think it?' Then, in a rush he said, 'You will come, won't you?'

'If you really want me to. But let's combine it with doing something nice, like taking Liesbeth, Sofie and Tante Else for a trip to the Hoge Veluwe. We could go for a walk across the heath and the sand dunes, which is a lot more exciting than just poking around in those gloomy woods,' she said, kissing his hand.

The train slowed as it approached Kampenveld station and there was Else waving from the platform. She hurried alongside their carriage till it came to a halt. Wouter tumbled out with their suitcases, followed by Laura.

'You made it!' Else held Laura at arm's length so she could take a good look. 'You're looking well, really well. Oh, Laura, when I heard you'd fallen ill, I was so worried about you. Wouter must have taken great care of you.'

Laura blushed and reached out to take Wouter's hand. 'I dread to think what would have happened to me if he hadn't turned up.'

Wouter shrugged, muttering he only did what he could.

'Come here, Wouter. It's been too long, really it has.' Else stretched out her arms to embrace the two of them. 'Now let's go,' she said, picking up Laura's bag and moving off.

'Here, let me,' said Wouter, catching up with her so he could take the bag. Drawing level, he asked, 'How is Sofie coping?'

'You'll see. There's so much to tell,' said Else. 'Now, you won't believe it but I'm still driving the old delivery van. It'll be a bit of a squash but we should all fit in the front.'

The van, battered and rusty, was parked in a side street. When Wouter saw it he was overcome with a wave of nostalgia. 'Can I drive it? For old times' sake,' he said, kicking one of the tyres like he used to.

He took it slowly as he familiarised himself with the controls, marvelling that it was still in working order. It even started at the first attempt. There was more traffic on the roads now and when they arrived at Else's house he was forced to park a little way down the street.

'Most of the neighbours have moved away and a lot of the new tenants have cars,' said Else, pursing her lips.

Inside, everything was the same, even down to the faint cinnamon smell of baking that always hung around the kitchen.

'Coffee?' said Else, busying herself with the kettle at the stove.

'That would be lovely, and, oh, I've brought something to go with it,' said Laura, digging into her bag. 'They're a bit squashed as I bought them at the station before we set off. They were fresh.' Laura held open a paper bag and her face fell. 'I see now that *oliebollen* don't travel well,' she said, observing the grease from the Dutch-style doughnuts that had seeped into the bag, making it transparent.

'I'm sure they'll taste good.' Else tipped them onto a plate and found some icing sugar to sprinkle over them.

Wouter bit into one and declared it to be delicious. 'I

remember how we once all sat round this table yearning for all the things we missed.'

'And *oliebollen* were my favourite. Still are,' said Laura, taking a bite of hers.

'But we never went short of real coffee, did we, Else?' said Wouter with a wink. 'Are you going to tell us where you got it from?'

'I thought you knew. It was Henk, of course,' said Else, pouring steaming coffee into her best cups. 'But he never would reveal his sources. It just wasn't done. Probably it came from one of the German officers he was friendly with.'

'So they must have known about Berkenhout and turned a blind eye,' said Wouter.

'They knew Henk was working on building projects for Dick involving moving materials and goods around the woods, but Henk would never have let on about Berkenhout.'

'Do you really believe that?' said Wouter with a frown.

Else looked at him in surprise. 'Why wouldn't I?'

They were interrupted by the arrival of Liesbeth, stepping through the door with a bundle in her arms.

'I can't believe you're actually here,' she cried, awkwardly kissing Wouter and Laura in turn as the baby squirmed in her arms. 'And this is Marieke. Lively little thing, she is,' she said, staring affectionately at the baby who gazed up at Liesbeth with a toothless smile.

'Here, let me take her from you so you can say hello properly,' said Else, cradling and fussing over the baby.

Four months had elapsed since the end of the war and there was a lot to catch up on. Liesbeth now had the baby to look after, which meant she'd had to put on hold her plans to finish her schooling and go to university. 'There'll always be time when Marieke's older, but I am keeping up with my studies when she sleeps,' she said wistfully.

'But what about Sofie? Doesn't she help you at all?' asked Laura.

'Oh yes, she sends money when she can, but her job doesn't pay that well so I don't like to ask.'

Wouter couldn't help but shake his head. 'I'm sure we can spare a little ...'

'No, it's not necessary,' said Liesbeth sharply. 'We manage quite well, thank you. Really.' She jumped up to take the baby who had started to cry, and jiggled her against her shoulder till she settled. When she turned round she had tears in her eyes. 'It's nothing. I have no regrets at all, but it's Sofie. She still harbours such hatred for what that *mof* did to her that she can't move beyond it and see the beautiful baby she's produced. It's so sad that she gave her up so readily. Don't get me wrong, she's doing everything she can to support us but she won't visit us. It's hard.' Her sniffing seemed to set Marieke off again, a little whimper that became a cry. 'She's hungry, that's all,' said Liesbeth, taking a bottle of milk she'd brought with her and warming it in a bowl of hot water provided by Else. She cooed over the baby while the others sat around, listening to the infant's persistent cries. As they waited till the bottle was ready, Laura asked to hold her, lifting her gently into her arms.

'She's beautiful. What a head of hair she has. Just like Sofie's.' She smiled, gently smoothing the springy dark curls on top of the baby's head. She rocked the baby while speaking to her softly, but her efforts only made the crying worse.

The tension in the room grew. Wouter stood by, at a loss what to say or do. Laura was now upset and handed back the baby. Everyone was in turmoil, all because of this helpless baby. Nothing about this seemed right. Fortunately, the bottle was ready and the baby immediately stopped her crying as she latched on, and the mood amongst them lifted. Their relief was palpable when Liesbeth announced she needed to get to an appointment at the baby clinic.

'Do you think Sofie would see me?' Laura asked Else after Liesbeth had left.

'Yes, I think it could be just the boost she needs.'

FIFTY

LAURA

Even though her face isn't visible, the woman sitting in the window of the café is unmistakable from the halo of dark curls and tilt of her head as she stirs her coffee.

I check my watch, worried I might be late, and quicken my step across the street. Through the glass frontage, I can see the café is packed. I push open the door and am greeted by the warm fug of cigar smoke and hum of voices. I thread my way between the tables and tap Sofie softly on the shoulder.

'Oh, you came!' Sofie looks round with a start.

'Of course I came. I'm so happy to see you.' I hug her for a long moment.

Sofie's eyes are shining. 'I can't believe you're here. I thought I'd never see you again.' She gazes at me, drinking me in. 'But you've changed. You look so much more grown-up. Different.'

I tip my head back and laugh. 'Do I? I suppose it's been a long time. Too long.' But Sofie is also changed; she has shadows beneath her eyes and what looks like a silver thread in one of her curls. I'm embarrassed I can't find any positive words. What had happened to the lively, feisty, often confrontational person I used to look up to? I remove my jacket and sit down as the wait-ress arrives to take my order.

'I'll have a coffee. And *appelgebak*. What about you, Sofie?'

'Yes, why not? I'll have one too.'

'This is nice. Do you come here much?' I ask, looking around at the clusters of people enjoying a treat out.

'Me? No,' scoffs Sofie, her smile now gone and replaced by a closed, guarded look. 'I avoid going out if I can help it. Just to work each morning. Did you know I worked as a bank teller?'

'Yes, Liesbeth did tell me.' I watch Sofie carefully for her reaction, but there's none. 'Do you enjoy it?' I ask, not really believing she can. I remember our conversations, how Sofie had been so keen to go university and make something of her life. It had always been Sofie who'd kept me going through our darkest times. I'm filled with sadness for the girl I thought I knew, always so full of ambition and a determination to succeed.

Sofie stares out of the window as she contemplates her answer. 'It's a job and brings in some money so I can pay for the baby.' Her voice sounds flat, devoid of any emotion.

I have to stop herself from shaking my head. 'Liesbeth brought Marieke for us to meet her. She's quite a feisty little thing and has such a mass of curls already. She's so like you.' I give what I think is an encouraging laugh and try to catch Sofie's eye, but she keeps her eyes on something just beyond the window.

'Laura, I know what you're trying to do and why you wanted to see me, but there's nothing that will change my mind about the baby. I'm grateful that Liesbeth has been kind enough to look after her and wish them both well. But I have to get on with my life now, can't you see?' From the fiery look in her eye, I see that she hasn't lost her old passionate side.

The waitress interrupts the conversation with the arrival of our order and seems to take an age in setting the items in front of us. 'Thank you,' I say abruptly, wishing she'd leave us in peace. After she's left, we sit in silence as we sugar our coffee. Sofie then takes a tiny fork and tastes her cake. 'This is nice. I haven't had *appelgebak* in ages,' she says brightly.

She's trying to close off the conversation, but I won't allow it. 'Sofie, you can't keep pretending it never happened. It was awful, what happened, it must have been. But you have a beautiful daughter who deserves better. She deserves to have you, her mother, can't you see?'

'I don't expect you to understand.' Sofie prods her cake. 'I mean, look at you. You have Wouter, you have a new life. You're so fortunate. I'm pleased it all worked out for you but I lost everything and all because I was too scared. I don't know what I was thinking, but by the time everyone was gone it was too late. That's when the *moffen* came back for me. I've gone over it so many times, but always come to the same conclusion. I should have fled with the others and faced the consequences, even if it meant being shot. That would have been preferable to what I was left with.'

'You can't think like that,' I tell her, horrified. 'What about Marieke? Don't you care what happens to her?'

Sofie scoffs but I can see she's trying to hold back her tears. 'Do I need to spell it out to you? Instead of being able to scrub myself clean and put the whole terrible thing behind me, the child is a constant reminder of how I was violated by an evil Nazi. Her father. And not just that... he was the one who shot Karl dead. At least Karl never had to suffer seeing me with that monster's child.'

I'm now also close to tears and don't know how to respond. During the last weeks at Berkenhout, I'd grown fond of Karl and had thought he and Sofie made the perfect couple. Now all of it has been swept away: Karl is dead and Sofie, the victim, has been left to pick up the pieces of her life.

As Sofie gazes at me, she appears to soften, letting a glimpse of her old self shine through. 'I've started evening classes in bookkeeping. I can make more money with a qualification. Maybe I'll move to Hilversum and get a proper job. It's the best I can do for now and I need to get through this on my own. And one day, I sincerely hope she'll forgive me. Do you understand?'

I'm not sure I do and wish I could do or say something to make it right between us. I understand that the most important thing is to part company as friends with the promise to meet regularly. So when it's time to go, I give her a big hug and am relieved she returns it. I watch her as she walks away and my heart breaks for her.

FIFTY-ONE

WOUTER

Before setting out, Wouter spent a long time fiddling under the bonnet of the van ensuring it was capable of making it along the rutted tracks. In all the time he'd used the van during the war, lack of oil and spare parts had made it difficult to keep it roadworthy. Now, after a little tinkering, he found it was running as well as ever.

'All done,' he said triumphantly, checking the oil levels and wiping the dipstick clean on a greasy rag. He tried to kiss Laura, but she squirmed away, telling him he should clean up first. She'd already made it quite clear that she was coming with him on sufferance and was growing impatient to get this rendezvous over and done with.

'Come on, let's go,' said Wouter, wiping his hands on his handkerchief before walking round to the passenger door. On her seat, he'd placed a cushion for her back and a rug should it turn chilly. 'See, I've even made it more comfortable for you.'

'Thank you,' said Laura, suppressing a giggle.

This time she let him kiss her. As he held her and looked into those dark eyes that had haunted him for so long, he still could hardly believe she was by his side and actually wanted to be with him. His breath caught in his throat as he realised how close he'd been to losing her. Going back was the only way he could imagine erasing that memory.

'I've heard the track is virtually impassable beyond the crossroads, so we'll park the car by old Hendrik's house,' he said on the long stretch before they entered the woods.

'I never met him in all the times I went to fetch water from the pump,' said Laura, starting to relax and reminisce over old times. 'We knew he was there and sometimes I'd glimpse a dark shadow of someone moving in the window.'

'I don't think he realised quite what a lifesaver he was. Living by himself in the woods must have been pretty lonely and I think he liked being part of the operation. When Klaus and I started running errands for Else, we called in on him one time. Foolishly, I left the van in full view of the road and of course a couple of *moffen* turned up. It was a near thing and only because old Hendrik warned them off. I hadn't thought to park the van round the back. My mind was all over the place at the time. I imagined that anyone I came into contact with would have news about you.' Wouter went quiet as he gripped the steering wheel and concentrated on steering the van along the rutted track.

The house looked almost exactly the same as Wouter had last seen it – dilapidated and abandoned. The garden didn't seem to have been tended for some time and a creeper had wrapped itself round the doorframe, twisting long tendrils onto the handle. Wouter blew out his breath. 'It doesn't look very hopeful.' They knocked, just in case, and walked round to the back of the property, but there was nothing to see except a few rusty garden implements half buried in weeds. Wouter hoped the old man hadn't had his comeuppance and been hauled off by the Germans for his insolent behaviour. Or maybe they'd found evidence that he'd been colluding with Dick Foppen and had him shot too. Wouter wanted to get away.

'There's nothing here. He was really quite old and probably just passed away,' said Laura, as if she knew what he was thinking.

Wouter was silent as they set off down the track both had taken so often in the past. Laura chatted about inconsequential things, leaving him to his thoughts. He was beginning to regret this whole exercise, which was turning into a complete waste of time. Everything was so different now and all anyone associated with Berkenhout wanted to do was to forget and move on. That was certainly Laura's wish and he should have respected that. She had her own terrible memories, losing family members to the Nazis, being wrenched from her family to go to live in Berkenhout, then finally the discovery that her parents had never made it across the border to Switzerland and been hauled off to perish in Auschwitz. He so wished he'd been there to comfort her when she'd needed him most. Now, whenever he gently probed her about her past, she would shake her head with a sad smile and change the subject. One day, he hoped she'd be able to open up to him and share her pain.

They arrived at a clearing but with no discernible path. 'Look, shall we turn back? It's all changed and there's nothing left anymore,' said Wouter, doubt in his voice.

'But it can't be far. You don't want to give up now,' said Laura, striding on till the track veered away to the left. Instinctively, they both knew they must turn right along a faint path that seemed to go deeper into the woods.

'It's here, isn't it?' said Laura, who was walking a little way ahead. The sides of the path were quite overgrown with no sign that anyone had been there recently.

Unsure, Wouter looked about him. 'Didn't there used to be a big oak tree just here?'

'It's not there now.' Laura pointed to a stump covered in vegetation. 'And see, others have been chopped down. It looks as if someone had the idea of clearing a way through and gave up on the idea.'

'You're right, but now we know we're heading in the right direction, it can't be far.'

They swished through the long grass that petered out when they reached a denser patch of wood. The terrain was now more familiar to Wouter, but there was a new sandy path that came in from their right. 'Let's see if it takes us there,' he said, buoyed up by Laura's encouragement. The new path narrowed and disappeared off between tall trees opposite a clearing they both recognised next to a gnarled oak tree with spreading branches.

Laura spotted it first and let out a cry. She ran forward over the empty plot dotted with low bushes and began poking around with her foot. 'I'm sure that's where the reception hut was.' Bending down, she pulled out a stick of charred wood half buried in the undergrowth. 'I can't believe they did this.' She dropped the blackened stick to the ground. They scanned the area all around them, but there was no evidence of any of the five huts that had stood above the surface.

'Wait, I bet we'll find they didn't destroy the underground huts. If I'm right, then your hut should be here,' said Wouter, surveying the area before his gaze settled on a tangle of undergrowth in shadow beneath a sprawling beech tree. The hut was hard to make out, as it should be. It was almost completely hidden from view apart from a significant dip where the entrance must have been. Together, they tore away at the creepers and tugged the branches till they could peer down into the gloomy hollow they'd created. But there was nothing more to see.

'It must have been here,' cried Laura, on hands and knees. She kept scrabbling at the vegetation that blocked the entrance.

The crack of a twig from behind caused them both to look round in alarm. It was pure instinct. They were back in the camp, reacting to any unusual noise that might indicate discovery by the enemy. His heart beating fast, Wouter grabbed Laura to him as he spied a tall man dressed in a long overcoat come striding towards them through the trees, looking for all the world like a German in SS uniform.

'It's Henk,' said Laura in a relieved whisper.

'Henk?' Wouter relaxed his grip on Laura and took a step forward. 'I really didn't expect to see you here,' he said more in surprise at himself for not guessing that Henk would be prowling around the area like he always did. The woods were the forester's natural habitat and he knew them better than anyone. It was more surprising that Wouter had never bumped into him during those weeks when he was fleeing from the Germans.

'So you found Berkenhout. Not quite what it was, is it?' said Henk, ignoring Wouter's comment.

And pleased to see you too after all this time, Wouter didn't say. *As gruff and unfriendly as ever*, he thought. He felt all the old animosity rise in his chest, but kept his voice calm and even. 'They said it had been burned down but I didn't believe there'd be nothing here. Not even something to show that it existed.'

Henk took a crumpled cigarette pack from his pocket, hooked one out and lit it. He drew on it deeply before answering. 'It's best that way, don't you think? People don't want to talk about the war anymore, least of all what happened here.' He paused to drag on his cigarette as he stared at the ground. 'Isn't that so?' he mumbled.

'You might think that, but I believe it's wrong to pretend it never happened.' Wouter swallowed hard. 'People lost their lives here. They were my friends, innocent people who had committed no crime but were forced to flee their homes and family. And we,' he flung an arm round Laura's shoulder and pulled her to him, 'were the lucky ones. It's up to us to make sure that this shameful episode isn't swept aside just because it makes others feel uncomfortable.'

When Henk didn't answer, Wouter walked over and picked up the charred wood Laura had found. 'The Germans did a pretty good job in destroying this place. It's as if nothing was ever here.' He threw it back down in disgust. 'You must have known it was happening. Maybe you even had a hand in it.' He moved a couple of steps towards Henk, his hands balled up by his sides.

'Wouter, please,' whispered Laura in an urgent voice, with a restraining hand on his arm.

'No, Laura, leave me to say what I think. It's about time someone did. I never did believe it was only chance the *moffen* were passing. After all those months of scouring the woods and never turning up anything. Or maybe they had a tip-off. Well, Henk, tell us what you know.'

Henk gave Wouter a strange look, somewhere in between surprise and indignation. He paced slowly up and down. 'I can't tell you exactly, not because I don't want to say, but because I don't know.'

'I don't believe you,' retorted Wouter, losing patience with the man.

'Let him speak,' pleaded Laura, and Wouter gave her a reluctant nod.

Henk stood, then half turned away from them, as if he couldn't bear to look them in the eye. 'Not long after I started to build the first huts, I was returning home when a German officer appeared from the trees and waved me down. Luckily, he wasn't interested in searching the van, not that he'd have found anything. I always made sure I kept any tools buried near my place of work. I told him about my work as a forester and he seemed pleased to hear how well I knew the woods. His men were stationed at the *landhuis* on the edge of the woods. They were having problems sourcing enough food. Their local delivery boy was unreliable, blaming the lack of supplies on how little there was on the black market. I could see where this conversation was heading. The officer suddenly dropped his friendly manner and pushed his face right up to mine. He insisted that I use my van to bring groceries to their headquarters, or else. Now, I'm not a man to put up with that kind of behaviour, but I realised pretty quick I shouldn't argue with this thug. I had no choice but to comply.'

Henk paused for a long moment, still staring at the ground. It was as if he'd forgotten Wouter and Laura standing there, watching him.

'It wasn't simple getting hold of the stuff at first, but as soon as the first people moved into Berkenhout it got easier. The shopkeepers in Kampenveld all wanted to help. It was their way of getting one up on the Germans, but little did they know that my requests for more provisions were...' – he searched for the word – 'less than honourable. Then everything changed one evening when the officer came knocking at my door with a box full of *jenever* bottles. He shook my hand vigorously and said I should call him Manfred. I was suspicious. He stood there smiling and I wasn't sure if he was about to make another of his demands or was being genuinely friendly. He seemed a bit tipsy but I thought I should invite him in and we ended up sharing a half bottle of the stuff. I was relieved he didn't go on about their failed attempts to find the Jewish refugee camp; it was just friendly chat. But when he got up to go, he slapped me on the shoulder and said he was so grateful for me helping the Nazi cause for the future of the Fatherland. He said we'd soon be free of all the dirty Jews. I was cringing inside with fury. It was my chance to tell him what I really thought, but I somehow couldn't bring myself to say it.'

As he continued his story, Henk almost spat out the words. 'My mind was in turmoil. I hated this man and everything he stood for. He was forcing me to do something against my will, but how else could I help Dick and the *onderduikers*? Believe me, I wouldn't have chosen to agree to his demands. He didn't even notice I was silent. He was used to that.' Henk gave a snort. 'Then he told me that in return for keeping up deliveries he would grant me the freedom of the woods without any inter-ference.'

At last Henk lifted an anguished face towards Wouter.

'Did you tell anyone?' Wouter said in a quiet voice.

Henk shook his head. 'I intended to go to Dick and tell him everything, but what good would it do? No one ever asked any questions as long as I brought them what they needed. In return, I'd get my *jenever*, coffee and my freedom. Manfred was as good as his word and they never once searched my van all the times I was transporting goods to Berkenhout. I admit I some-times took a few risks, but I always made sure they never knew about my connections with Berkenhout. I regret what happened that day, but I swear it was nothing to do with me. It was a coincidence those Germans were snooping around and got lucky.'

'Did you never tell Dick and Else about this?' said Wouter, scrutinising Henk's face.

Henk lit another cigarette before answering. 'They must have known but we never spoke about it. They had my trust and that was enough.'

Wouter remembered one of his conversations with Else and how she appeared to defend Henk's actions. Perhaps they were all at it. But there was something about the way Henk spoke, more softly and with a hoarse emotion that gave Wouter reason to believe that, maybe, he'd underestimated the man.

'Henk,' said Laura hesitantly. 'I never had a chance to thank you for getting me out and for all you did getting us to safety.'

'It was nothing.' He shrugged. 'I could have done more but that would have endangered everyone. It's why I had to turn you out so you could get as far away from Berkenhout as possible. Those children you took – I don't suppose they ever saw their parents again?'

'I can't say. I was forced to move on without them not long after – it was almost more than I could bear. But I had no choice,' she said sadly. 'I don't think any of us had. My parents...' She took a faltering breath. Wouter squeezed her hand and she regained her composure. 'I was one of the lucky ones but it doesn't make it any easier. We didn't know at the time, but if we hadn't put our trust in strangers, there would have been no future for any of us.' Laura took a deep breath and moved towards Henk and embraced him briefly.

'What will you do now?' she asked.

'Me?' said Henk as if such a thought had never occurred to him. He darted a look behind him into the woods. 'I've still got my job. I'll carry on as normal. I must go,' he murmured. He nodded at both of them without saying goodbye and walked away, his shoulders slightly stooping.

Wouter ran his hand through his hair, bemused by all he'd heard.

'Don't be too hard on him,' said Laura, staring after Henk. 'He made mistakes... we all did, but that doesn't make us bad, does it?'

'No, I don't suppose it does.' Wouter sighed, taking a long look at the rough ground that bore virtually no signs of their hidden village. He swallowed down hard. Nostalgia for everything good that it had represented mixed with a lingering sense of regret.

He was turning to go when his eye caught sight of something poking out of the ground in the shadow of a beech tree. He hadn't noticed it before as it lay hidden in the undergrowth close to the hut they'd been investigating. His heart quickened as he rushed forward to take a closer look.

'What's the matter?' said Laura.

'It can't be. It's...' Wouter fell to his knees and scrabbled the grass and soil away so he could lift out the object, crawling with woodlice. Carefully, almost lovingly, he brushed the dirt and insects aside and ran his fingers around the rim.

'It needs a bit more work doing on it, but nothing I can't sort out.' He smiled up at Laura who had a quizzical look on her face. 'Do you see? It's the bowl I was carving you when we were ambushed. The peace offering I never managed to give you. I lost it in the chaos to get out and never imagined I'd see it again. Laura, will you now accept my gift?' Standing up, he held it out to her in both hands.

'It's perfect,' she said, taking it with a laugh, and she stroked its smooth surface and marvelled at the swirl of the dark rings against the blond wood. Still holding the bowl, she moved closer to Wouter. 'And worth coming back for. But are you ready to leave now?' she said, searching his eyes as she stretched up to kiss him.

'I'm ready,' he said, and taking her firmly by the hand, he led her away without a backward glance.

A LETTER FROM IMOGEN

I want to say a huge thank you for choosing to read *Hidden in the Shadows*. If you did enjoy it and want to keep up to date with all my latest releases, just sign up at the following link. Your email address will never be shared, and you can unsubscribe at any time.

www.bookouture.com/imogen-matthews

I hope you loved *Hidden in the Shadows*, and if you did I would be very grateful if you could write a review. I'd love to hear what you think, and it makes such a difference helping new readers to discover one of my books for the first time.

I love hearing from my readers – you can get in touch on my Facebook page, through Twitter, Goodreads or my website.

Thanks,

Imogen

www.imogenmatthewsbooks.com

facebook.com/TheHiddenVillagenovel
twitter.com/ImogenMatthews3
instagram.com/oxfordnovelist

GLOSSARY OF WORDS AND PHRASES

Dutch

Appelgebak - Apple cake/tart

Appelmoes - Apple sauce

Dank je wel - Thank you

Dolle Dinsdag - Mad Tuesday

Eet smakelijk - Enjoy (your food)

Gezellig - Cosy, sociable

Godverdomme - God damn it

Goedendag - Good day

Goed zo - Well done

Grote Kerk - Great Church

Hoi - Hi

Jenever - Dutch gin

Kachel - Stove, heater

Kalverlaan - Kalver lane

Kerkstraat - Church Street

Landhuis - Country house

LO: Landelijke Organisatie voor hulp - National Organisation for Aid

aan Onderduikers - to Those in Hiding

Mof(s); moffen(pl) - Derogatory slang for Germans

Onderduiker - Someone in hiding

Tante - Aunt

Meneer, de Heer - Mr, sir

Mevrouw - Mrs, madam

NSB: Nationaal-Socialistische Beweging - National Socialist Movement

in Nederland - in the Netherlands

Olibollen - Doughnuts

Proost - Cheers

Schatje - Darling

Verdorie - Damn it

Vrij Nederland - Free the Netherlands (name of an underground newspaper established during the German occupation)

German

Halt! Absteigen! - Stop! Get down!

Aufmachen! - Open Up!

Ersatz - Substitute

Heil Hitler - Hail Hitler

Unglaublich - Unbelievable

Hier gibt es nichts zu sehen - There's nothing to see here

Verdammt - Damn it

Was machen Sie hier? - What are you doing here?

ACKNOWLEDGEMENTS

After I'd finished writing *The Hidden Village*, the thought didn't occur to me to write a second book: everything about the story, the place and the characters I'd created were so personal to me that I couldn't envisage doing justice to the memory again. Readers thought otherwise, and as reviews for *The Hidden Village* started coming in, I noticed that many of them wanted more. So it is to those readers that I would like to extend my gratitude for making me realise that I had in me another story waiting to be told. Grateful thanks also to Liesbeth Heenk, my mentor and erstwhile publisher, who brainstormed ideas with me and set me on the path to writing this next book.

There have been many people who have listened to, encouraged and critiqued my writing along the way. I appreciate all their comments and support. I have many writing buddies built up over the years, who understand what it's like to get down to the business of writing a novel – thank you to each and every one of them. I'd especially like to name Sue Clark, Anna Pitt, Louise Ludlow, Steve Sheppard, Jennifer Anton, Keith McClellan, Peter Perugia, Sheila Johnson and Brian Reynolds, along with everyone in the Aynho Writers group.

Thank you to Jennifer Hunt at Bookouture, who first approached me about publishing my wartime Holland stories, and has been such a support to me on my writing journey towards publication.

This is my third book with Bookouture and my admiration for their dedication and attention to detail keeps on growing.

Thank you to everyone at Bookouture, and especially to Susannah Hamilton, Jess Readett, Rhianna Louise, Alba Proko and Alex Crow, but there are countless others working tirelessly behind the scenes who are deserving of my thanks.

Last but by no means least, a big thank you to my family for supporting and putting up with me when I'm in the throes of writing or rushing to meet a publishing deadline. It's a great comfort to know you're always there.

Made in the USA
Columbia, SC
06 July 2024